WHO ARE YOU?

A LAKE SUPERIOR MYSTERY

R.T. LUND

LITTLE CREEK PRESS®
AND BOOK DESIGN
MINERAL POINT, WISCONSIN

Little Creek Press
5341 Sunny Ridge Road
Mineral Point, WI 53565

ORDERING INFORMATION
Quantity sales. Special discounts are available on quantity purchases by corporations, associations, and others.
For details, contact info@littlecreekpress.com

Orders by US trade bookstores and wholesalers.
Please contact Little Creek Press or Ingram for details.

Printed in the United States of America

Cataloging-in-Publication Data
Name: Lund, R.T., author
Title: Who Are You? / R.T. Lund
Description: Mineral Point, WI: Little Creek Press, 2022
Identifiers: LCCN: 2022918136 | ISBN: 978-1-955656-34-4
Subjects: FICTION / Thrillers / Romance

Book design by Mimi Bark and Little Creek Press

Cover photos:
Sky: shutterstock_162721421
Pavilion: shutterstock_657791428
Reeds: shutterstock_1767912215

The evil that men do lives after them;
The good is oft interred with their bones

—SHAKESPEARE

For Ann, whose appetite for
mysteries is an inspiration.

CHAPTER 1

Uncertainty is in the air. It's ten past five in the morning on the second Saturday in March. It's between winter and spring, between night and day, between freezing and thawing. But one look at the slender female form sprawled across the concrete steps of the Lake Harriet band shell is enough for me to know: It's definitely murder.

I get the call at four forty-five from Minneapolis dispatch. With no traffic, the drive from my place in Linden Hills to Lake Harriet Parkway takes less than five minutes. A city squad and a medi-van from Hennepin County Medical Center are already at the scene. It's cold enough for vapor to rise from congealing blood that frames the victim's torso. I recognize one of two uniformed officers having an animated discussion with a paramedic twenty feet from the body.

"Hey, Barnes," calls Officer Mickey Stanich, a stout, middle-aged pro, one of the few female beat cops on the force. "Where's Lindy?"

Warren Lindquist, aka Lindy, is my partner.

"On his way," I say. "Dispatch said a guy walking his dog discovered a dead woman at the band shell. What else do we know?"

"This is Rick Pearson," Stanich says. "Fresh from the academy three weeks ago. It's his first death case. He didn't touch anything but got a close-up of the victim while shadowing the EMTs."

Pearson is a baby-faced beanpole who can't be more than middle twenties. I'm hoping he can say something worthwhile before losing his breakfast.

"Are you okay, Rick?" I ask. "I'm Detective Barnes. Lincoln Barnes."

He extends a long, bony hand that's as cold and clammy as a lizard, but I shake it to be polite, even though protocol discourages it these days.

"I'll be fine. Just a little shook up by all the blood and the look on her face. I know you'll see for yourself, Detective, but she was stabbed right in the middle of her forehead and then multiple times in the neck and chest."

"Any ID?" I ask.

Stanich hands me a plastic bag from the pocket of her leather jacket. "The paramedic who checked her vitals came across this iPhone on the steps near the body. I'm sure it's password protected, but one of our IT guys or someone at the BCA might be able to break into it."

I decide to wait for Lindquist before examining the body. The MPD windbreaker I'm wearing over a hooded sweatshirt was not a good choice, and I'm freezing my ass off.

"Any missing person reports in the area that might match her description?" I ask.

"I checked the database and with downtown ten minutes ago, and there's nothing even close," says Stanich, "but one of the paramedics said she looks really familiar, like someone on TV."

Before I can ask about the forensics team, Lindquist's bulky six-foot frame emerges from his ancient Mazda 280Z. Warren has been my partner since my promotion to homicide four years ago, and I love him like a much-older brother. He hates the name Lindy, so I call him Warren. I don't know what I'll do when he retires at the end of the year.

Stanich and Pearson exchange a few words with him on the way back to their squad. Their shift ends at six. Homicide and forensics will finish securing, investigating, and documenting the scene.

"Kind of a nice neighborhood for this kind of shit," Warren says, handing me a steaming cup of dark roast from a local bean shop that opens at five. He's wearing a long wool coat with leather gloves and a black watch cap. At least one of us came prepared for a frigid morning.

"I brought the good camera," I say. I always take my own photos, not to use as evidence but to pin up in my cubicle for inspiration. "The lighting will be sketchy till the sun comes up, but we should get started. Someone from the ME's office will be out with the van."

Lake Harriet is one of five urban lakes connected by parkways and bike paths in the more affluent neighborhoods of the city. The band shell resembles a Disney cartoon-castle with turrets flanking a covered stage. Patrons sit on portable chairs or the grass to enjoy plays, concerts, weddings, and other spectacles during the six or seven months of the year that aren't winter. A paved trail circumscribing the lake is a magnet for walkers and runners. Though not so much in the winter, especially between midnight and dawn, when the park is closed.

I take latex gloves, a surgical mask, and a penlight out of my backpack as we dodge patches of ice and snow on our way to the band shell. Friday was a glorious day with temperatures in the forties, but a cold front brought rain that turned to sleet and snow overnight. This morning, winter is back. I kneel on a slushy concrete step next to the body. Warren opens his spiral notebook and uncaps a new felt-tip pen. Warren has a thing for pens.

"The knife wound in the forehead is about two inches long and deep," I say.

"Whoever stabbed her was powerful and probably a lot taller," Warren says as he shines his flashlight in her face and then scribbles in his notebook. "Even with the headband and that gash, she looks familiar. Has anyone found an ID?"

"The EMTs found her cell phone. It was on the upper step, next to her body, but it's password protected, of course."

Pearson mentioned the haunting look on her face, and he was right. Her eyes are locked wide open, her thin, colorless lips slightly apart and turned down in a grimace. I sense a combination of shock and agony. She's got dark-brown hair streaked with gray in a pixie cut. I'm a compulsive runner, so I feel an immediate kinship as I inspect her outfit—newer, expensive shoes, high-end Asics, with gray compression tights, a long-sleeved mock neck top, and a navy, quilted vest that is ripped in several places and stained with blood.

"This seems pretty fresh to me, Warren. I'm thinking the guy walking his dog didn't miss the action by much. At least a dozen stab wounds to the chest and neck, though the one in her forehead might have been enough."

"Okay," Warren replies, "but if she's jogging around the lake, how did she get on the band shell? The trail runs behind the stage, along the lakeshore. Was she trying to escape her assailant? Or maybe she'd left the trail and was running away from the lake when she was attacked?"

"Or she was just arriving," I say. "I run around Harriet at least once a week, and often access the trail near the band shell. Sometimes I drive over here, park in the neighborhood, and run two or three of the lakes."

"There aren't any cars in the lot, but she could have parked somewhere else," he says. "If she were attacked anywhere near the band shell, the park's video surveillance cameras above the snack shop should give us a decent look at the assailant. I'll call in and order everything they've got over the past twenty-four hours."

"Good idea," I say.

Warren manages a baby grin. He's always quick to give me credit for the few good ideas I have, so I try to reciprocate.

I never run at night without carrying some form of identification, usually my driver's license, and a can of pepper spray, so I check the pockets on her vest and leggings, but there's nothing, no keys and no ID. Then I remember something my sister used to do when she'd go for long runs in college.

"What is it?" Warren asks after I find a plastic card wedged between her right ankle and wool sweat sock.

"Looks like a driver's license. A Minnesota driver's license. Her name is Kathryn Patterson Bagley. She lives on York Avenue South, less than a mile from me. It says she's five feet six inches tall and a hundred twenty pounds. Born May 23, 1972, so she's forty-nine years old. I'd have guessed younger."

"Don't you recognize the name Kate Patterson?" Warren asks, as if I'm a complete dumbshit.

"Should I?"

"If she's who I think she is, she's president of the Minneapolis City Council, representing your ward in Linden Hills."

Warren's a big shot in the Minneapolis police union, so he's more in touch with the local political scene than a thirty-something detective who's only lived in this frozen wasteland for six years. Before I can think of a good comeback, the forensics van drives up, and we all dive into the science and mystery of an urban homicide.

CHAPTER 2

It's another working Saturday in Murderapolis. My precinct, the fifth, has the fewest homicides in the city. Last year, there were ninety-seven murders in Minneapolis—eight in my precinct, all investigated by Warren and me. Only twenty-eight of the ninety-seven have been cleared, but seven out of our eight. A seventeen-year-old runaway, a homeschooled transgender female from a wealthy family in Edina, was raped and strangled on the hottest night of the summer. Someone dumped her broken body in a pond in Loring Park. That's our unsolved case. Kate Patterson could become our second.

Warren's right, of course. Patterson's a big deal, a successful businesswoman and three-term council member with aspirations to be mayor and maybe governor.

We divide the work. I'll track down her next of kin and prepare a report for external communications, who'll inform the media. Warren will roust somebody from park and rec to show him the surveillance video. Guess who drew the short straw.

It doesn't take long to learn that Kate Patterson is or was married to Paul Bagley, a cardiologist with a lucrative practice treating rich people with fibrillations and clogged arteries at Southdale Medical Center. They have a son, Paul Jr., who's a senior at Saint John's University north of St. Cloud.

I drive my old-but-reliable Wrangler from the precinct station on Nicollet to the Patterson-Bagley home on Forty-Second and York. It's nine o'clock, nearly four hours after his wife's mutilated body was discovered, and I'm betting Dr. Bagley can conjure up a dozen reasons why his wife hasn't returned home, but none of them is close to the truth.

The house is a stucco-and-stone mini-mansion with three stories and a red tile roof. I park in the spacious driveway, empty except for a portable basketball hoop stationed in front of the middle of three garage doors. Sliding my cell into the breast pocket of my jacket, I grab a notebook from the front passenger seat and exit the Wrangler. I notice closed blinds and curtains in all the first-floor windows as I stride up a paver walkway to a small, concrete portico and oak double-entry doors. I press the lighted doorbell button several times and then knock, but no barking dog, no footsteps, no answer. There's no one home.

Though it's a difficult, thankless task, I prefer—and it's department protocol—to notify families of the worst possible news in person. But sometimes circumstances don't permit it. Still on the porch, I call the weekend number for Bagley's clinic. After listening to a recorded menu of options, I decide not to call 911, even though some might call this an emergency, and press zero to speak to a live person.

"Southdale Cardiac Partners, how may I help you?"

"Good morning." I try to be polite. "This is Detective Barnes with the Minneapolis Police. I need to speak with Dr. Paul Bagley. He's not home, so I'm wondering if he's at his office."

"I'm so sorry, Detective," says a youngish female with a sweet but insincere voice. "Dr. Bagley won't be in this weekend. He's attending a conference in Tucson until Tuesday."

"That's great," I say sarcastically. "Could you please give me his cell phone number and the name of his hotel? This is a family emergency."

There's a five-second pause. "No one is supposed to have that number, Detective, but I'll get it for you under the circumstances."

"Thanks. I really do appreciate it."

I return to the relative warmth of my SUV to contact Bagley with the horrible news. Warren calls before I get situated.

"What do you know?" I ask.

"A couple things. I just viewed the video from the cameras at Harriet. I'll send you a copy, but for the most part, it's not very enlightening. The attack didn't happen at the band shell. At three fifty, our victim comes into view from the northeast. She's bent over and staggering and then collapses on the steps. It almost looks like she was trying to make a call, maybe to 911, and then drops the phone on her way to oblivion. No one else is visible from three o'clock until a little old man with a beagle walks by and does a double take at four fifteen.

"I'll canvass the neighborhood around the parkway this afternoon and see if anyone saw or heard anything between midnight and five. Forensics isn't optimistic there's any useful DNA. No hair and she was wearing gloves, so she didn't scratch the killer with her fingernails. They circled the lake looking for a knife and any other physical evidence but only picked up an old jacket and a cloth glove that had probably been out there for days. How did Dr. Bagley take the news?"

"He's not home or at his office," I say. "Apparently, he's on some boondoggle in Tucson. I was about to call him when I took your call."

"Sorry to interrupt. I heard the mayor was in his office this morning. We should let him know after you talk to Bagley but before the department releases her ID to the media. The generic story was reported on local news and websites at eight. We didn't know whether the attacker was still in the neighborhood and what kind of ongoing threat there might be, so we had to get the word out."

"Got it. I'll be in touch as soon as I've talked to Bagley. We need to give him time to tell their son too."

With three twenty-something daughters, Warren understands this better than I.

"Of course."

CHAPTER 3

Bagley doesn't answer his cell. I leave a message to call me and then call Ventana Canyon Resort and Conference Center. I ask for Dr. Paul Bagley's room and, wonder of wonders, a pleasant gentleman with an accent connects me without asking a single question.

"Hello, who the hell is this?"

I'm surprised by a groggy female voice. It's eight thirty Arizona time, but my call must have awakened her. The good doctor must be treating patients in his hotel suite.

"This is Detective Lincoln Barnes with the Minneapolis Police Department. I need to speak with Dr. Bagley if he's there."

"Why do you need to talk to Dr.—"

"This is Paul Bagley. Who is this?"

"Sorry to disturb you, Dr. Bagley. This is Detective Barnes with the Minneapolis PD. I have some very bad news, sir." There's really no good way to say this, so I get right to the point. "It's about your spouse, Kathryn Patterson Bagley. We believe she went out for a run early this morning, before five, and someone attacked and killed her near the Lake Harriet band shell."

"Oh my god. Oh, Christ. I told her not to run in the dark, but when she feels the need, nothing can stop her. I can't believe this. How did it happen?"

Even though the question is probably rhetorical, I try to give him an answer. "She was attacked by someone with a knife, Dr. Bagley. There's no obvious evidence of sexual assault or robbery, so right now it seems like a random act of violence. But it's early in the investigation, so that may not be the case. We don't have any suspects at this time."

"What about my son? Does he know?"

"No, sir. I thought you'd want to tell him. Because your wife is a public figure, there is additional pressure to disclose her identity to the media. Normally, we'd give you an opportunity to see her first, but I don't think that will be possible, given you're in Arizona."

"That's fine. I'll talk to Paul as soon as we're through and fly back to Minnesota later today. Will we be able to view the body?"

"Of course. Someone from victim and family relations will contact you later today, and either my partner or I will want to meet with you soon as part of our investigation. I'm assuming you don't know anyone who'd have reason to harm your wife. Any political rivals, enemies, or angry constituents who could have turned violent." I don't need to go there so soon, but he's got another woman in his bed, so I do.

"Everyone in politics has enemies, Detective, but Kate and I don't associate with violent people. She's a loving mother and dedicated public servant. I can't think of anyone who would attack her with a knife. That's barbaric."

He sounds more like a publicist than a grieving spouse. I'll wait until he's back to probe deeper. I share my cell and email information and, still sitting in his driveway, ask a logistical question.

"One last thing before I let you go. We didn't find a house or car key in your wife's possession, and it's important for us to know whether she drove somewhere first or ran directly from your home. What was her usual practice?"

"She always ran from the house, often going more than five miles. If I wasn't home, she'd leave the key to the front door under a mat on our deck."

"That's probably what she did." I'll check for myself in a minute. "Again, Dr. Bagley, I'm very sorry for your loss."

He hangs up after "sorry." There's something I don't like about Paul Bagley, and it's not just the other woman.

———

Warren and I touch base late in the afternoon. Local media outlets, from the *Star Tribune* to talk radio, are reporting the "brutal murder" of Minneapolis City Council President Kate Patterson. I tell him about my conversation with Dr. Bagley and about the woman who answered his phone and presumably shared his bed. Warren says none of the neighbors he interviewed in the vicinity of Harriet Park heard any screams or saw anything suspicious. Most were sleeping.

We have no murder weapon, no suspects, and no physical evidence, yet. There's always the possibility the medical examiner's office will find the killer's blood or DNA on the victim. Now that Patterson's identity is public, we'll get calls and emails from citizens who "saw something." Ninety-five percent of them will be dead ends. Discerning the five percent that aren't is like panning for gold in the ocean. Warren has set up two meetings for Monday morning, one with Mayor Sampson and the other with Kate Patterson's staff at city hall.

I finish some paperwork in the office and head back to my apartment for a quick shower and change of clothes. My younger sister lives in a three-bedroom Dutch colonial in the Highland Park neighborhood of Saint Paul, about a mile from the Mississippi. She's invited me for dinner. The new murder case gives me an excuse to cancel, but I don't.

The front door's unlocked, and I don't bother to knock. The twins are watching an animated movie, maybe one of the *Toy Stories*, on a small, flat-screen TV in the living room while their mom and dad sit at the dining room table, each holding a bottle of Summit Pale Ale.

"Hi, Auntie Lee," says Henry, one of the five-year-old Decker twins. "Lee" is easier to say than "Lincoln," and "Linc" is stupid, so "Lee" has become an acceptable shorthand for Henry and Theo, my favorite little guys. I hand each of them a bag of chocolate-covered gummy bears.

"Thanks, Auntie Lee," says my sister, Wanda. She and Craig have been married for ten years. They're both teachers at a Saint Paul high school. He's also the boys' basketball coach.

"Wow, what a spread," I say, eying an array of my favorite Mexican dishes on the buffet.

"There's beer and soda in the fridge," Craig says. I'm six feet tall, and Craig, the center on his D2 college hoops team, towers over me and has the deepest voice I've ever heard. He's also the nicest man I know.

"The kids have already eaten," says Wanda, "so you can grab a plate and start us off."

"I thought Mom was coming," I say, surprised she isn't already here.

"She's stuck in Chicago. They're getting hammered with snow," Wanda explains. She hands me a plate after I pop the cap off a Dos Equis.

Our mother has been a flight attendant with United since before I was born. She had enough seniority to move from Chicago to the Twin Cities when Wanda's twins were born.. She and my dad never married but lived together in a one-story, three-bedroom house built over a hundred years ago in the Irving Park neighborhood.

John Hayes grew up in Louisville and played center field for the Illinois State Redbirds. By the time he met my mom, his split-second stint in the minors was over and he'd embarked on a thirty-year career as a firefighter with the CFD. I don't know much about my family tree. In fact, I learned more from Ancestry.com than I ever learned from Lucy Barnes or John Hayes. Wanda and I are mostly English and African-American. Our grandparents died before we were born, and neither one of our parents had siblings.

My dad really wanted a son, a son he could name Lincoln after his hero. He left a few months after Wanda was born and stayed in touch on birthdays, holidays, and a few weekends each year. I loved him desperately and tried to be the son he'd wanted, earning a softball scholarship to Illinois State and getting into the police academy in Chicago, always hoping to be closer to him. He contracted COVID-19 while helping to evacuate a nursing home infiltrated by the insidious virus. He never recovered.

"The story of her life," I say while filling my plate with rice, black beans, chips and salsa, chicken enchiladas, and bean tostadas. I've hardly eaten today, and Wanda makes the best comfort food in town. Given the hectic, lonely life I've chosen, I love spending time with the Decker family.

We sit at the dining room table, Wanda and I on one side and Craig on the other. Craig recites a familiar prayer he learned in Sunday school. Then he leans across the table and speaks in a half whisper, so the kids won't hear. "We heard about the city councilwoman on MPR this afternoon. Murdered near Lake Harriet. Is that yours, Lincoln?"

Henry and Theo suddenly appear, vying for my lap.

"Let's just say I'm familiar with the case. You think your team will make it to state this year?"

CHAPTER 4

I decide to take Sunday off. Diane's in Florida with her mother, so Warren will go back to Harriet and snoop around. On a caffeine-and-sugar high after consuming a chai latte and cinnamon scone from the neighborhood Starbucks, I drive to my fitness club, one of the big chains, in St. Louis Park. Belonging here is an extravagance for a lowly detective, but I have workout needs that can't be met in my one-bedroom apartment. I'm dressed in outdoor running gear. I only use the locker room and shower in the dead of winter or when I swim laps. After playing DI softball for four years, I should be used to women's locker rooms, but I've never liked to be ogled by other women in various stages of undress. For the most part, men just go about their business; women judge and compare.

The club is bustling at seven fifteen on Sunday morning. I remove a nylon pullover and complete a circuit of strengthening exercises, leg extensions, curls, and lat raises, and then spend five minutes on an elliptical before stretching on the floor near one of the exits. As usual, I'm so lost in random thoughts, from my running route to my grocery list, that a baritone voice above my head startles me.

"Going for a run?"

I don't know if he sees me flinch, but a handsome, middle-aged man wearing a black-and-purple Vikings cap is hovering over me, his tanned, clean-shaven face about a foot from mine. He obviously didn't get the memo on social distancing.

"Do I know you?" I ask from an awkward kneeling position. I stand to level the playing field and to get a better look at this guy.

"I don't think so," he says. "My name's Rob. Robin Gildemeister. I was on the Cedar trail for a long run, and nature called about a half mile from here. Luckily, I'm a member or they wouldn't have let me in. Anyway, I saw you stretching by the door, so I thought you might be heading outside. I wouldn't mind some company, but I totally understand if you'd prefer to run alone."

The name sounds familiar, but I can't recall why. His face is glistening with perspiration. He's a few inches taller than me and looks like Harrison Ford with a longer nose and darker hair. I'd peg him at forty-five or a well-preserved fifty. Intrigued, I take the bait, confident he won't be able to keep up for long.

"I'm Lincoln, Rob. Nice to meet you." People rarely shake hands with strangers these days, so I just give him a nod. "I usually run alone, but today I'd be happy to have some company. Where do you want to go?"

"How about taking the Cedar trail over to Lake of the Isles and then downtown along the river?"

"Perfect." I'm training for a big race, so a ten- to twelve-miler sounds good. I follow Rob out to Cedar Lake Road, and he starts jogging at a leisurely nine-minute-mile pace, which is fine for a warmup half mile. His stride is smooth and athletic.

"Do you run the lakes often?" he asks.

"Two or three times a week if I can," I say. "How about you?"

"I hate to admit that I usually run on a treadmill. I run the river more than the lakes on weekends. Feel free to pick up the pace if you'd like."

By the time we hit Isles, I'm moving at three-quarter speed, about a seven-and-a-half-minute-mile pace, and old Rob has no trouble keeping up. He keeps the conversation going without laboring. He usually runs on a treadmill? Hmmmm.

We pass Walker Art Center and the sculpture garden and climb the steps to the pedestrian bridge over Hennepin Avenue. He activates an internal accelerator as the downtown skyline comes into view, and now I'm struggling to keep up.

"I've lived downtown forever," he says, still not breathing heavily.

We're racing through Loring Park, and I notice two young women kneeling on a patch of grass between Loring Pond and the walking path, setting a white cross near the spot where Billie Holloway's battered, lifeless body was discovered eight months ago. I put on the brakes and tap his right forearm with my left hand.

"You go ahead, Rob. I have to check something out."

I jog over to the pond and crouch down to their level, trying to think of something to say.

"Good morning." It's all I can muster on short notice.

The signs and flowers that covered the area last fall must have been removed after the first snowfall in November. Dressed in down parkas and blue jeans, these two girls are teenagers. They've just finished planting a solitary white cross, about three feet high with artfully painted black-and-gold lettering on the horizontal axis:

Billie Jordan Holloway
May 4, 2004 – August 24, 2021
In peace forever

I'm afraid of startling them, but they barely move at the sound of my voice. The shorter, dark-haired girl acknowledges me with her eyes and then says, "Hi."

Her friend has been crying. She wipes away tears on her cheek with a woolen mitten. "Who are you?" she asks. "Did you know Billie?"

"I'm so sorry to intrude," I say. "My name is Lincoln. I'm one of the police officers assigned to find out what happened the night Billie was attacked."

"You mean to find the killer?"

"Yes, that's what I mean," I say, trying to build some rapport with the girls. "Did you know Billie?"

"We live in Billie's neighborhood in Edina. She's Brianna, and I'm Holly. We were friends with Billie in grade school. He was a shy little guy who liked to ride his bike in our cul-de-sac and play Pokémon. We used to play night games in the summer. He'd join in whenever he could. I guess you'd say he presented as a boy back then. His parents were super strict and religious. When he grew out his hair and tried to dress more like a girl because that's what he was inside, his mom started homeschooling him. Some neighborhood kids teased her a lot. We didn't see much of her after that until we heard she ran away."

"I got my license a few months ago," Brianna says. "I came downtown for a music lesson at MacPhail and drove by the park. When I saw that all the candles, dolls, and signs were gone, I thought we should put something more permanent here for Billie. She didn't deserve what happened to her, Officer Lincoln. I know she had a horrible life."

I interviewed some of the family's friends and neighbors last fall, but not these girls. I commend them for their thoughtfulness and, lifting my phone from my sweats, exchange contact information with them. They promise to call or text me if they think of anything that might help the case. I'll follow up with them because if they feel this strongly about Billie several months after her death, they might know something significant.

Returning to the walking path, I'm surprised to see Rob sitting on a park bench facing the pond, his arms folded across his chest.

"You look like you're ready for a nap," I say. I worry that I'm actually glad he waited for me. There's something about him other than his good looks, a quiet confidence maybe. "Did I wear you out, or don't you have anything better to do on a Sunday morning?"

"You're right on both counts," he says, joining me on the path. "But, to be honest, I'm curious why you stopped to talk to those two young ladies."

"I'm starting to freeze from standing here. Can we move while we talk?" It's a lame attempt at changing the subject, so I fess up to being a cop as we jog out of Loring Park and toward downtown.

"I'm a homicide detective with the Minneapolis PD. One of my unsolved cases involves a young trans woman who was murdered in the area and found near where those girls planted the cross. I wanted to see if they knew anything that might be helpful."

"And did they?"

"Not sure. They grew up in the same neighborhood as the victim." He's taking me through downtown Minneapolis on busy Hennepin Avenue.

"Are you referring to the Billie Holloway case?"

"Yeah. You have a good memory." There've been scores of murders in Loring Park over the years.

"Not really. I'm a judge in Hennepin County, so maybe I pay closer attention to the Minneapolis crime scene than most people. Anyway, even I was shocked by the brutality of that poor girl's murder."

"Judge Gildemeister. Sure, I've heard of you." It's a lie, and he knows it. "I'm sorry I didn't recognize the name when you introduced yourself." He probably thinks I'm an idiot.

"There are over sixty district judges in the county. I don't think you've appeared in my courtroom—I would have remembered—so I'm not surprised you haven't heard of Robin Gildemeister, the hanging judge."

He playfully shoves my shoulder with his hand, and we both laugh. It's hard to get to know someone on a run, but I'm enjoying this more than I should. When we get to the Mississippi, he stops at the entrance to the Hennepin Avenue Bridge and starts jogging in place.

"I live in that brick high-rise across the river," he says, pointing to a twenty-plus-story building looming over the river in the gentrified Nicollet Island neighborhood. "I'll make you the best cup of coffee you've ever had and give you a ride back to your club if you join me for breakfast at my place."

A voice inside tells me to politely decline and run back to the club, but I ignore it.

"Okay, now I'm curious. I'll sample your coffee, Judge."

"Great," he says, starting to trot over the four-lane suspended span that arches high above the fast-moving Mississippi, "but please call me Rob."

We get on the elevator, and I get a better look at him while he's watching the floor indicators light up and stop at seventeen. I'm guessing late forties because he's a judge, though he looks closer to forty. A few gray hairs are mixed in with the brown, and his eyes are an unnatural green, which means he's wearing tinted contact lenses. He flashes a key card and leads me into 1704. It's an open floor plan with a kitchen on the left and a spacious great room straight ahead. The ceilings are high, maybe twelve feet. The walls are painted taupe with white enameled trim and built-ins, made brighter by floor-to-ceiling windows that provide a panoramic view of the river and downtown skyline. The room is dominated by three items: a black Steinway baby grand, a spiral metal stairway leading to an upper level, and a dark-brown leather sectional. I'm impressed and embarrassed at the same time, comparing this place to my Spartan living quarters.

"Nice place," I say, trying to downplay my true reaction as I take in the hardwood floors, paintings on the walls, and expensive furnishings throughout. Though I've never really cared about such things, I can't help but appreciate them. In another life, I'll be a realtor or interior decorator.

"Thanks," he says, taking off a nylon pullover and draping it over the back of the sectional. He's trim but well-muscled in a tight navy T-shirt. "I moved here three years ago from a condo in Uptown. Other than this couch, everything else has been accumulated over many years of bachelorhood." He sounds wistful, not proud of his status.

"Would you like to sit in here or out on the terrace? I have a couple of propane heaters out there to take the edge off." He's standing less than a foot from me, looking directly into my eyes, which most men don't do. I feel weirdly drawn to him but assume he's thinking more about coffee than me. And then his right hand softly caresses the small of my back, perhaps inadvertently, and I lean in and kiss him gently on the lips.

We start out on the sectional, removing each other's running wear while kissing and exploring. I haven't had sex or any form of intimacy for two years, and he seems just as hungry for a physical connection. He feels and smells so good, like a man, and he's not in a hurry, which I like.

We move off the couch and onto a plush ivory rug. He hesitates momentarily and asks, "Is this okay?"

I nod, and we continue.

I shower in the guest bathroom on the upper level of his condo. He's left a hair dryer, extra bath towels, and a pair of comfy cotton sweats and socks on the bed in the guest room. I walk down the spiral staircase and see him sitting at a glass table on the terrace. He's showered, changed into khakis and a sweater, made coffee and egg-and-cheese breakfast sandwiches, and set out a plate of food and a mug filled with steaming coffee for me. There's also a bowl of fresh fruit in the center of the table.

"Did you find everything okay?" he asks, taking a sip of coffee from a red-and-white Wisconsin Badgers mug.

I run a hand through my ultra-short black mane and decide not to tell him about the time I wasted searching for a brush. "The shower felt great. Thanks. You've been busy."

"I hope it's not too cold out here. I wanted you to experience the view."

I try the coffee. It's hot and strong, and the propane contraption next to my fancy sling chair is spewing plenty of heat. I look out over the river and see the downtown skyscrapers, the IDS Tower and Wells Fargo Center. To the south, I can see the lakes and Bloomington skyline, and to the east, downtown Saint Paul. Part of me can't believe what's happening this morning; another part has always rolled with the punches. I cut the bagel sandwich in half and take a bite. "Oh my, this is good. I'm usually lucky to eat a slice of peanut butter toast on the run."

"I enjoyed this morning very much," he says. He's so cool and in control but also polite and interested. He doesn't wait for my response. "Are you from the Twin Cities, Lincoln?"

"No. I grew up in Chicago and started out with the Chicago PD. I moved up here and joined the Minneapolis force about seven years ago."

"Chicago's been a vortex of violent crime for as long as I can remember. I don't blame you for leaving."

Even though I don't know what "vortex" means, I get it and hesitate to delve into more personal matters with someone I barely know, except intimately, but what the hell. "I didn't leave because of the violence—there's plenty in Minneapolis as well. I left to put some distance between me and my ex-husband, who's also a Chicago cop. He's an alcoholic who hasn't come to terms with his illness. The whole situation was too uncomfortable to continue. What about you, Rob, are you from around here?"

I can tell he wants to pursue more about my past, but that's all he's getting for now. He refills our mugs and then clasps his hands together and rests them on the table as he bends at the waist and leans toward me like he's got something important to say. "I'm originally from a small town on the north shore of Lake Superior, but I've lived in the Cities for over twenty years."

Now it's my turn to pry, both because I'm curious and because it's an occupational habit. "Looks like you live here alone. Has that always been the case?" That's pretty bold, but after an initial shudder, he seems more amused than irritated.

"I've never been married—you can interpret that any way you like. As for girlfriends, I've had a few, but none serious enough to marry. I'm not proud of being a bachelor, Lincoln, not at all, but I love my job, and I spend a lot of time lecturing at the law schools and mentoring at the Boys & Girls Clubs in Minneapolis. It's not the same as having your own kids, but it can be rewarding."

"I know what you mean," I say. "I get my kid fix vicariously through my sister's twin boys."

Rob looks out over the city and leans back in his chair. "The murder of Kate Patterson, the city council president," he says out of the blue. "I saw the headline on the front page of the paper while you were in the shower and scanned the article. I was out of town yesterday, so that's the first I've heard about it. What a shocker."

"It's not just a shocker. It's my case."

I'm relieved that he knows enough not to ask about the investigation. Our conversation ends a few moments later when I hear the bells in the clock tower above city hall. It's noon, and I tell him I need to go. At first I decline his offer to drive me back to the club, but I'm glad he insists. I'm not dressed for a long walk, and I don't feel like running, especially with a bag of damp clothes. We take the elevator to an underground parking garage. He explains that he rarely drives anymore; he walks or bikes to work and uses Uber or Lyft when he can.

We get into an older Mercedes sedan. It's clean and comfortable but too stodgy for me. We drive by Target Field, and he asks if I'm a Twins fan. I tell him I love baseball and the Cubs, though I can't help but follow the Twins after seven years. He's a season ticket holder. I like him even more.

When we get to the club, he looks into my eyes and smiles, placing his right hand over my left. "You can keep or toss those sweats, but I'd like to see you again."

"Sure," I say. "I'd like that too."

We exchange phone numbers even though I doubt he'll ever contact me. I unbuckle my seat belt, and we kiss, and then kiss again.

"Thanks for the ride and a better Sunday morning than I've had in a while."

CHAPTER 5

I get home at about one thirty and open my laptop and a cold beer to work on the Holloway case. The first thing I see is an email from Warren. Mayor Sampson has canceled our interview Monday morning "on the advice of counsel." He'll call to reschedule later in the week. Warren says he can't disclose the "real" reason in an email but will fill me in when he picks me up in the morning for our meeting with Patterson's aides. I'll let Warren soak up the gossip and rumors percolating among the minions in city hall while I delve into the private lives of the victim and her spouse. But first things first: who is Robin Gildemeister?

I google every permutation, combination, and abbreviation of Judge Robin Gildemeister and quickly conclude the man has no presence on social media. Unless he's got a pseudonym, he's not on Twitter, Instagram, Facebook, or even LinkedIn. He shows up in several newspaper articles reporting on criminal and civil trials, but there's nothing personal or controversial.

I click on his biography on the Minnesota judicial website. I'm familiar with the site because I've studied the bios of the two judges in whose courtrooms I've had to appear for homicide cases that went to trial. Rob's is the shortest by far. He received a BA from Union College in Schenectady, New York, and a law degree from the University of

Wisconsin. He was "engaged in the private practice of law" in Minneapolis before being appointed to the bench in 2012. That is it. Nothing about his law firm, private life, affiliations, family, hobbies, interests—nothing. He's a ghost on the World Wide Web.

I want to see him again.

More than once, I've spent a half hour or so watching the monitor in the control room. Gerald "Jerry" Wikelius paces like a caged animal in a Hennepin County jail cell, awaiting trial on a string of sexual assaults that occurred between July and November of last year. According to the mainstream media, he doesn't fit the profile of a serial rapist, though I think makes his profile is even creepier. A married, thirty-five-year-old father of two young children, Wikelius worked out of his home in Arden Hills as a bookkeeper for several small businesses. Prior to Thanksgiving weekend, he had no criminal record, not even a parking ticket.

According to the charging attorney's complaint, Wikelius abducted a nineteen-year-old woman as she left a dormitory on the U of M campus near the intersection of Oak and Washington shortly before midnight. He approached her from behind and pressed a massive forearm against her throat, nearly crushing her windpipe. He whispered in her ear that he had a knife and would use it if she screamed or didn't do exactly as he said. A bear of a man, he wore black leather gloves and a ski mask. His maroon Econoline van was parked less than a half block from the dorm. After struggling more than usual to maneuver her into the passenger seat, he confiscated her cell phone and tied her wrists together behind her back with a heavy zip tie, something she was sure he'd done before. Stuffing a handkerchief in her mouth and covering her eyes and most of her face with a thick cotton scarf, he flipped her phone into a dense boxwood hedge before climbing into the driver's seat. He threatened to slash her throat if she tried anything as he started the van and drove off.

Wikelius parked in a dark, vacant lot adjacent to an abandoned warehouse near the Milwaukee Road railroad depot. He was in control, his voice calm. He reminded her again to cooperate if she wanted to live. They'd be moving onto a mattress. He'd carefully planned everything, except that his victim was a U of M varsity hockey player, a goalie and the strongest woman on the team. As soon as he'd started the van, she began stretching and twisting the zip tie. She freed her hands in transit and used the time to devise a plan to escape, assuming he was telling the truth about the knife.

When he grabbed her by the shoulders to toss her into the back of the van, she lowered her blindfold, getting a good look at his startled mug a second before kicking it as hard as she could with the heel of a SOREL boot. While he cupped a bloody nose with his hands, she jumped out of the van, barely hearing him call her a "fucking bitch" because she was already two blocks away, running full throttle out of the warehouse district and toward the lights and action of downtown.

Her testimony will be critical to the prosecution's case. All of Jerry's other alleged victims, nine in total, were sexually assaulted in a van and then dumped alive but in shock in Loring Park between one and three in the morning, blindfolded, their wrists zip-tied behind them, their rescue depending on the goodness of strangers in the middle of the night. A few sobbed for hours before help came. Others screamed and howled.

Wikelius is a sick fuck who needs to go away forever, but I don't think he killed Billie Holloway. Warren does. Without a confession, we'll never prove it. There's no physical evidence—no DNA, no blindfold, and no zip tie. No need to blindfold a dead girl.

CHAPTER 6

Warren picks me up in the unmarked, black Explorer we share for work. He usually drives because, like most men, he likes to think he's in control and because I'd prefer to have my nose in my phone or laptop. I'm so keyed up to ask him something that I forget to thank him for the steaming cup of Colombian Reserve he's placed in my cupholder.

"What do you know about Judge Gildemeister, Robin Gildemeister?" I ask coyly, hoping not to get the deep Warren probe in return.

"One of the best, in my view," he replies without any hesitation, turning toward me with a look that asks why I want to know. Then he continues. "He's fair and treats everyone with respect. Some cops and prosecutors think he's too lenient on nonviolent offenders, but I like that he imposes severe consequences for blowing second chances. I've heard that his private life is a mystery. He's not married, and he doesn't socialize with court personnel."

"Wow, how do you know so much about him?"

"My nephew who works for the state public defender clerked for Gildemeister for a year. He was impressed with his intelligence and demeanor but calls him 'Judge Enigma' because he's so damn private. He even speculated the judge could have a double life as a spy or something nefarious. Now, the obvious question, what's your interest in Judge

Gildemeister?"

"I went for a long run yesterday morning. We nearly ran into each other in one of the tunnels a mile from downtown. He introduced himself and was very personable." I'm not quite ready to tell Warren that I'm having sex with a judge.

"So you were stalking him and now you want to get the lowdown before moving in for the kill." There's a bit of an edge to Warren's voice. He's tried to set me up with a few "eligible" men, but I've politely declined because they were either cops or parole officers. No, thank you.

"That's exactly right," I say. "I should have called you yesterday. We'd be married by now."

"Hey, all kidding aside," he says, "Sampson begged off our meeting. He claims his personal lawyer, not the city attorney, can't make it."

"Why would he need his personal lawyer?"

Marcus Sampson, a charismatic former federal prosecutor, is the first Black man to lead the city of Minneapolis. Only a few months in office, he's ripped apart and rebuilt the MPD in response to a hundred fifty years of systemic racism and, most recently, the killing of two defenseless Black men by a handful of my former colleagues, now convicted felons—killing caught on camera, unjustified killing, murder. And even though both Warren and I are beneficiaries of many of the reforms at what is now the Minneapolis Peacekeeping and Public Safety Department, the MPPSD, I prefer MPD, and I still call it the MPD.

"I think the mayor is hiding something," Warren says as he turns into the Fourth Street ramp across from city hall. "He and Patterson were on opposite sides of disemboweling the department, and he kicked her ass. She should have learned that if rich white folks want a voice in politics in this city, they better fall in line. There's a presumption down here today that white equals racist."

"Take it easy, Warren. You don't really mean that."

He's out of the squad before I finish the sentence and doesn't respond. Maybe he didn't hear me. I grab a nylon portfolio from the back seat and follow him to a bank of elevators on the fifth level of the ramp, where there's a line forming to get into one working elevator. It's seven forty-five on Monday morning, and the city is humming with activity. Warren hates crowds. He admits he's claustrophobic.

"Let's take the stairs," he suggests, opening the metal exit door for me.

We're both wearing our "dress" uniforms—blue blazer, white oxford cloth shirt (no tie), and gray wool pants for Warren, and the same for me except I've substituted a pencil skirt for the pants. I'm dressed for the seventy-degree skyway, not the twenty-degree sidewalk, but the skyway doesn't connect to city hall so, like a couple of true Minnesotans, we walk outside with our heads down, not saying a word but freezing our butts off.

———

Offices of the mayor and city council are on the third floor of city hall, a stately red-granite building that's over a hundred years old and seems to be in a constant state of restoration and repair. It's worth the trouble, I think. There's a statue of Hubert Humphrey, a former mayor, senator, and vice president, whose bronze likeness no one's tried to topple, and a rogues' gallery of former mayors near the two-story council chambers. A tall, attractive blonde woman wearing an expensive blue business suit with matching, blue-rimmed glasses is waiting for us near the third-floor elevator.

"Good morning. You must be Detectives Barnes and Lindquist. I'm Natalie Brinkman. I'm—or I was—Council President Patterson's chief policy aide. We're meeting in a conference room just down the hall. I apologize for not telling you earlier, but Josh Cummins, my colleague, couldn't make it this morning." She talks while leading us down a narrow corridor inside the cavernous city offices. "He and his partner had a baby a few weeks ago."

"That's understandable," Warren says, but we give each other a WTF look, signifying that maybe the death of your boss is important enough to give up a few hours of paternity leave.

Natalie stops at a conference room near the end of the corridor. There's a coffee dispenser, bottled water and juices, and a tray of bagels and pastries on a serving cart to the left of the entrance. To the right is a rectangular oak conference table, circa 1960, surrounded by eight matching oak chairs, designed for work, not comfort.

"I see you already have coffee, but please help yourself to something to eat," Natalie offers while refilling a coffee mug. "Sit wherever you like. It'll just be the three of us."

I grab a bottle of water, and Warren uses a napkin to slide a chocolate donut filled with custard onto a paper plate. We sit across the table from Natalie. It appears she's been crying. Her glasses can't hide the redness and swelling under her eyes, and her hair is pulled back in a tight bun that's practical but seems unnatural.

"Thanks for meeting with us this morning," I say. "I'm sure this is a difficult time for you."

"I just don't get it," she says, looking up from her mug. "I've been with Councilwoman Patterson for five years. I've been on her campaign and council staff through an election cycle. I know a lot of people have disagreed with her positions on issues. Some think she's aloof and condescending, but that's politics. I can't think of anyone who would do this, who would attack her physically."

"Tell us about her relationship with her husband, Dr. Bagley," Warren asks, deciding to get more information before attacking the helpless donut hiding under his napkin.

"I'm going to be brutally honest about this because it might be important and because she's gone. She and Paul had an arrangement. They stayed together for their son and their careers, but they both had discreet relationships with other people, Paul won't deny it. He's not an easy man to like, in my view."

"Bad temper?" I ask.

"Not really. Just a gigantic, brittle ego coupled with an inability to admit mistakes. Some might call it a God complex."

"Others might call him an asshole," Warren says. There's nothing Warren hates more than an empty suit who's blinded by his own ego.

"Maybe. You'll judge for yourselves, I'm sure, but I never saw him treat Kate with hostility or even disrespect. He's a conservative Republican, so they're on opposite ends of the political spectrum, but in my opinion, what pulled them apart was her ambition. He wanted her to be a homemaker, to volunteer at the local hospital and nursery school. He's five years older. Early in their marriage, I think she deferred to him and was content to work part time in a bookstore in Linden Hills and to focus on their home and his growing medical practice. But when Paul Jr. started school, that wasn't enough. She became more interested in social issues and politics and opened a boutique public relations firm in Minneapolis. By the time she hired me, she and Paul were not a happy couple." There's something about her little speech that seems rehearsed and manipulative.

"When I called Dr. Bagley to tell him the terrible news about his wife, a woman answered the phone in his hotel room in Arizona. It was eight in the morning. Any idea who that might have been?" I'm glad she introduced the couple's infidelity but not confident it will lead to anything worthwhile.

"According to Kate, he's been seeing a sales rep from a medical device company that makes stents. She's just one in a long line of mistresses, each one a little younger and prettier than her predecessor."

"What about your boss?" Warren asks. "Did she have a love interest?" The phrase "love interest" coming from Warren sounds weird.

Natalie stares at her cup for several seconds. "Not currently," she finally says.

"How 'not currently'?" Warren probes.

Natalie is a cool customer, but she's squirming like a perp about to confess. I just can't tell whether it's all an act. Even the red eyes don't seem real. "She made me swear not to tell anyone, and I think it was over before this past weekend." Having made the decision to unload, she regains her composure, as Warren and I anticipate a bombshell. "If this becomes public knowledge, it could destroy a family and a political career." Natalie's eyes search mine for some kind of reassurance, but none is coming. "Kate was having an affair with Marcus Sampson."

Warren appears stunned by the revelation. I'm not.

"You said you thought it was over. Why?" I ask.

"Christie Sampson gave birth to twin boys a week ago. Kate told me then that she and Marcus agreed things had to end. I didn't see the mayor at all last week until Friday. I saw him sneak into her office and close the door late in the afternoon. I waited until six thirty for him to leave so I could talk to her, but I had to meet a friend for dinner at seven. I texted and called her later that night, but we never connected."

"Tell us more about this relationship," Warren says. "When and how did it start?"

"It began about two months ago. They had marathon meetings over the dismantling of the police department. As everybody knows, the mayor wanted to fire the chief and deputy chiefs and create a new leadership team patterned after the Camden, New Jersey, community policing model. Kate admired the chief and wanted to keep him and most of the current structure but rip up the union contract. The council was divided. As you know, the mayor's vision won out. What nobody knows is that those intense late-night meetings led to an intimate relationship."

"How did they keep this relationship so secret?" I ask, wondering if Natalie was really the only one who knew about it.

"The mayor had a lot to lose both personally and professionally if word of their affair got out. Sleeping with a rival wouldn't play well with his base or his young wife. And Kate has always been fiercely protective of her private life. She said the only places they'd meet were Sampson's office and her family's cabin near Hayward. No hotels, restaurants, or other public places where someone could spot them. Of course, I can't be a hundred percent sure that no one else suspects or knows, but I'm sure Kate told no one."

"What about Sampson's wife?" Warren asks. "What do you know about her?"

"I know the state DFL party hired her as a community organizer right out of college. She grew up in the Hawthorne neighborhood and must have made a lot of friends. She developed a reputation for getting out the vote in places that traditionally didn't. She started working for Sampson as an aide a year ago and may have been responsible for his messy divorce last year. They've only been married for six months, and their baby boys are the mayor's only children. She's twenty-five, smart, attractive and, I've heard, concerned about her husband's fidelity. If she found out, or finds out, that he was unfaithful with Kate Patterson, there will be fireworks, or at least flying dishes and utensils. Even so, I can't imagine her attacking Kate, especially in the horrible way it happened. It seems more like the random, violent act of a stranger, don't you think?"

"It might have been exactly that," I say, "but there's some evidence, I can't say what, that Councilwoman Patterson knew her killer. In any case, it's way too early to draw any conclusions about that, so we need to cast a wide net and gather as much information as we can."

She seems disappointed by my response. "I wish I could be more helpful," she says insincerely. "I'm probably forgetting something important, but the news about Kate came as such a shock."

"Of course," says Warren with an empathetic nod. "To your knowledge, did your boss have any other close friends to whom she might have confided about her relationship with the mayor?"

"Not anymore." Natalie sighs. "Her best friend from college died a couple years ago. Other than me, she was the only person to whom Kate would have disclosed intimate personal details. She had hundreds of connections and colleagues, but she kept them all at arm's length. Her rivals called her cold and calculating. That's because she was an incredibly ambitious woman who wanted to change the world. She didn't trust many people."

"Did she make a habit of running in the dark?" I ask, wondering whether a stalker could have anticipated Patterson's predawn jog.

"Running was her stress reliever. She ran two out of every three days, twenty to thirty miles a week. Depending on her schedule, she might run from her office around Lake of the Isles or along the river at noon, or on a treadmill at her club after work. It was more haphazard than planned, but when she could, she ran. She once told me that when she couldn't sleep, she'd get up, meditate for fifteen minutes, and then head for the lakes. That's probably what happened last Saturday."

"Could be," Warren says, thinking out loud. "When did you last communicate with your boss, and what was the gist of that conversation?" Warren is getting antsy. He's ready to wrap this up.

"We had a quick lunch together last Friday at Turbo Taco. That's the last time we talked, but Josh was with us, so it was strictly city business, except for discussing his new bundle of joy. As I said, the mayor spent most of Friday afternoon in her office. I tried calling her at about eight Friday night and left a message on her cell. Her only response was a cryptic text just after midnight. I didn't see it until Saturday morning."

Before delivering the punch line, Natalie loses it, covering her face with her hands and sobbing. Warren's about to say something, but I grab his wrist and give him the "not now" shake of my head, knowing that Natalie will compose herself and continue. I hand her a paper napkin, which she uses to wipe her face and dab her eyes.

"I honestly don't know why she sent it or what she was referring to, but her text was in caps. She never did that. I'll just show it to you." She lifts her iPhone from the table and, after a few seconds of searching, hands it to me.

WE NEED TO TALK!!!

Warren waits until we leave city hall to comment on our meeting with Natalie. Her preppy, rich-girl look and persona are a bit hard to stomach, but it's tough to be normal when your dad is the owner of the largest commercial real estate developer in the country. There's something about her description of Patterson's affair that doesn't ring true. She's definitely cunning and manipulative, yet I have a feeling she'll be a critical link to the truth before this is over.

"Do you think she's telling us everything she knows about Patterson's relationship with the mayor?" Warren asks as he sets a brisk pace back to the parking ramp. "I mean, forgetting the bullshit display of emotion, don't you think that last little disclosure about the text should have been the first thing she told us?"

"I think she's grieving in her own aloof, I-don't-really-give-a-fuck-about-anybody-else way," I say, not disagreeing with my partner but wondering whether he had a bad night. "I also think I need to remind the BCA we need Patterson's cell phone records and last thirty days of text messages ASAP. I say we interview each council member to get a better feel for her world."

"Good idea. Let's transition to divide-and-conquer mode this afternoon. We'll each take half the council and then compare notes. I'm meeting Dr. Bagley at his office at noon. Maybe you can set something up with Sampson's office for later this week. We'll need to double-team him and his lawyer."

"I don't look forward to that meeting," I say as we buckle up in the Explorer. "He's self-righteous and can be downright hostile. Not a good combo when we're asking about extramarital activities. I wonder who'll be representing him."

"I have no idea," Warren says, "but they'll be no match for Lincoln Barnes."

CHAPTER 7

Warren drops me off at my apartment on his way to Edina. Like most detectives in the metro, I work from home about fifty percent of the time, up from twenty percent prior to COVID and down from eighty percent at the height of the pandemic. I change into sweats and check my phone. Two messages and a text grab my attention. One of the messages is from the Hennepin County medical examiner's office, wanting to schedule a meeting for later in the week to review preliminary autopsy results on Patterson. The other is from our admin in homicide. Some guy called the tip line, left his name and number, which is unusual, and said he saw something suspicious near Lake Harriet early Saturday morning and thought the police might be interested. I make a note to call him.

The text stuns me, but in a good way. It's from Brianna, one of the girls rebuilding Billie Holloway's memorial in Loring Park on Sunday morning.

Could you meet me at the Starbucks on France & 75th @ 4? I need to talk before I lose courage. Thx. Bri

I don't hesitate.

Yes. I'll be there.

Detective Barnes

Suddenly hungry, I slice a banana and some fresh strawberries and dump the fruit and a few cashews in a bowl of Greek yogurt. I spend most of the afternoon setting up appointments with the six council members on my list, five Democrats and a Green Party guy. The Minneapolis City Council has not included a Republican for over a decade. I can honestly say I don't know any personally, though I think Warren, who claims to be an unaffiliated independent, leans that way. We share a belief that few politicians are worthy of respect these days, a sad state of affairs in a democracy.

When I was growing up in Chicago, I thought all Republicans were white and rich. Raising two mixed-race girls and working full time, my mom never said much about politics, although she belonged to a union and always voted for Democrats. My dad was an ardent supporter of Jesse Jackson. He liked Bill Clinton but said he'd be a better leader if somebody lopped off his dick. He was wary of anyone named Daley and passionate about Chicago's favorite adopted son, Barack Obama.

A warm front brings clearing skies and temperatures in the low forties by midafternoon. I decide to pack a bag with running gear. I'll get in a quick ten-miler around Normandale Lake and the Hyland Park Reserve after meeting with Brianna. Maybe I'll hear from the judge.

I spot Brianna sitting at a table for two in a corner of a Starbucks that's not much larger than a kiosk. Slender and pretty, with short brown hair and olive skin, she looks older than I recall from Sunday. She's wearing a gray wool skirt with a red-and-white crewneck sweater. The button pinned just below her collarbone says, "Go Red Knights." She's cradling a clear plastic cup filled with an iced coffee drink. I approach and set my phone and spiral notebook on the table.

"Hi, Brianna. I'm going to order a cup of coffee. Can I get you anything?"

"No, thank you, Officer Barnes."

I get a tall decaf and return to the table.

"I see you go to Benilde," I say. Benilde-St. Margaret's is a private Catholic high school in St. Louis Park where students don't wear uniforms but have a strict dress code.

"That's right," she says. "I wanted to go to Edina, but my dad went to

Benilde, and both my parents are Catholic. It's been a better experience than I thought, especially basketball. I'm on the varsity, and we play DeLaSalle in a big game tonight. I only have about fifteen minutes to talk."

"Understood. Well, I hope you win your game. I played a little basketball in high school myself, and my brother-in-law coaches the Highland Park boys. I really appreciate that you reached out to me, Brianna. I'm here to listen and help if I can."

She's nervous, chewing on ice and staring at her cup like it's a crystal ball. "I made a decision after it happened, after Billie died, that I wouldn't tell anyone what I know. I hoped that someone else would know something and come forward, but that hasn't happened. I was so scared back then and so, so sad." Two rivulets of tears stream down her face, but she wipes them away with her napkin before I can react. She clears her throat and looks up, staring at my coffee cup as she speaks. "But now I feel more guilt than fear, and when you told us you were investigating Billie's murder, I made the decision to tell you what maybe nobody else knows, except the man who killed her. If you've talked to Billie's parents, you know they're weird."

"I've talked to them many times, Brianna. I know they're deeply religious and didn't approve of Billie's lifestyle. I also know they made it difficult for Billie to live in their house, but I think at least her mom regrets that. Why do you say they're weird?"

"Her dad is a television evangelist. I don't understand how he can go on TV every Sunday morning and tell everyone to come to Jesus, put their trust in Jesus, try to be like Jesus while he's not anything like Jesus. Jesus wouldn't have given Billie an ultimatum—stop trying to be a girl, undergo therapy, and act like a man or get out. He's made millions of dollars being a hypocrite."

I'm surprised by Brianna's hostility and maturity. Noel Henry Holloway is senior pastor of Riverwood Church in Eden Prairie, one of the exploding mega-churches with a congregation approaching forty thousand and ten campuses in the metro. Each location watches Holloway's weekly message via digital technology and audiovisual equipment rivaling those of any theater or sports arena in the country. Each campus has its own gospel rock band and drama group, and Riverwood's main Sunday service is broadcast to thousands more on cable television. With an annual budget exceeding a hundred million dollars, Riverwood pays its senior pastor a million dollars a year plus incentives for new members and collections. His wife makes about half that as director of music and drama. I know all this because I've done exhaustive research on the family, hoping to discover some connection between them and Billie's killer.

"That might be true, but I don't think either of Billie's parents had anything to do with her abduction, at least not directly." Billie had lived in a one-bedroom apartment in a rundown brick tenement a block off University Avenue, about a mile from the U of M. She'd moved out of her parents' place during the summer before her senior year, lying about her age and living with a staffer from the Gender and Sexuality Center for Queer and Trans Life at the university.

"I think Billie's landlord killed her." Brianna looks me straight in the eyes for the first time. The burden of keeping her secret has been lifted.

"Her landlord? I interviewed her landlord six months ago. She's a woman in her early forties who inherited the building from her father. She drives an MTC bus and lives in South Minneapolis with her boyfriend. You think she killed Billie?"

"I've never met her. I visited Billie at her place at least once a week. I lied to my parents. Told them I was going to the community center to play ball or to a friend's house in Edina or wherever I made up at the time. I was Billie's closest friend, and no one knew. Billie's roommate, Maura, always dealt with the landlord. It was her apartment. Three months before Billie died, Maura moved to Madison, and Billie was on her own. One night when I was over, a tall man with a scruffy beard pounded on the door and said he was there to collect the rent. His name was Ken. That's all she ever called him. She had the money that night, but she told me later she was afraid of him. He said if she couldn't come up with the money, he'd let her pay in other ways. Then she lost her job cleaning rooms at a hotel that went bankrupt and got a part-time job as a server at the Thai café on Oak Street. After that, I Venmoed money to her when I could.

"Billie's mom really wanted her to come home and secretly sent her cash but was too afraid to visit, thinking her dad would find out. A week before she died, Billie told me she thought Ken was following her in his car, a rusted out minivan with a noisy engine. That's all I know, Detective.

I thought for sure someone else would know about this guy. I really did!" Tears start streaming down her cheeks, and she wipes them away with the back of her hand.

"No one could blame you, Brianna. No one. I'm so proud of you for telling me. I promise to investigate this guy, and I'll try my best not to involve you in any way. I think it would be wise for you to tell your parents about your friendship with Billie and your conversation with me, but I will respect your decision not to for as long as I can."

Brianna glances at her phone and lifts her jacket from the back of a chair. "I need to go now," she says. "Please let me know what you find out."

I can't stop myself from getting up to give her a hug. "I'll be in touch," I say. "Call or text me if you need anything or just want to talk."

Working at the kitchen table while inhaling a gourmet dinner of tomato soup out of a can and a grilled cheese sandwich, I call Warren and tell him about my conversation with Brianna. He's home after spending some quality time with Paul Bagley.

"Sheila never mentioned that her boyfriend collected rents at Billie's building," he says. Sheila Bjore was Billie's landlord.

"I suspect his collection activities were focused on one apartment. I interviewed every tenant in the building and not one mentioned anything about an intimidating, bearded rent collector."

"One of us could call Sheila to get some background on this guy," Warren muses, "but she might alert him."

"I'm already working it," I say. "Before I left Starbucks, I ran a check on any 911 calls made by Bjore since 2018. Only one. A domestic against one Ken Tarnowski. She claimed he choked her in a drunken rage in December of 2019."

"Fast work."

"I just called Marci—she's the one who's fast. Tarnowski has a DUI and a couple of stalking charges involving teenage girls in addition to this 2019 assault. No jail time. The stalking charges were both dropped. He's ten years younger than Sheila and, unlike his girlfriend, is active on social media, YouTube and Twitch to be specific."

"Twitch?"

"I'll explain later. For now, it looks like this guy's a professional gamer, as in video games."

"That's a real job?"

"Let me do a little more research, and we can discuss tomorrow." I don't have enough time to explain to Warren how someone can make a decent living playing Call of Duty or Fortnite.

"I guess Wikelius might not be the guy after all," Warren says, half to himself.

"This is a real lead, Warren. In fact, I think we may want to get a warrant to search Tarnowski's van."

"You want me to take care of that?" Warren has developed a rapport with a few of the more experienced judges in Hennepin County. "Or maybe your new friend will want to help?"

"He might. He knows the facts of the case for sure." I decide to change the subject. "How'd it go with Bagley?"

"The good doctor was more upset than I thought he'd be. Probably because Paul Jr. is devastated, though I sense senior still has feelings for her. I've never understood how an open marriage could last, but he claims it worked for them, or maybe for him. He also swears he didn't know about her relationship with Sampson, which I told him has never been confirmed and is highly confidential. Anyway, he doesn't believe it ever happened. He thought his wife was taking a break from relationships after the sudden end of a long, discreet affair with a former state legislator. Have you ever heard of Tom Amdahl?"

"The name sounds familiar," I say with no confidence. I'm a casual follower of state politics, not a wonk like Warren. "Didn't he die recently?"

"He was a lifelong bachelor who taught courses in politics and public affairs at the Humphrey Institute. Apparently, he was on the Minneapolis Charter Commission with Kate Patterson, and they enjoyed each other's company. According to Dr. Bagley, Amdahl died in bed *in flagrante delicto* with the council president at his cabin up on Gull Lake. A massive heart attack. He was only seventy."

"Not a pleasant thought or image," I say.

"That was two months ago," Warren says. "I don't know how Patterson finessed it, but her relationship with Amdahl was never public knowledge as far as I can tell."

"Then it never happened."

"I suppose. Bagley also mentioned how odd it was that his wife's best friend was also killed two years ago."

"Murdered?"

"He claimed it was a suspicious death during a vacation. Apparently, Patterson and her college roommate married two medical-school students who were also roommates. One of them was Bagley. He claims his old roommate hasn't been himself since his wife's death."

"Do you think Dr. Bagley will be grieving two weeks from now?" I can't shake that bad first impression.

"That's harsh, Lincoln. Though, given his attitude and narcissism, I don't think there's room for an intelligent, opinionated woman in his life."

"Speaking of huge egos," I say, "I got us a meeting with Sampson. Wednesday afternoon at three thirty in Freddie Tyler's office."

"Freddie Tyler? Hired gun for the rich and famous when they're in deep shit? The mayor must have something to hide."

"Let's hope he knows something because my half of the council gave me zilch. Not one admitted a relationship with Patterson beyond council business. One called her the ice lady and another a heartless witch. They all said she was organized and sharp but distant and condescending. She outworked everyone and was everyone's second choice for council president. Not a sympathetic group."

"And each of them was their first choice," Warren says. "I'll start on my half in the morning. Then we'll compare notes and decide if we should do any in-person interviews. I'm pretty familiar with this cast of characters, and I can't think of anyone who wouldn't have come forward by now if they knew something."

"I'll work on a warrant for Ken Tarnowski and call you tomorrow."

A text message sends a shot of adrenaline mixed with testosterone down my spine and brings back feelings from better times. It's from the judge.

Another run tomorrow night? Dinner?

Rob

CHAPTER 8

I hate swimming. Unfortunately, a competitive triathlete must be a competent, if not elite, swimmer. Training for the Campeche Half IRONMAN, I need to swim over a mile in under thirty-five minutes, bike fifty-six miles in under three hours, and run a half marathon in under an hour and fifty minutes. Accomplish all three and I finish in under six hours. That's my goal.

I'm running thirty miles a week now and, when the streets aren't covered in ice and snow, biking sixty. On Tuesday and Thursday mornings, I drive to the club at five and force myself to gulp, gasp, slap, kick, and splash for ninety minutes. Then I throw up.

I spend the day drafting an application for a warrant to search Tarnowski's van and prepping for the meeting with Sampson. As a federal prosecutor, Sampson gained hero status in Minneapolis when he successfully prosecuted one of my former colleagues for violating the civil rights of a Black man who'd inadvertently locked himself out of a tiny bungalow on the north side before a night of heavy drinking at a dive bar a few blocks away. Patrolling the neighborhood at one in the morning, the officers spied a man trying to maintain his balance atop an arborvitae bush while prying a window open with a screwdriver.

Startling him with a spotlight while "step away from the house and put your hands in the air" bellowed through a loudspeaker, the lead officer shot him through the heart with his Glock because, instead of raising his hands, he'd reached into the back pocket of his jeans to pull out a wallet that contained his driver's license, proof that the bungalow was his home. The police union's hired gun was no match for Assistant US Attorney Marcus Sampson, so her client will spend the next twelve years in Marion federal penitentiary. Less than a year later, Sampson, his campaign bankrolled by some unknown benefactors, beat the incumbent, one-term mayor, also a Democrat, by a landslide.

There's quite a contrast between Marcus, the big-time politician, and Kenny, the big-time gamer with a small-time but disturbing rap sheet. Ken Tarnowski has a history of hanging around high schools and middle schools, making people uncomfortable. I track down the two stalking complaints, one involving a sixteen-year-old at North High and the other a junior at Washburn. He's a giant of a man with perverted, predatory instincts that he hadn't acted upon until maybe he did and with the most horrible of consequences.

The judge and I meet in the lobby of Alumni Gymnasium on the campus of Macalester College in Saint Paul. Highland Park plays Richfield High at six o'clock in a sectional semifinal game, with the winner playing Saint Thomas Academy on Friday for a berth in the state tournament. The judge looks corporate and handsome in a charcoal, fitted wool sport coat over a powder-blue oxford cloth shirt and blood-red silk tie covered with tiny gold scales of justice. He smiles warmly and hands me a ticket and program.

"Thanks," I say, thinking he looks even younger all duded up than he did over the weekend. "Nice tie."

"It's totally inappropriate," he says, shaking his head, "but it was a Christmas gift from my two law clerks, and it's usually covered by a robe."

"Oh, c'mon," I tease as I walk ahead of him into the gym. I'm wearing jeans and a red, hooded sweatshirt with the Highland Park Scots logo, a gift from my brother-in-law, Coach Decker. "I like it. I hope you came straight from court though. Otherwise, you're way too fancy-pants to hang with me."

I climb the bleachers two steps at a time, searching for a spot at least ten rows behind my sister and mother, who are two rows behind the

Highland bench. There's been an incredible resurgence in school spirit since the COVID restrictions were cautiously lifted. It's fifteen minutes before game time, and there aren't many open seats. The Scots haven't been to the state tournament for forty years, and there's a feeling that this team has a chance.

In his fourth year as head coach, Craig has rebuilt the program from the bottom up, with summer camps, clinics for AAU coaches, and involvement in youth programs throughout the district. During the season, he invites middle-school players to Saturday-morning practices to participate in drills and scrimmage with the varsity. It's old school, but it works, especially when you combine an infectious love of the game with the most positive attitude I've ever seen.

"I hate to say this," says the judge, studying his program while watching the teams run pregame drills, "but I think Highland is going to get creamed."

"What are you talking about?" I protest, waving to my mom, who won't stop staring at us. I'll have to introduce her to the judge at halftime, and I'm already nervous.

He points to the teams' rosters in the program. "Highland starts a freshman and two sophomores, and their front court averages about six two Richfield has a six-eight post who's committed to the Badgers next year. Hey, Highland's had a great year, but Richfield only has two losses, and they're ranked third in their class."

"You are a frickin' Mr. Know-It-All, Judge Gildemeister, but I say Richfield won't know what to do with our full-court zone press."

Richfield's up by sixteen at half. Their lead is twenty when we leave, with five minutes to go. Unfortunately, my attraction to the judge grows by the minute. Subjected to cross-examination by my mom during halftime, he admitted he "played a little ball" in high school. Otherwise, he listens more than he talks, preferring to ask me questions about triathlon training and to watch the game with genuine interest, even cheering for the Scots for my benefit. Occasionally, he touches me subtly but intentionally on the shoulder, the knee, and the wrist. It makes me smile inside.

Though we're not dressed for the pelting sleet outside, we decide to brave it and rendezvous for a late dinner at Brasa on Grand Avenue. We each order the smothered chicken bowl and split a basket of tortilla chips with guacamole. I order a Diet Coke but change to Castle Danger

Ale on tap after he orders one in a frosted glass. We briefly commiserate about the game. He reminds me of the Scots' youth, and I don't feel so bad for Craig. Next year.

I'm relieved when he asks about Brianna. I didn't want to ruin a nice evening with work, but I would have.

"She reached out to me, Rob, so I met with her yesterday. She provided new information about a person of interest, a man who had scared Billie and has a history as a stalker. He wasn't even on our radar."

"Why now?" he asks, sitting back in his chair with a fixed gaze that signals his full attention.

"At first she was scared and didn't want her parents to find out she was spending time with Billie. She was sure someone else would identify this guy, but when no one did, she became distraught, still afraid to get involved but wanting to do something to avenge her friend's death. Plus, she trusts me to shield her identity, if that's possible."

"So, you think this guy did it?"

"I think there's enough evidence to merit searching his place and vehicle for traces of the victim. I spent part of today digging into his past and preparing an application."

"If you've got it, I'll take a look after we eat."

"Thanks. I really appreciate it."

The food is delicious, especially the chicken. The judge asks about my family. He's especially interested in my parents' relationship, which I don't mind discussing with a man who wants to get to know me. But when I try to turn the tables and ask about his family, he doesn't mention parents.

"I have an older half-sister who teaches English and smokes a lot of pot in Colorado Springs. She supports a guy who's a part-time poet and part-time handyman, though I don't think he's made any money doing either."

When I ask if his mom and dad are still living, he's almost defensive.

"Let's just say I was raised by my grandmother, and she died over twenty years ago."

I decide not to probe, not yet.

We finish eating after nine, and he takes some time to review and sign the Tarnowski warrant.

"Very thorough, Detective," he says, handing it back to me. As we put on our coats, I'm wondering whether the evening will continue after Brasa, but not for long.

"I'm in the middle of a murder trial, Lincoln. It should be over Friday, but I need to review a few motions for court tomorrow." We walk to our cars, and he curls an arm around my waist, drawing me close. "How about we go for an early-evening run on Friday and then I make dinner at my place?"

"I'll have to check my calendar," I say coyly. "Do you want to meet at the Target Center club?"

"Since I'm not sure when the case will go to the jury, why don't you come to the Government Center around five thirty? I might be done by then, but you can bring a laptop or book and wait in my chambers on the ninth floor. I'll leave the door unlocked. Text me tomorrow if you can make it."

A book? He pulls me towards him and kisses me gently on the lips. I've never been attracted to anyone or anything tender. I kiss him again like I mean it.

"I'll be there," I say.

CHAPTER 9

Sheila Bjore lives in a comfortable three-bedroom rambler in the Diamond Lake neighborhood of South Minneapolis. According to Warren, the homes in this area were built before World War II. This one has been updated with white vinyl siding and blue metal shutters. Sheila's a landlord and property manager, so I'm not surprised her place has street appeal. We bring a team from the property division to search every inch of Sheila's home at seven in the morning. Three of them walk around to the detached garage facing a back alley in the rear of the property. The garage is a two-story affair, with an apartment or studio on the second floor.

Some might consider this a "high-risk" warrant under the MPD's revised guidelines for no-knock entries, but Warren and I agree to announce our presence at least three times before resorting to force. Several body cams will record our actions. It's a clear, cold day in the city, a good day to follow the rules.

Sheila opens the door within seconds of the first knock wearing a white terry-cloth robe and maybe some panties. She's a few years past forty but appears younger with a slim figure and perfect, round breasts that may have been purchased. Her chestnut hair is streaked with gray and gathered in a ponytail that shoots out a slot in the back of a Twins cap and dangles between her shoulder blades. She could use a little makeup around tired smoker's eyes, but I'm thinking she aspires to play the part of the tough working broad, and she's succeeding. Anyone who drives an MTC bus in the inner city has to be tough.

"What's this about, Warren?"

The first-name basis surprises me. Warren interviewed her twice about five months ago and got nothing—she said she never met Billie and was in Duluth, visiting her mother, on the night of the abduction. Because Warren knows her, he'll serve the warrant.

"Good morning, Ms. Bjore. We've got a warrant to search your property and to take possession of a 2006 Dodge Caravan, Minnesota plate number GSX 441, in connection with the kidnapping and murder of Billie Holloway on August 24, 2021." Warren hands her a copy of the warrant, and three officers move past her and into the house.

"I already told you I wasn't even here that day, Detective, and that vehicle belongs to my boyfriend, Ken, not me."

"We're aware of that, ma'am. We'd also like to interview Kenneth Tarnowski. Is he in the house?" Warren is all business this morning, but I sense he might have been less formal with Sheila out of my presence.

"Why would you want to question Kenny? He's a tech guy who's got nothing to do with my properties. Besides, he's in Vegas at a gamers' convention. I don't expect him back until tomorrow night. You're wasting your time on him, Warren. He was with me in Duluth on that day anyway."

"I'll make a note of that, Ms. Bjore," Warren says, using his most patronizing voice. It's time for me to step in.

"I'm Detective Barnes, Ms. Bjore. Here's my card. I'd appreciate a call when Mr. Tarnowski returns. Or you can ask him to call me. If I don't hear anything by Thursday morning, I'll be back."

"This is total bullshit, Warren, and you know it," she says, completely ignoring me.

The search at Sheila's is pretty much a bust. Either she or Kenny is a complete neat freak. Warren and I agree on which one. The floors and walls are spotless, the furniture dusted and clean. Every cupboard, every drawer, and every closet is pristine. Clothes are laundered and folded, and business files are organized and put away. There's a smell in the air, a combination of ammonia and bleach. There's no way any of Billie's clothing, personal effects, or blood could survive for six months in this environment.

The garage is a different story. The second-floor addition, a twenty-by-thirty-foot room with exposed beams and an open ceiling to the roof, is clearly Tarnowski's workspace. Thousands of dollars in computer and broadcasting equipment—modems, monitors, microphones, webcams, and computer mouses—are strewn and stacked on and under a long metal table. A flat-screen TV hangs from a wooden beam above the gaming table, and a ripped leather executive chair is stationed between the tallest monitor and a blinking webcam. Bags of potato chips (some opened) and empty beer, energy drink, and soda cans are scattered about the tiled floor along with various items of men's clothing, from dirty boxers to down vests. A single bed with an extra-long mattress is unmade and reeks of BO.

Our team rifles through everything but only takes the hard drive from his desktop computer and the minivan for further inspection and testing. I know Warren is getting skeptical. While I haven't seen anything definitive, my hyperactive senses tell me there's a connection between Kenneth Tarnowski and Billie Holloway's murder. I can smell it.

CHAPTER 10

Freddie Tyler's office occupies the entire third floor of a historic stone-and-brick building on Hennepin Avenue in the heart of the Minneapolis entertainment district. According to Warren, Freddie has a dozen investigators and paralegals on his staff but has always been a sole practitioner, preferring not to share cases, fees, or the marquee with other lawyers. I can't say I'm familiar with many lawyers in the Twin Cities, but unless you're living in a van down by the river with no access to the outside world, you've heard of Freddie Tyler, or as his home page reads, "Freddie Tyler for the Defense."

During my seven years here, I can't recall a high-profile criminal case involving the rich or infamous that didn't involve Tyler—from U of M athletes accused of sexual assault to serial entrepreneurs accused of Ponzi schemes, from big-shot CEOs charged with killing their wives to the owner of a strip club indicted for running a Russian sex-slave operation. Freddie Tyler, a poor Black kid from East Texas who lost a track scholarship at Ohio State after ripping an Achilles and then graduated Order of the Coif from law school, is THE MAN.

Freddie's tall male receptionist escorts Warren and me into an intimate conference room with washed-brick walls and a view of Target Center out of floor-to-ceiling, double-pane windows. We sit in white leather chairs on the same side of a boat-shaped mahogany table. Standing in the doorway, he mentions that coffee, water, and soda are available in the mini-fridge in the back of the room.

"Mr. Tyler will be with you shortly," the polite, twenty-something, white man says, and then disappears.

Before we can get our phones and legal pads out, Freddie and the mayor fill up the small room, handle introductions, and sit across from us, Tyler with a leather folio and Sampson with a can of Diet Coke. I'm struck by the resemblance between two men separated in age by thirty years. Both are strikingly handsome, both well over six feet tall and tapered, both wearing silk three-piece suits worth more than my entire wardrobe, and both with closely trimmed goatees. The biggest difference: Freddie's hair and goatee are mostly white, whereas Sampson's are black. Freddie sets the mood with a peremptory speech.

"Being a public figure, my client has a reputation to preserve as well as a young family to protect. Of course, he had nothing to do with Council President Patterson's tragic death—his relationship with her was always professional in every way. He is here today to answer your relevant questions about that relationship."

I admit I'm intimidated by Tyler, but I know Warren isn't.

"Is it relevant that you were having an affair with Kate Patterson, Mayor?" Warren asks right out of the gate.

"It would be relevant," Sampson quickly replies, "but it's not true."

"But didn't you meet with her, alone in her office, for over three hours last Friday afternoon, hours before she was murdered?" I ask, taking the indirect approach.

"I met with her about city business last Friday. Is there something wrong with that?"

"Of course not," I say, "but Ms. Patterson confided in at least one other person that your relationship with her was more than collegial, that it was intimate."

Sampson barely reacts to the bait, taking a sip of his Diet Coke. Freddie calmly takes notes while his client shifts in his chair and leans in toward me with a cold stare.

"Someone other than Councilwoman Patterson may have told you that in order to defame me, but it's a fabrication, pure bullshit. All of my dealings and communication with Kate Patterson were about city business, period."

"And I strongly advise you not to spread that vicious lie beyond this room," says Tyler in his deepest, most authoritative voice.

I'm surprised that Sampson doesn't admit the affair, figuring that's why he's retained Tyler.

Warren gives me a subtle "what the hell?" look and gets the most obvious questions out of the way. "We're conducting a murder investigation, counsel, and we'll go wherever the facts take us. So, Mayor Sampson, what time did your meeting with Councilwoman Patterson end, and where were you between that time and six o'clock the next morning?"

"That's easy," says Sampson. "I left Kate Patterson's office at about six forty-five and returned to mine for fifteen or twenty minutes before going home. I was home with my wife, mother-in-law, and twin babies until eight on Saturday morning. In fact, I was up most of the night with my mother-in-law and the twins, trying to let Christie get some sleep between feedings."

I make a note to follow up with Sampson's mother-in-law after doing some research on her. I know the answer to my next question, but one of us needs to ask. "Can we get your cell phone records for the last sixty days, so we can corroborate your claim that your relationship with Council President Patterson was strictly business?"

"Not without a warrant, Detective Barnes," Tyler says. "However, if you divulge the identity of the liar who's been slandering Mayor Sampson, we'll consider giving you a redacted copy of his cell phone records, removing sensitive and confidential information that is irrelevant to your investigation."

Sampson's tight lips form a smirk at his lawyer's offer.

"We'll look into a warrant, Mr. Tyler," Warren says, "and we appreciate the offer. Let's shift gears and discuss Ms. Patterson's other relationships. Given your background as a federal prosecutor, I respect your perspective and opinion on this. Are you aware of anyone with personal animus toward the council president? Anyone you think might have committed this violent act or hired someone else to do it?"

Sampson considers the questions for at least twenty seconds before responding. "Detective, I'm going to assume there's evidence, something related to the victim or the manner in which this crime was carried out, that makes you think it was other than the unplanned, random act of a stranger, motivated by robbery, hate, or mental illness. When I heard the news of the horrible slaughter, that's where my thoughts went immediately. Kate Patterson was a brilliant, opinionated woman who was not afraid to confront the opposition, including me from time to time, but I can't think of anyone, political opponent or personal enemy, who would plan and then execute her murder. But keep in mind, I've been mayor of this city for a few months. She was on the council for more than a decade. Some others on the council and city staff might have a different perspective."

"We've been interviewing them, Mayor," I say, "but so far, we don't have any strong leads."

"Would you tell us if you did?" asks Tyler, a wry smile on this face.

"Probably not," says Warren, "but we appreciate your time and cooperation today." That familiar phrase means the meeting is over.

"Someone's lying," says Warren as he navigates heavy rush-hour traffic between downtown and my apartment.

"Why would Natalie Brinkman lie about Patterson's affair?" I ask. "That makes no sense."

"You think Patterson might have had a reason to make it up, to tell Brinkman she was having an affair with Sampson when she wasn't?"

"That's crazy too," I say.

"Precisely. Sampson is a bald-faced liar, and a convincing one at that."

"He's a professional," I say. "It won't be easy to prove the affair or to get a warrant."

"We're professionals too," says Warren, waiting for a red light to turn green. "We're goddamn professionals too. And there's something not right about Brinkman."

Kate Patterson is dead. I need to learn more about Natalie Brinkman.

CHAPTER 11

I hear nothing from Sheila or Tarnowski on Wednesday, so I plan to visit them after an early-morning run. It's still dark at five thirty, but a light southwest wind makes it feel like spring. I make a deal with myself to run to the paved trail along Minnehaha Creek and head east to see the sunrise—six miles total. Though I'm not afraid to run in the dark, even after what happened to Kate Patterson, I take precautions. A mini-canister of mace and my phone share a vest pocket. As a cop, I've had martial arts training, but I've rarely used it, preferring the techniques my dad taught me: a quick knee to the groin or a punch with the heel of my hand to the nose. Both have worked against uncooperative suspects and perps. To be honest, I'm a strong, tough, determined woman. But if all else fails, I can outrun most men.

My running route is highlighted by views of a magnificent morning sky, transitioning from black to blue. I'm amazed at how my brain and the rising sun can create nature's version of time-lapse photography.

It's nearly seven when I strip out of running clothes and hop in the shower. Warren is meeting with the medical examiner's office at nine thirty to discuss preliminary results of Patterson's autopsy, so when my phone starts whining before I'm fully dressed, I'm surprised to see his name on the caller ID.

"What's up? Didn't expect to hear from you this early."

"Didn't expect to be calling, but I've got some news, and I'm not sure if it's good or bad."

"I'm about to leave for Sheila's place, so let's hear it."

"I'll save you the trip," Warren says. "Sheila called distraught at six this morning. She said Kenny barely reacted to the news that we took his van and hard drive and rummaged through his stuff. She was suspicious when he told her he was going for a walk, something he never did. She went to bed, thinking he'd join her at some point and they'd talk. She woke up at four, and he wasn't back, so she went out to the garage, where she found him dangling from the rafters. He used his belt and a chain to hang himself. She called 911, and the overnight squad in the area responded. Then she called me."

"Holy shit, Warren. I knew it. I knew that fucking predator killed Billie Holloway. I feel bad for Sheila. She doesn't deserve this, and we still need to tie up any loose ends with her."

"I don't disagree, but I told her we'd give her a few days to deal with the nightmare." Warren's a softy at heart, especially when it comes to women.

"That's fine," I say. "By then our team will have processed the vehicle and hopefully retrieved something of value from his computer. I'll check with them this afternoon. Is that all your news?"

"No. A woman who lives on the corner of West Forty-Fourth and Lake Harriet Parkway left us a tip-line message on the Patterson case. She claims she was taking her new puppy out to do his business at about four in the morning last Saturday when she saw a tall man wearing dark sweats with a hood jogging south on the path along the lake. I called her last night. Her name's Mary Gordon. She's a widow and retired school principal. She said if it's above zero, it's not unusual to see an occasional jogger or walker on the path even after midnight, but this guy gave her the creeps."

"Because of the hood?" I ask, thinking that's typical racial profiling by older whites.

"That might have been part of it, but she said he was singing in a deep, raspy voice. The only phrase she could understand was 'your day of reckoning.' When she read about Patterson's murder, she thought there might be a connection."

"My ex was a big Megadeth and Metallica fan. I think that phrase is from one of their songs. Kate Patterson's killer could have been a nutjob who would have killed anyone he crossed paths with that night. Maybe we should knock on every door along the parkway from Forty-Fourth to the band shell and see if anyone else saw this guy."

"Whoever he is, he never ran or walked by the band shell, since he was never picked up by the surveillance cameras. Plus, I've already talked to a dozen residents in the two blocks closest to the trail of blood and got nothing, but I'm game to hit the rest of the neighborhood. Let's wait for the autopsy findings and Patterson's phone records before making people nervous about a killer on the loose."

"Okay, Chief," I say, knowing I'll get a reaction.

"Please don't call me that," he says, which is music to my ears.

"Yes, boss."

I meet Brianna at four in the afternoon at the same Starbucks in Edina. This time, I arrive first and get a small dark roast for me and a white mocha Frappuccino for her. Not only did BCA forensics find Billie's hair and pieces of a ripped tank top in Tarnowski's filthy van, but their techies discovered enough teen porn photos and videos to entertain the sickos on Jeffrey Epstein's Island for weeks and to put Kenny away for years, even without the murder.

We sit at the same corner table, and I explain what happened with Tarnowski in general terms. Brianna's eyes widen as I tell her we have definitive proof that he was the perpetrator and that he will never hurt anyone again.

"I feel bad that someone else died, even though he did such a horrible thing," she says, clearly relieved that the case will be over without her having to testify or tell her parents.

"You're the hero in all this, Brianna. Tarnowski is responsible for himself—no one else is. Your love for your friend and sense of justice made you come forward when you didn't have to and when it could have put you in danger and created problems with your family. I admire your bravery and your parents should as well. It's still my advice that you tell them about all of this, but I'll respect your decision, whatever it is."

Brianna's wearing a letter jacket over a white cotton sweater. With her hair in braids, she looks young and vulnerable, once again wiping tears from her pale cheeks with a napkin. "I'll think about that," she says. "I'm so glad we met and that you were handling the case. Not to change the subject, but I've been thinking that I really admire what you do, Detective, and might try to major in criminal justice in college. Do you think we could stay in touch?"

"You'll be one of the chosen few who have my personal cell number, Brianna. I hope you'll reach out from time to time. I'd really like that."

She stands, cup in hand, ready to leave, her world returning to basketball, college applications, and the future, not fear, anxiety, and murder. I wonder whether I'll ever hear from her again.

I spend the rest of the afternoon in my cubicle at the precinct trying to track down Patterson's cell phone records. She had two phones, one personal under a family plan with the good doctor and her son and a business phone issued and paid for by the city. I have a pleasant phone conversation with Dr. Bagley, who makes a joint call with me to Verizon, after which they send me an encrypted file containing a record of all calls and texts made to or from her phone over two billing cycles, about two months. Bagley had already agreed to leave her personal phone in the custody of the MPD for as long as we needed it. Maybe he's not as big a prick as I thought.

I'll drive over to BCA headquarters in Saint Paul in the morning to pick up a thumb drive containing voicemail, texts, and email messages siphoned off Patterson's work phone and laptop from the bureau's IT division, but only after the city attorney conducts a privacy and security check.

I leave the office for home shortly before six, but a voice within compels me to take a quick detour to the Harriet band shell. I can't get two disturbing images out of my brain: Tarnowski's lifeless body dangling from the rafters and the hooded jogger singing about revenge. I walk the path, now clear of ice and snow, from the band shell to the presumed area of the confrontation and stabbing, about sixty yards. I'm not looking for anything specific, simply trying to recreate the crime in my mind's eye. It's an exercise in futility. Plus, it's getting dark. Having the autopsy results would help, but Warren hasn't communicated with me despite two texts and a voicemail. If he has a major flaw as a partner, it's lack of communication. He would turn the tables and say I should investigate more and communicate less.

Warren rarely texts, but I get one while enjoying my Lean Cuisine chicken and rice in peanut sauce with a glass of Butter Chardonnay. I pause the episode of *Game of Thrones*, my current binging fetish, to retrieve my pinging phone from the charger.

Having family dinner out; autopsy confirms theory; call you tomorrow to discuss.

Warren

Warren is big on family dinners and gatherings, especially around the holidays. I like my independence but am envious of both him and my sister for having the kind of family life that Americans used to take for granted but is rare these days, in my opinion. I'm amped up, thinking about the case and my evening with the judge tomorrow. Might need a couple of Xanax to get some sleep.

CHAPTER 12

"The lead pathologist has never seen anything like it," Warren says, showing me two gruesome photos and some kind of X-ray or magnetic imaging that highlights the angle of the knife wound on Patterson's forehead. Warren is lucky I was up at six o'clock to let him into the lobby of my building. As usual, he didn't call first, thinking he'd let me sleep an extra fifteen minutes. I was up at five. We share reheated coffee and my last bagel, toasted, with honey and peanut butter.

"What is it with you?" I ask, slapping his bicep with the back of my hand.

"What are you talking about?"

"You say you're going to retire at the end of the year, yet you're at my door before sunrise like an eager rookie."

Warren looks hurt, but I know he's not. "Just because I've got thirty years in and want to move to a warmer climate to write my memoir doesn't mean I don't love this job, Lincoln. In fact, in spite of my partner, I love it now more than ever."

"That's sweet, Warren. Now tell me more about the ME's confirming your brilliant hypothesis."

"According to Dr. Atkinson, the blow to Patterson's forehead was made with incredible force by someone much taller than she, who was either extraordinarily strong, aided by adrenaline, or both. He said the knife wound was made perpendicular to her hairline while she was upright, either sitting or standing. It penetrated her skull and sank two and a half inches into her cranium. The killer then removed the knife, probably as or after she fell to the ground. There's also one stab wound in the chest that penetrated her heart. Atkinson said either that wound or the forehead gash would have been sufficient to kill her, but the attacker stabbed her over twenty times in the chest, neck, and abdomen, signifying a crazed individual or the premeditated actions of someone trying to portray a crazed individual."

"Hmmm," I say, digesting the information in light of my own preconceived scenarios. "So, it's likely she faced her killer toe-to-toe and was attacked after a confrontation or argument. How does that happen in the dark at four or five in the morning? I've been there, Warren. I can tell you, I wouldn't stop and chat with someone I didn't know. He'd have to either catch me first and tackle me, or stab me while I was moving. Do you think someone like Patterson would stop and talk to a stranger?"

"It's unlikely," Warren says. "Highly unlikely. But she was a politician, so who knows? I'm still betting she knew the killer. Maybe our hooded singer was out for blood and recognized her. He could have had a flashlight or headlamp as well as a knife."

"That's possible," I say without conviction. "Was there any evidence of resistance by Patterson?"

"No physical signs—no cuts or bruising on her hands, wrists, or forearms. The strangest thing to me is that she got up and staggered fifty yards to the band shell. Atkinson said a combination of adrenaline and the cold temperature could have provided the stimulus to give her a brief surge of energy until her major organs shut down forever."

"That's almost poetic in a sick way. I say she knew her killer and was desperate to expose him with her last breath, so she played possum after being mutilated. Once the attacker was sure she was dead, he ran off in the other direction. Unfortunately, her last gasps didn't include a text or call."

"I can buy into that theory. Now we just need the perfect suspect to prove it."

Before his current stint as a homicide detective, Warren spent ten years investigating white-collar crimes, sometimes partnering with the FBI or IRS. It was the kind of work that could turn a saint into a cynic, but Warren was already a cynic. He wouldn't admit it, but he's a numbers guy, majoring in finance in college and responsible for millions as treasurer of the Minneapolis police union. He and Diane, an emergency room nurse he met on the job thirty years ago, established college funds for each of their daughters, and I know he wants to spend more time managing their retirement accounts, preferably from a beach on Marco Island.

That's all relevant because Warren believes greed and power are stronger motivators for crime than love and lust. He also believes that most politicians are either corrupt or corruptible. Hence, to the extent it's possible without a warrant, he'll be looking into Mayor Sampson's finances. "By indirection find direction out" should be Warren's motto, though I think somebody famous beat him to it.

Sitting at the kitchen table with my laptop and a vegetable smoothie, I organize and start poring over all the phone and email records in the Patterson case. My first impression is, she didn't like texting. By far, the most frequent recipient of her texts is her son, Paul Jr., and I feel a pang of sadness reading the running dialogue between concerned (and somewhat-helicopter) mom and loving (yet evasive) college student.

News flash to the file: not one text or voicemail message between Patterson and Mayor Sampson during the past two months. There are several emails, but most of them are to the mayor and city council or the mayor and various staff members. And every one is about city business. There are differences of opinion and disagreements, but all civil and no personal attacks. In fact, there are no personal conversations between Kate Patterson and Marcus Sampson. Most of her texts are to Natalie Brinkman or Natalie and Josh Cummins. A few are to other friends and family, including a handful to and from her spouse. There's nothing threatening or suspicious. It's what you'd expect from a city council president who represents the wealthiest ward in Minneapolis, has a background in public relations, and usually gets what she wants.

No matter how smart and careful Patterson and Sampson were, if they were having an extramarital affair, there is a trail of evidence somewhere that proves it. I have no doubt about that. The mayor's official cell number shows up on Patterson's phone records a few times each week, and there are several numbers on both her personal and city records that we can't identify, so they may have talked using a burner phone, but these records alone don't support the allegation that Patterson and the mayor were having an affair. Now I'm sure I need to reconnect with Natalie Brinkman. And what does Josh Cummins know?

CHAPTER 13

My backpack passes through the scanner at the security checkpoint. I know one of the deputies guarding the entrance to the court tower, so I might be able to flash my badge and be on my way, but I don't attempt to avoid security and am gratified my fellow peace officers don't dispense with protocol. At 5:20 on a Friday afternoon, the Hennepin County Government Center has pretty much emptied out for the weekend, but there's still some activity because, as Joe Friday always said, justice never sleeps.

Dressed in a light ski jacket over winter running gear, I've packed a change of clothes along with my laptop and other essentials for a sleepover at the judge's place. I took a Lyft downtown, figuring I'll catch a ride back later tonight if things don't work out.

I ride an empty elevator to the ninth floor and poke my head into the judge's courtroom for less than a minute. A few jurors look my way, but most are fixated on the prosecuting attorney, a young woman with short dark hair and glasses, wearing a beige pantsuit and using a laser pointer to emphasize something on a whiteboard. Her voice is loud and confident, and based on the chorus of nods I see in the jury box, things aren't going well for the defendant. I can only see the back of his bald head. He's sitting between two well-tailored, gray-haired defense lawyers who are definitely not public defenders. There might be a dozen people seated in the gallery. The judge acknowledges my presence with his eyes, but I'm sure no one else notices, and I let the door swing shut and head down the hall to his chambers.

I set my backpack on the floor and remove my laptop. Before setting up at a round, glass-top conference table, I scan the judge's spacious quarters. He's scored a corner office with windows on two sides overlooking downtown near U.S. Bank Stadium. I admire nicely framed black-and-white photos of the Capitol in Saint Paul and Minneapolis City Hall over an upholstered beige loveseat, but there are no family photos, diplomas, or pictures of the judge anywhere. Describing his chambers as "sterile" would be an understatement. A black modular desk and credenza are bare, except for a computer keyboard, two large monitors, and an office phone. The long credenza has file drawers below and a wall of bookshelves above, where something catches my eye. Among four rows of legal books, case reports, Minnesota Statutes, court rules, and jury instructions is a complete outlier. It's blood red and oversized, in the shape of a coffee-table cookbook or travelogue. It sticks out from the legal volumes by at least six inches, and its title, *Minnesota's Black Community*, doesn't fit any better.

I grab it from the shelf and sit back on the couch for a closer look. It was published in 1976, about a decade before I was born, by Walter R. Scott Sr. and his son, two serious-looking Black men whose photos are included in a long publisher's statement. Apparently, Minnesota had an interracial commission back in the 1940s that issued a report on the condition of Blacks in the state, titled "The Negro Worker in Minnesota." Thirty years later, the report was out of print and the Scotts endeavored to chronicle, in words and photos, the progress, if that's the right word, of Blacks in Minnesota between World War II and the Bicentennial. According to the publisher, this new report covered Black leaders in all walks of life, from business to entertainment, from government to professional sports. Most of the people highlighted in the book have three things in common: a bad hairdo, a date of death, and a name that means nothing to me, except for Rod Carew, Tony Oliva, and Alan Page, and that's not to say the others weren't outstanding people who made valuable contributions to the state. But that all begs the question, why is this book prominently displayed in Judge Gildemeister's chambers? I intend to ask but decide to return it to the shelf for now.

It's a stretch to reach that high, and when I attempt to slide the heavy book between two law books, I inadvertently knock several volumes of the *North Western Reporter, 2d* off the shelf, revealing a brown, leather-bound book that is wedged sideways between the law books and the wall. Curious, I stand on the judge's office chair and carefully lift it from the shelf.

Back on the couch, I open what appears to be a diary or scrapbook that includes newspaper articles, letters, photos, and even plane tickets glued or stapled to the pages. There are also handwritten notes everywhere. The first page has a handwritten letter stapled to it. It's dated February 9, 1992, and contains the salutation "Dear J. R." Concerned the judge could enter at any moment, and assuming this book belongs to him, I start snapping photos of pages with my phone, capturing the '92 letter and then random pages at the beginning, in the middle, and at the end of what must be a hundred pages. The last few pages include an article from the *Milwaukee Journal* from a couple years ago. The final entry is a handwritten note in black marker: "It's over."

I hear voices from the hallway and frantically put the diary back where I found it, cover it with the legal books, and slide *Minnesota's Black Community* back into place just as the judge walks in with the prosecuting attorney, two defense lawyers, and a court reporter.

He definitely sees me stuffing the law books back on the shelf but acts like he doesn't, turning to the three lawyers to make introductions.

"Everyone, this is my good friend, Lincoln Barnes. Lincoln, this is Jill Kasting, my court reporter, and these three respected members of the bar are the lawyers who tried a case before a jury over the past week and now have asked to put a plea agreement on the record. I apologize for the intrusion, but I think we can get this done in fifteen minutes if you could wait on one of the benches in the hallway."

"Of course," I say, relieved he didn't catch me with the diary. "Very nice to meet all of you. I'll gather my things and let you get to it."

The three lawyers leave the judge's chambers ten minutes later, giving me time to return a few calls and read an email from Warren letting me know that Kate Patterson's memorial service will be at ten on Monday morning at the First Universalist Church of Minneapolis, where she was a member. "It's the nonchurch church for rich agnostics who prefer poetry readings and string quartets to Bible verses and hymns," he editorializes. Warren says we should go, and I agree.

The judge and court reporter emerge five minutes after the lawyers. He looks and smells good, though I'm disappointed when I see a briefcase but no gym bag.

"Good night, Jill," he says as she walks down the hall toward the bank of elevators. "Thanks for staying late." Then he spontaneously gives me a one-armed hug. "And thank you for waiting. That young prosecutor kicked some ass this week and forced those self-absorbed, old warhorses to convince their client that a manslaughter plea and fifteen-year sentence was a good deal. But enough about that. Are you ready for a moonlit run on this beautiful night?"

"I am," I say, "but are you going to wear that suit?"

"If it's okay with you, I thought we'd walk over to my place and run from there rather than take the skyway to the Target club."

"That's fine with me," I say, wondering why he didn't suggest that in the first place.

We settle on a five-mile route from his condo, down Nicollet Mall to Loring Park, across the pedestrian bridge to the Kenwood neighborhood, around Lake of the Isles, and back the same way. It's closer to six miles according to my Apple watch, and we finish in under forty minutes, which I can't believe. Neither of us said a word after the first mile. Before we started, the judge asked me to set a pace for a triathlon training run. He'd tell me if it was too fast. I don't think he struggled any more than I did, and I'm getting suspicious of his claim that he runs twenty miles a week at an eight-minute-mile pace.

It's close to eight thirty by the time I've showered and changed into jeans and a cable knit sweater. I'm the opposite of a primper, but when I descend the stairs from the loft, I see the judge has already set out a bottle of water and glass of red wine for me on the kitchen counter. He's standing over a sizzling wok on the stove, stirring with one hand while holding a glass with the other.

"I thought we were doing takeout," I say, the smell of chicken, onions, and garlic frying in peanut sauce making me insanely hungry. "Not that

I'm disappointed. It just seems like a lot of work after your busy week in court."

"I love winding down by making a simple meal, and it'll take less time than waiting for takeout on a Friday night. There's a bag of brown rice finishing in the microwave and frozen egg rolls that should be done in the oven, if you want to be my sous-chef."

Working together, we're eating in ten minutes, sitting at a pub table overlooking the river. Except for two flickering candles on the table, nothing interferes with our view of the city or of each other. I'm already on my second glass of wine.

"This is great," I say, "so much better than takeout." I'm still wondering what he saw in his chambers, but he didn't mention it on the walk from the courthouse. All we talked about was my training schedule for the triathlon.

"So after signing your warrant, I'm curious about the Billie Holloway case. Anything you can tell me?"

"Tarnowski hanged himself in his garage yesterday morning. The MPD will release that news and the bastard's connection to Billie's murder to the media tonight. We have solid evidence of guilt, but that's not the way I wanted things to go."

"Of course not, but it's a form of justice nonetheless, don't you agree?"

"Sure, it is," I quickly agree. "It'll provide closure for the people involved, but in a truly just world, Billie's father might be charged as an accomplice in her murder."

"I don't disagree, but our judicial system isn't the forum for that kind of justice."

I want to delve into that response, but for now, I'd rather turn the spotlight on him. "So tell me about the kind of justice given to the defendant in your trial today."

When he stands abruptly, I'm concerned I've said the wrong thing, but if that's how he reacts to a fair question, good to know it now.

"Let's continue this conversation where we can be more comfortable," he says. "Why don't we move to the great room?"

"What about these dishes?" I ask, wanting to help with the cleanup.

"You flip on the gas fireplace and find a comfortable spot on the couch, and I'll clear the table. I've got all day tomorrow to take care of these dishes. I like a glass of Irish whiskey after dinner, but I've got bourbon, scotch, and a few different cordials if you'd prefer. Does anything sound good?"

My unsophisticated liquor resume includes beer, wine, and a few mixed drinks, but I'm game. "I'll try the Irish whiskey," I say as I carry a few dishes to the small kitchen, rinse them off, and deposit them in the dishwasher. I turn and nearly run into the judge, who juggles but doesn't drop a full bottle of Irish whiskey with the name Green Spot on the label.

"Sorry," I say, "I couldn't help myself."

He kisses me with meaning on the lips. "I couldn't help myself either."

I smile when Ray Charles starts singing "Georgia" through hidden speakers. Feeling a pleasant buzz, I'm slowly sinking into the leather sectional and alternating my gaze between dancing flames in the fireplace and twinkling stars and city lights through floor-to-ceiling windows. Before I drift into dreamland, the judge sets a wooden serving tray on an ottoman in front of us and hands me a heavy, crystal glass half filled with ice and brown liquor.

"Thanks, but why no ice in yours?" I ask.

"The ice cuts the burn a bit. I started drinking whiskey with ice and, over time, decided I enjoy it more without." He sits and nestles close to me, stretching an arm around my back.

"That makes sense," I say, taking a sip. It warms my throat and insides and has a subtle, sweet finish.

"The Strib and MPR are reporting there are no suspects in your other big case, suggesting it might have been the random act of a deranged killer. Is that what you're thinking?"

His question catches me off guard. "The reporting is accurate, but the investigation continues. Did you know her—Kate Patterson?"

He pauses, staring at the fire for a few moments before responding. "Not really. I think I met her at some county function some years back, so I'd nod or say hello when we passed each other in the skyway. I can't get involved in city politics even if I were interested."

"Hey, I'm not letting you off the hook. You were going to tell me more about your trial. I saw Lou Harrington from the BCA in the courtroom, so I assume there was a break-in or robbery involved."

"A burglary and a tragedy. The defendant was a football star at

Minnehaha Academy. He blew out a knee in his sophomore year at St. Cloud State, became addicted to pain pills, and dropped out of school. He was living with his parents in South Minneapolis, working part time at Target, and promising mom and dad that he'd go back to school last fall. They didn't know about his addiction, which expanded to meth and crack when he couldn't score any pills. Desperate for money to feed the habit, he and a buddy from the neighborhood started casing nice homes in the western suburbs, in Eden Prairie and Wayzata and on Lake Minnetonka. At first they'd scope out empty garages, looking for families on vacation, and then try to break in at night. They'd take electronics and jewelry, but what they really wanted was cash. When they figured out that people on vacation don't leave a lot of cash around, they started targeting occupied homes during early-morning hours. They'd search for unlocked back doors and climb decks, looking for unlocked sliders to gain entrance while the residents were sleeping. Often high on meth, crack, or opioids, they'd take stupid risks and search closets and bedrooms for wallets, purses, and wads of cash on dressers and counters.

"Unfortunately, they got away with it for a few weeks, until one night in early September. They climbed a tree to access a second-story deck off a multimillion-dollar house on Lake Minnetonka. There were two sliding glass doors—one was locked, and the other, leading to the master bedroom, was not. It was between two and three in the morning when they entered that bedroom while Mr. and Mrs. Murphy slept in their king bed. They had the audacity to snatch a laptop at the foot of the bed and then creep from the master bathroom into a walk-in closet, where the defendant found Mr. Murphy's billfold with six hundred dollars in cash on a shelf with other personal items: gold cuff links, a Rolex watch, and the keys to the Porsche 911 in the garage. He put them all in his backpack while his partner lifted a purse from a hook in the kitchen and a bottle of vodka from the liquor cabinet. As the defendant was about to exit the closet, Mr. Murphy grabbed his forearm with his left hand while wielding a golf club with his right.

"I don't know if Murphy said anything. He probably didn't have time. The defendant picked up a ten-pound dumbbell from the floor and swung it at Murphy, hitting him in the side of the head with such force that it split his skull and caused a brain bleed and, ultimately, his death.

"The defendant and his accomplice figured they'd get away faster stealing the Porsche instead of running four blocks to the church parking lot where they'd parked their car. They didn't know that Mrs. Murphy had called 911 when she was awakened by strange noises and noticed the sliding door to the deck was open. They backed the Porsche into a Wayzata patrol car.

"The defendant's parents took out a second mortgage to pay the retainer for his defense lawyers. Probably twenty-five grand. The defense admitted the burglary but argued the felony murder was self-defense. Mrs. Murphy was a compelling witness, and after a brilliant closing argument by the young prosecutor, the defense lawyers asked for a brief recess before final jury instructions.

"The defendant pleaded guilty to manslaughter and a recommended sentence of no more than fifteen years versus the twenty-five he could have received after a felony murder conviction. Sentencing won't be for a few weeks."

"So, where's the justice in this?" he asks. "What do you think?"

"I agree it's a tragedy. But for the football injury, your defendant might still be in college and none of this happens. But if we're not held accountable for our actions, there is no justice system. The kid's parents and Mrs. Murphy probably don't agree on what the outcome should be. What do you think?"

He takes a sip of whiskey, and so do I.

"This young man still has a chance to make something of his life, but he'll spend at least eight to ten years in prison, so it's more likely than not that he won't. Another tragedy. Over the years, I've learned that our justice system, as good as it is, is inadequate to deal with certain issues, especially matters of the heart."

I'm not exactly sure what he means by that, but this conversation is getting too heavy for someone drinking Irish whiskey in front of a fire. He catches me off guard by changing the subject.

"I think you would be a great prosecutor."

"What makes you say that?" I ask, flattered and curious.

"Because you're smart, and you possess a good balance of empathy and toughness. Hey, didn't I see you returning a few of my law books to the shelves this afternoon? What case were you reading?"

I thought he saw me, and I'm kind of relieved he's bringing it up.

"I was paging through a book, but it wasn't a law book. Robin, you've got rows and rows of legal books and one that doesn't fit—a big, red picture book from the 1970s called *Minnesota's Black Community*. It's nothing but political propaganda sponsored by the state to show what a great place Minnesota is for Blacks. I don't know who'd be co-opted into publishing a book like that today, fifty years later."

"You're right about that," he agrees without hesitation. "But there's a good reason it's in my chambers. One of the Black leaders pictured in the book is William Posten, Judge William Posten. When the Government Center was built in the seventies, Judge Posten was the first district court judge to occupy my current chambers. When he retired, he left the book as a memento for his successor, who then left it for me."

That explanation takes the wind out of my sails, and I down the rest of my drink. The alcohol and the momentum of the evening make me forget about the diary and what revelations it might hold. I nod after he pours himself a second and suspends the bottle of Green Spot over my glass. He picks up a plate of chocolates from the tray and holds it in front of me.

"Dark chocolate, sea salt caramels and Irish whiskey, the best combination since peanut butter and jelly." Dark chocolate is one of my weaknesses. I take a caramel and hope the caffeine will counteract my light-headedness, but it doesn't.

I should stop drinking, but the warmth of the fire and my rising libido ignore that fleeting thought. We gradually melt into an embrace on the couch and then somehow stumble intertwined into the bedroom.

The note on the kitchen table and the text on my phone are the same.

Coffee made, yogurt and fruit in the fridge. Had to respond to small emergency.

Sorry. Call you later. Rob

It's six in the morning. I grab a robe from his closet and cover my nakedness while surveying the scene of our crimes. My head is throbbing, but what do I expect after last night's debauchery and four hours sleep? Everything, every single thing, has been cleaned and returned to its place. No dishes in the sink or dishwasher, no bottles of wine or whiskey in the great room. He must have been up for at least an hour before leaving. And what could the emergency be?

Sipping a cup of his coffee (and it's so good too, dammit), I feel the need to get home, so I dress quickly, gather my things, and write the judge a brief note before ordering a Lyft.

> *Hope everything is OK. Thanks for a great night.*
> *Talk soon.*
> *LB*

CHAPTER 14

2/9/92

Dear J. R.,

Patty and I just got home from a party at Shaler after we beat Beloit by three in overtime. It should have been a fun night, but the whole time, I was struggling with how to tell you. I know I should call you, Jason, but I'm not strong enough to do that. Please forgive me. I have decided to accept an offer from my adviser to edit her new book and spend the summer after graduation here at Ripon. What that really means is that I won't be spending the summer in Minnesota and won't be moving to Upstate New York when you head to Cornell next fall.

I always thought we'd be together forever, but I've changed a lot in the past few years and feel it's best for both of us if we go our separate ways. I never discussed our relationship much with anyone before Patty. She's made me reflect on the fact we've been a couple since we were sixteen, limiting our life experiences. We're much different people today than we were in high school and, while we've had many wonderful, unforgettable times together, and I have great admiration and respect for you, I'm not as committed to "us" as I need to be to take the next step.

Jason, I know I was the first to say, "I love you," and in some ways, I still do, just not enough. I want you to know there is no one else. That's not what this is about. It's about growing in different directions and experiencing new and different things.

Please, please don't try to change my mind. It's been absolutely gut-wrenching for me to make this decision and then muster the courage to tell you. I need time and space to redirect my life. I know how much heartache you've already experienced in your life, so I'm very worried about how you'll react, but I hope ultimately you'll realize that this is for the best.

All the best to you, Jason,
Sara

This letter was stapled to the first page. Someone wrote the word "lie" in red marker after "I want you to know there is no one else." I managed to take photos of a dozen pages of what I'm calling a diary. Whatever it is, it's disturbing, especially because I might be in love with the person who created it, whatever his name is. J.R.? Jason? And who is Sara?

On the very next page is an engagement announcement from the May 23, 1992, edition of the *Lake County News Chronicle*.

Wheaton, Hyatt

Sara Wheaton of Two Harbors, Minnesota, and Timothy Hyatt Jr. of Milwaukee, Wisconsin, plan to be married July 18, 1992, at St. Mary's Catholic Church in Lake Forest, Illinois.

Her parents are Jack and Margaret Wheaton of Two Harbors, Minnesota. His parents are Marilyn and the late Dr. Timothy Hyatt of Lake Forest, Illinois.

The future bride, a 1992 graduate of Ripon College in Ripon, Wisconsin, has accepted a position as an editor with Seaworthy Publications in Port Washington, Wisconsin.

The future groom is a recent graduate of the Medical College of Wisconsin and will begin a residency in general and orthopedic surgery at Rush-Presbyterian-St. Luke's Medical Center in Chicago, where the couple will reside.

I'm no relationship genius, but I'm guessing Sara Wheaton was the judge's high school sweetheart. The diary had over a hundred pages; I only have images of ten more. Even so, I'm shocked by what comes next: a round-trip plane ticket from Minneapolis to Orlando, departing on March 21, 1999, returning March 26, 1999. The passenger's name is Robin Gildemeister. There are miniature color photos pasted on the page, all of a young, attractive Caucasian family, a mother and father and two children, a boy about six and a girl about four. They're at Disney World, enjoying rides, playing in a pool, and sitting at a table at an outdoor bistro.

Two pages from a trip to Big Sky, Montana, in February of 2006 are filled with photos of the same family. Dad's put on a few pounds, mom is still beautiful, and the kids are growing into adolescence. There's a close-up shot of mom and dad on the balcony of a third-story condo. How did he get these? Why? Why?

There's another family vacation in Italy in 2012 and a destination wedding on the Big Island in Hawaii in 2018. I'm guessing the bride, Whitney Hyatt, is Sara's daughter. Was the judge invited? Was he a wedding crasher? Bizarre. In each case, a round-trip plane ticket is surrounded by photos of the family, until the last trip. A round-trip ticket from Minneapolis to Cancun, departing March 2 and returning March 6, 2020, is followed by an article from the March 6, 2020, edition of the *Milwaukee Journal Sentinel*.

Authorities Investigating Mysterious
Death of Brookfield Woman
By ALAN ACKERMAN, ASSOCIATED PRESS
March 6, 2020—6:30 a.m.
PLAYA DEL CARMEN, MEXICO—Local tourist police and Mexican state authorities are investigating the death of a prominent Brookfield, Wisconsin, woman in the early-morning hours of March 5. Sara Wheaton Hyatt, a forty-eight-year-old author of popular travel books, was vacationing in Playa del Carmen, Mexico, with her husband, Dr. Timothy Hyatt, an orthopedic surgeon. The couple was staying at the Fairmont Mayakoba Resort, where Dr. Hyatt was attending a conference. According to Dr. Hyatt, his wife went for a walk

on the beach at about 10:00 p.m., saying she'd be back before midnight. When she hadn't returned three hours later, he became concerned and alerted resort management, who contacted police.

According to a spokesman from the state police, someone staying at a property about a mile from the Fairmont discovered Ms. Hyatt's body washed up on the beach at approximately 3:30 a.m. and contacted authorities, indicating she was unresponsive. There was evidence at the scene that Ms. Hyatt's body might have been moved from some other location and either placed on the beach or deposited in the ocean. As of this morning, there is no official cause of death, but the investigation continues.

Besides her spouse, Sara Hyatt is survived by two adult children and their spouses.

What does all this mean? There were a few pages with handwritten notes between this article and the last entry, a handwritten statement in heavy black marker: "It's over." What could that mean? I need to see those pages. I need to fill in the blanks, but how?

———————

It's ten in the morning. A cold rain puts a damper on my mood, which had already swung from elation to confusion. I decide to scrap a planned thirty-mile bike ride around the lakes. I have texts from my sister (Sunday dinner invite) and my mom (asking about my date with the judge) but nothing from Warren. It is the weekend, after all, and now that Brianna Holloway's murder has been cleared, I decide to put Kate Patterson on the back burner for at least a few hours and concentrate my efforts on Robin Gildemeister. Or is it Jason Robin Gildemeister? No combination of these names yields anything new on the World Wide Web, so I research Sara Wheaton Hyatt and get a cornucopia of hits— author, Junior League, philanthropy, even highly ranked amateur tennis player—but nothing connecting her with Jason or Robin Gildemeister. Apparently, they're both from Two Harbors, a place I've barely heard of and never visited. I could confront the judge with the "evidence" I have and ask for an explanation. That approach would end our relationship, and I don't think I want to give it up. Not yet.

There's something romantic about a man who can't stop pursuing the woman he loves, even after he's rejected. It reminds me of *Love in the Time of Cholera*, a book I read for a class in college. But that guy wasn't a stalker. That's what's really bothering me. Not only following her but taking photos of her family on vacation. How did he know when and where they were going? She never knew or suspected, all those years? And does he know how she died? Was he involved? Did he kill his former girlfriend? So many questions.

Still suffering from the throbbing fog of a hangover from a night that seems like a week ago, I mix Fresca and orange juice over ice and take two naproxen, the only OTC pain reliever that works for me. Then a name pops into my head: Sam MacDonald. He was the featured speaker at the Peace Officers Association annual meeting in January, talking about the wave of violent and unusual crimes that he and his small staff up in Lake County have faced over the past few years. I recall two things about MacDonald. First, he was a big shot in the Secret Service before moving back to Minnesota, and second, he grew up in Two Harbors, the seat of Lake County. I'm guessing he's a few years older than the judge, but I'm desperate, and he's my best source for some answers.

CHAPTER 15

The trip to Two Harbors is mostly a straight shot up I-35. About three hours of gently rolling hills, farm fields, pine forests, rest stops, and sleepy little towns like Sandstone, Finlayson, and Barnum. "Why haven't I been up here before?" I ask myself sarcastically.

It's a pleasant-enough drive, but gloomy skies and a steady rain contribute to my dark mood. I silence my phone and listen to a CD I made for my dad a decade before he died. Nat King Cole, Oscar Peterson, John Coltrane, Louis Armstrong, and Earth, Wind & Fire. The scenery gets more interesting the farther north I travel.

I drive over the crest of a steep incline, and there it is, the city of Duluth stretching for miles along the shores of Lake Superior. It's hard to believe the population is only 85,915, but that's what the road sign says. I take the Superior Street exit and drive through downtown. Tired old buildings, a few vacant, mixed with recent attempts at urban renewal and some modern health-care facilities. It reminds me of Elgin, only whiter.

I haven't eaten all day, so I stop at a supper club on the east side of town called the Pickwick. It must be happy hour because the place is packed and reverberating with loud voices, an Eagles' song blasting through an ancient sound system, and laughter. The host, a gangly kid with more acne than whiskers, leads me to the lone empty seat at a well-stocked mahogany bar that looks like it's been around since Prohibition. A friendly, heavy-set bartender seems offended when I order a club soda with a lime. Couples on my left and right are engaged in flirtatious banter, but I sense things could escalate to an uncomfortable (for me) suck-face level soon. I try to ignore them by focusing on the second half of a Big Ten Tournament game on a flat-screen TV behind the bar while devouring a cheeseburger and the best onion rings I've ever had.

Sheriff MacDonald returned my call within fifteen minutes this morning. When I asked whether he knew Robin Gildemeister, he said he did but not well and asked for context. Was I investigating him with respect to a crime? Was he presiding over one of my cases? When I hesitated and then awkwardly blurted, "It's personal," he suggested a face-to-face meeting, especially if I'd never been up the North Shore.

I plug "Bob's Breezy Point Cabins" into my GPS and follow directions through the Lakeside neighborhood of Duluth and then up Scenic Highway 61 along the lake. Despite warmer temperatures and a steady rain, there's still a layer of snow on the ground. It's dusk when I pass through a tiny village called Knife River and, five minutes later, see Bob's decrepit wooden sign and turn down a snirt (snow and dirt) driveway to my destination. MacDonald recommended the place, and a last-minute cancellation opened one of the twelve lakefront log cabins for my Saturday-night stay.

After getting instructions and a key from Bob, who reminds me of Grizzly Adams, I park the Jeep behind cabin eight, grab my backpack, and hop up a couple stairs onto a porch and wraparound deck. I'm instantly in awe. I grew up near Lake Michigan. It's a big, impressive body of water, but Lake Superior is an ocean, seemingly flowing forever to the north and east. But that's not all. It's windy up here, and my cabin can't be more than twenty feet from the rocky shore and forty feet from the lake. Huge waves create whitecaps as far as I can see and crash against the rocks, sending a cold spray all the way to my deck. Bob said the lake was mostly frozen in mid-March two years ago but has been ice-free for most of this winter.

There's a firepit with a pile of wood between the deck and the rocks. Bob said if the wind dies down tonight, he'll come by and build a fire, even if I prefer to admire it from the warmth of my cabin.

The inside is perfect—small but perfect. It's one room with a separate bathroom the size of a closet. A king bed dominates the space, but a vaulted, cedar-lined ceiling, wood plank flooring, picture windows framing the lake, and a gas fireplace make it seem bigger and give it rustic charm. There's even a full kitchen with miniature appliances.

I unpack my stuff, including a six-pack of Diet Coke and some fruit, and sit in front of the fireplace with my laptop. It doesn't sound like the wind will subside anytime soon, and that's fine with me. The rhythmic roar of giant waves rushing in evokes a kind of primitive solace deep in my core. I turn my phone back on after a three-hour hiatus. A text from the judge makes me shudder.

Sorry about this morning. Judge Hansen had a stroke last night and died this afternoon at HCMC. Only 54. I'm her on-call backup this weekend. Brunch tomorrow?

Robin

It was sent at four. I need to reply. I need to lie.

No need to apologize. Terrible news about the judge. A rain check on brunch? Promised my mom I'd spend the day with her. Thanks again for last night.

LB

———————

I don't sleep well and get up before sunrise. I'm anxious for some answers, but they'll have to wait until at least nine, when I'm meeting MacDonald. I need a run to calm my nerves and to stay in racing shape; the half IRONMAN is in a week.

I dress in winter running gear and attach traction cleats to the bottoms of my shoes. There are patches of ice on the roads and trails up here, and the outdoor thermometer on the kitchen window reads fifteen above. After stretching for ten minutes, I head north on Scenic 61 and am treated to the morning sun glistening across the big lake that comes in and out of my view. I push myself to cover ten miles before eight. There's minimal traffic and a handful of pedestrians on the streets of Two Harbors as I run through the middle of town and pass by the usual bars, motels, souvenir shops, and convenience stores that populate a tourist town.

I'm back at Bob's with five minutes to spare. After a rejuvenating shower, I dress, pack, and check my phone for messages. Nothing from

Warren, but this from the judge:

Have a great day with your mom. Hope to see you before the big race.
Rob

I'm early, which is usually the case, especially when I'm nervous. The tag line for Cedar Coffee Company is "off the beaten path," and it is. Nestled among tall cedars and pines about a quarter mile north of 61, the slope-roofed wood-and-glass building looks new and, according to the sheriff, is the best place in Lake County for a hot beverage and quick breakfast. A full parking lot confirms its popularity. I pay cash for a black coffee and raspberry scone at the register and sit at a two-person table in the back.

Five minutes later, a tall, broad-shouldered man wearing jeans and a bomber jacket enters the café. I recognize MacDonald's trimmed salt-and-pepper beard. Any doubt is dispelled when patrons greet him with either, "Hey, Mac," or, "Hey, Sheriff, how's it goin'?" A middle-aged guy in a UMD Bulldogs sweatshirt comes out of the kitchen, hands him a steaming mug, and slaps him on the shoulder. That's my cue to stand and wave to get his attention.

"Good morning, Sheriff," I say as he sets the mug on the table. I'll shake a hand now and then with the right person, and it feels right with MacDonald. I extend my hand, and he envelops it with a paw the size of a catcher's mitt. "Lincoln Barnes," I say, looking into his kind green eyes. "I really appreciate this."

"Great to meet you, Detective," he says, draping the bomber jacket over his chair before sitting. He knows I'm familiar with his background, so he asks how I came to be a detective with the MPD. I'm generally uncomfortable talking about myself, but he's clearly an interested listener, so I say more than I intended about my life in Chicago and my professional career in Minneapolis. I tell him a bit about the Kate Patterson case, which he's heard about, and then segue to my short history with Judge Robin Gildemeister, omitting some intimate details, but emphasizing what I learned from my accidental discovery of the diary.

"That's potentially very disturbing or even worse," he says, looking around to make sure no one's eavesdropping on our conversation. Then he leans in. "I'll tell you what I know about Judge Gildemeister. We both grew up around here, but I'm three or four years older. We were never friends, but that doesn't matter. Many of the folks who lived in Lake County at that time know the basics of what I'm about to tell you.

"His father's name was Jason Campbell. The judge's birth name was Jason Robin Campbell, but everyone called him J. R., hence the reference in the old letter you saw. His dad started out as a stockbroker in the Denver area. He and his first wife had a daughter, but his wife died from a fall during a camping trip to Glacier Park. After a brief, and probably inadequate, inquiry, her death was ruled accidental, even though there was a half-million-dollar term policy on her life. Campbell and his two-year-old daughter moved here in the late sixties to get a fresh start. He opened a Dain Bosworth investment office on First Avenue and, within a year, married Laura Gildemeister, a young nurse at Lake View Hospital. J. R. was born a year later."

"You've really done your homework," I interrupt. "Dates and a lot more specifics than I'd remember about someone who wasn't even a friend."

"No homework involved, Detective. When you hear the rest of the story, I think you'll understand why it's stuck with me. A few years after J. R. was born, the Campbells built a sprawling new house on one of the hills overlooking the lake north of town. Everyone figured they must be the richest family in Lake County, and Jason Campbell did everything he could to promote that notion. He donated thousands to local charities, advertised his investment business on billboards and the radio, and joined every business and civic group in town. He was a charismatic, fast-talking snake-oil salesman, and by the early eighties, when the stock market took off, he'd gained the trust and investment accounts of hundreds of folks in Two Harbors and Silver Bay and even some down in Duluth, where they invited him to join Northland Country Club.

"Like a lot of us who live on the North Shore, Campbell developed a fascination with Lake Superior. He bought a thirty-foot cabin cruiser and named it *Sunken Dividends*. I'm told he invested in scuba diving and sonar equipment so he could explore some of the sunken shipwrecks in the lake, hoping to recover lost treasure. I'm not sure whether that's true, but in early June of 1984, on their fifteenth wedding anniversary, Jason and Laura Campbell had dinner at the Lakeview Castle near Duluth and then drove to the Knife River Marina, where Jason rented a slip for his boat. The manager at the marina was the last person to see either of them alive. Jason's body was recovered the next morning, floating in shallow water a hundred yards from Reserve Mining's main facility in Silver Bay. He was wearing a dry suit, but he must have misjudged something because he drowned before making it to shore. The boat was found adrift three miles south of Two Harbors. Its fuel tanks were empty. Laura's body was never recovered.

"It turns out that Jason Campbell was a fraud, a swindler, and a sociopath, not to mention a killer. Like Bernie Madoff, he created fictitious accounts and statements and used his clients' money to fuel a lavish lifestyle, even though he could have had a very nice life if he'd played by the rules. He owed his clients over three million dollars. He'd taken out six different policies on Laura's life over a three-year period with a total death benefit of four million."

I'm stunned by what I'm hearing, but I'm not going to interrupt again. It strikes me as an odd coincidence that the judge's parents died in the year I was born.

"There were investigations and lawsuits, but in the end, there was nothing conclusive except that J. R. and Beth Campbell were orphaned. Beth had just graduated high school and was on her way to Colorado College. J. R. was in eighth grade. Fortunately for him, his maternal grandmother, who'd recently been widowed, decided to quit her job as a school librarian in Grand Rapids and move to Two Harbors to become his guardian.

"After the feds liquidated Jason's business and the family's lawyers settled with the insurance companies, J. R. and Beth each got a couple hundred thousand dollars, and as far as I know, Beth has never been back here. I don't know whether she and her half-brother have maintained a relationship. Hilda Gildemeister bought an old log cabin on the lake, north of town for her and her grandson.

"As I said, I didn't know J. R. well, but my mom was a nurse at Lake View. She worked with Laura for years and befriended Hilda when she came to town and didn't know anyone. They were in a book club together, and after my dad died, they became pretty close friends. Hence, I know more about your judge than I otherwise would. Unfortunately, Hilda died more than twenty years ago, and my mom is in a memory-care facility in Duluth, so my sources of current information are limited.

"J. R. Campbell was a big deal in this little town, and he and Sara Wheaton were together from the summer after his parents died until his senior year in college. He was an excellent student, an accomplished musician, and a talented athlete—one of those kids who was good at everything but not great at anything, except tennis. That was something he and Sara had in common. They each placed high in singles in state tennis tournaments and played mixed doubles together all over the Midwest. They were inseparable. Hilda loved Sara and felt she played a critical role in J. R.'s recovery. She was homecoming queen—bubbly, pretty, and athletic. I remember she had an infectious laugh and wanted to be a journalist. Her dad was one of two veterinarians in town, and her mom worked part time in his clinic. According to my mom, her parents believed J. R. and Sara would always be together. I recall Hilda was surprised when the couple decided to test the strength of their relationship by attending separate colleges a thousand miles apart.

"I was in the air force when they broke up, but my mom told me J. R. was so distraught he gave up a scholarship to Cornell Law School. He spent over a year living with Hilda at the cabin. She was terribly worried about him, claiming he was listless and depressed and would often break down and sob. I heard he wrote hundreds of letters to Sara but never sent any of them. Hilda helped him change his name from Jason Robin Campbell to Robin Gildemeister, which, given his father's misdeeds, was probably a good idea regardless of his reasons. Then out of the blue one day, he told her he was going to law school in Madison and wouldn't be coming back to Two Harbors—ever.

"Hilda moved back to Grand Rapids a short time later but never sold the cabin. I assume the judge inherited it, but as far as I know, he's not been back here since the mid-nineties. No one lives there, but clearly, someone's taking care of the place. It's kind of eerie.

"I heard Sara married a doctor in Milwaukee and worked for a magazine, but I hadn't given the Campbell saga much thought until I read a blurb in the local paper that Sara had died in an accident in Mexico."

My head is spinning trying to take everything in. I want to know more about Sara and the circumstances of her death. "Are Sara's parents still around?" I ask.

"They moved to Arizona after Doc Wheaton retired five years ago. Sara was their only child, so I'm sure they've had a difficult couple of years."

"What would you do if you were me, Sheriff? Confront Robin about the diary? Talk to Sara's husband? Run?"

"You obviously like him or you wouldn't be here. I assume you have enough on your plate in Minneapolis without snooping at the periphery of a cold case in the Yucatan. Talk about an exercise in futility.

"You have to ask yourself—if Robin Gildemeister were consumed with his feelings for Sara Hyatt, and he clearly was, but didn't cause her death, can I get past his obsession for another woman? I might be able to do it, but only if I were convinced, beyond any doubt, that he didn't kill her. The smartest thing to do, Detective, is move on, but it may not be the easiest."

I can't answer those questions right now, and I'm feeling guilty for taking up so much of his time. "Thanks for doing this, Sheriff. You've given me a lot to ponder." I stand and slip on my jacket.

He slowly rises, like a man who's experienced a lot in life and doesn't move fast without good reason. "Listen," he says, gently cupping my shoulder with his hand. "There might be someone up here who has stayed in contact with Gildemeister over the years and can shed more light on all this. I'll do some digging and let you know what I find. That diary you discovered has piqued my curiosity. But if I had to bet, I'd wager the judge was living life vicariously through Sara's family vacations, observing the life he wanted but could never have, and there's nothing more to it than that. It's unusual for sure but maybe not, considering his history."

Considering his history—I think about that phrase all the way home. His history includes a father who's a sociopath and a murderer. I should walk away, but I can't.

CHAPTER 16

Warren and I plan to meet in the parking lot of the First Universalist Church at nine thirty. The memorial service for Kate Patterson starts at ten. I arrive fifteen minutes early, hoping to have a brief discussion with my partner, and of course, he's fifteen minutes late. That gives me the opportunity to watch a parade of city and state officials, lobbyists, and other assorted big shots walk up concrete steps and into a sanctuary that is too small for the crowd that's assembling to pay respects to a woman who might have been on her way to the governor's mansion. Instead, her ashes occupy a decorative box.

I see Warren crossing Dupont. He couldn't find a place in the lot. The silver fox looks distinguished in a black suit and navy tie. Nobody needs a coat on this glorious spring day.

"Nice of you to show," I say, the words dripping with sarcasm. "Did it take a long time to decide what to wear?"

"Very funny," Warren says. "I got delayed tracking down some interesting info on our mayor. Have you seen him?"

"He's here with his wife. I've seen most of the council and even the lieutenant governor. I've been waiting for a half hour. I haven't seen Dr. Bagley or his son."

"I'm sure they're already here. We'd better go in. I'll fill you in on what I've found after the service."

As I suspected, there's no place to sit. The first two rows in the center section are roped off for family members, and a highway patrol officer appears to be reserving the front row of a side section for some dignitaries. Warren and I are relegated to the second row of standers in the back of the church. Fortunately, we're tall enough to see over the first row. There's some commotion at a side door to the sanctuary, and the governor appears and follows his security team to the saved seats in front.

Dr. Bagley and a half dozen family members enter from the same door a few minutes later. Paul Jr. is a tall, spindly, handsome kid with curly brown hair and a wispy goatee. He's sitting between his father and an even-taller man who could be an uncle or close family friend.

There's at least a fifty-fifty chance Kate Patterson's murderer is here. Warren claims some killers are compelled to attend their victim's funeral, stimulated by others' grieving, and gloating over conversations about the deceased and speculation about the means and manner of death. Some enjoy the thrill of the cat-and-mouse game with authorities.

The service is nice enough—eulogies by Patterson's former business partner and campaign manager and short speeches by two city council members and a constituent. They all convey the same message. Kate Patterson was a brilliant, tough, dedicated public servant who outworked and outmaneuvered her adversaries. Her husband doesn't speak, but Paul Jr. reads two poems by Emily Dickinson that were his mom's favorites and then reads one that he picked out by a poet named Henry van Dyke. He reads it haltingly, wiping away tears with his shirt sleeve.

Time is too slow for those who wait,
Too swift for those who fear,
Too long for those who grieve,
Too short for those who rejoice,
But for those who love, time is
Eternity.

"Thank you, Mom, for everything. I love you very, very much."

One of the Steeles delivers a mournful, understated rendition of "Amazing Grace" that gives me a gut ache. After standing for over an hour, I'm ready to nudge Warren and slip out the front door when Mayor

Sampson strides to the podium.

"What the fuck?" Warren whispers in my ear. "This isn't in the program."

"Patterson-Bagley family, governor, council, and fellow mourners. I didn't intend to speak today, but I need to say something about the unfathomable tragedy that's taken the life of the person I counted on, relied on, and respected more than anyone else in city government, a woman who had a vision for Minneapolis that didn't always align with my own. We often had to agree to disagree on policy issues but never on the bigger picture of creating a thriving and diverse community for our citizens. I want the family to understand that not only did I respect Kate Patterson—I truly loved her as a person. In my opinion, she is irreplaceable. We can't bring her back, but we can bring her justice. And we will."

We escape from the memorial service as soon as Sampson's self-serving, bullshit speech is over and agree to meet at the Uptown Diner to compare notes and eat unhealthy comfort food.

"So, tell me about your big find, Senior Detective Lindquist?"

"Did you see him?" Warren responds to my question with a question.

"See who?"

"Your boyfriend. The judge."

"Judge Gildemeister was at the service?"

"Sitting a few rows behind the governor, between the city attorney and Judge McFadden."

"Why would he do that?"

"That's a question for you. I assume it was out of respect for the city council president."

That might be true, but why didn't he tell me? He knew I'd be there. Time to change the subject. "You're probably right. Now, tell me about this new development in the Patterson case."

"You know I'm still the treasurer of the police union and its pension fund."

"Yes, Warren."

"I was meeting with our commercial banker at Union Bank & Trust, and she asked me about the Patterson murder. Did I think someone from the council or mayor's office could have done it? I say we haven't ruled anything out, that we're still investigating. Then she tells me, a month ago, Sampson came into the bank trying to borrow over a million dollars. He said he needed the money to pay off campaign debts. Turns out, he financed a lot of the media buys for his campaign with an undisclosed loan from a minority building contractor who was pressuring him for payment. The contractor was on the brink of bankruptcy and threatened to expose Sampson if he didn't pay up. Unfortunately for the mayor, he's got no equity in his house and no other collateral. The guy's been a government lawyer his whole career, and he just came through a messy divorce. She said he didn't qualify for half of what he wanted."

"Okay, so the mayor's in debt. Big surprise. Remember all the TV and radio ads his campaign ran? I'm no expert on campaign financing laws, but what's the connection to our case?"

"Maybe none, but two weeks ago, there was a wire transfer of over two million dollars into the mayor's personal checking account. It came from a bank in St. Louis and from a company called Plains Capital Group."

"The union's banker gave you all of this information? Why?"

"She didn't give me all the information, only that the bank denied Sampson's loan. I have another source for the rest of it, a source I can't disclose just yet, not even to you. But we might not need to use that source. We might be able to approach this from a different angle."

"You're losing me, Warren. I know you're a financial wizard, but please, tell me where you're going with this."

Plains Capital is a second-tier subsidiary of Brinkman, Jacobs & Company, the biggest commercial property developer in the country, whose chairman and CEO is Robert Brinkman, father of Natalie Brinkman."

"Holy shit, Warren."

"Now we have to figure out how we legally acquired this intel and how it's connected to Patterson's murder. Because my old bones say it is."

CHAPTER 17

"Please come in and have a seat at the dining room table. I just made a fresh pot of coffee. Could I get us each a cup before you interrogate me?"

Oliver Burns is the elderly gentleman who discovered Kate Patterson's body while walking his dog near the band shell. Officer Stanich interviewed him that morning, and her report indicates he lives less than two blocks from Lake Harriet on Forty-Seventh Street. He called her yesterday morning, saying he'd like to talk to the officer assigned to the case.

"Sure," I say, admiring the cozy, craftsman interior of Oliver's two-story stucco home, with hardwood floors, overstuffed furniture, and a wood-burning brick fireplace. A plump little man with a few thin strands of white hair combed over a balding head and a quick, toothy smile, Oliver returns with two cups of steaming black coffee.

"Cream or sugar?" he asks, handing me a cup.

"Black is good," I say.

"You can call me Ollie," he says, sliding into an antique oak chair across from me. "My wife is the only one who called me Oliver. She passed from cancer a few years ago."

"I'm sorry to hear that, Ollie. I really appreciate that you reached out to us. I understand you used to investigate fire losses for a big insurance company." I've done a little homework on Mr. Burns.

"Worked for the Travelers for twenty-five years and then ran my own adjusting company until 2010."

"So, you're used to paying attention to small details," I say.

"Better than most old farts my age, I guess," he says with a satisfied smile.

"Can you think back to last Saturday morning when you took your dog for a walk and came upon that awful scene?"

"I don't need to think back, Detective. I can't get that scene out of my mind."

"If it's really bothering you, Ollie, I can refer you to someone who might be able to help."

"No, no. I'll be fine," he says, waving a hand in my direction. "As I told Officer Stanich, I found something that morning. Something I didn't think was important at the time, but now I do."

"Tell me about it," I prod, hoping for a bombshell but expecting a dud.

"Right when Buster and I left the house, some guy in a hooded sweatshirt ran by us on Forty-Seventh. It was dark, so I didn't get a good look at his face, but he was tall and broad-shouldered. He got into a car halfway up the block and drove off. That happens all the time on this block, since we're so close to the lake, so I didn't think anything of it. When we got back here after talking to the police, it was between five and five thirty. On a March Saturday morning, there's usually no activity around here until at least seven or seven thirty. That's why I was surprised to find this on the street in front of my house."

He lifts a cellophane bag from the pocket of his flannel shirt and hands it to me. Inside is a white, plastic key card with "PROX IV" stamped in the middle on one side and a seven-digit number stamped in black near the bottom of the other. There is also a half-inch slit near the top of the card, probably to facilitate clipping it to a belt or lanyard.

"I think whoever ran by us that morning dropped this card," Ollie says with an air of authority. "I'm certain it wasn't there when Buster and I first left the house."

Bombshell.

Warren and I don't spend much time in Lieutenant Moe's office in city hall. The leader of the homicide-and-robbery division has confidence in his detectives and lets us work our cases with minimal supervision. A text from his admin summoning us to his office in the middle of the day is not a good sign. We don't have a chance to compare notes before sitting in the worn cloth chairs that face Moe's metal desk. A stocky former navy NCO with a crew cut from another era, Sherm Moe is a no-nonsense, by-the-book, rule-of-law cop but in the best sense of those tired phrases. In fact, he's the only "old-school" relic who's survived the most recent MPD regime change.

"I understand we still don't have any leads in the Patterson case," he says while scanning a status report on his desktop and looking alternately at Warren and me. "We've been hearing a lot from the residents near Lake Harriet. They're on edge, worried there could be a killer lurking in their neighborhood. I know the medical examiner thinks Patterson's wounds are inconsistent with a random attack. Do you two still agree with that theory? Because, from where I sit, it's not that persuasive."

I let Warren take the lead.

"It's certainly not airtight, if that's what you mean, Lieutenant, but I still believe it's more likely than not, based on the lack of any visible signs of a struggle by a tough, wiry woman and the angle of the first major wound."

"Barnes, what do you think?"

"I agree with Detective Lindquist." I recount my morning meeting with Ollie and his discovery of the key card in the street. "The research division at the BCA thinks they can track down the garage or building it can access and, eventually, who it was issued to. I believe there's a better than fifty-fifty chance a jogger in a hooded sweatshirt murdered Patterson. We now have two witnesses who've provided similar descriptions of such a person near the scene of the crime within the critical time frame."

"I guess we'll see about that," Moe says. "You know I trust you two to get it right, so let me get to the real reason I asked you to come down. Someone from the mayor's office has asked the chief for a status report on our investigation. In the confidential section of your report, you indicate that a senior member of Patterson's staff claims the council president was having an affair with Mayor Sampson but that he adamantly denies it.

Any third-party or other evidence that confirms who's telling the truth about that?"

I look over at Warren and get a subtle nod. "Patterson's smartphone records don't support an intimate personal relationship," I say. "No text messages between Patterson and the mayor, only council business matters in emails and infrequent phone calls. That doesn't mean they weren't having a discreet affair. We plan to follow up with Josh Cummins, Patterson's other senior aide, to see what he knows. He didn't show for our first interview because of the recent birth of a child. As for Natalie Brinkman, her credibility is suspect based on information Warren has uncovered."

"What the hell is wrong with this Cummins character?" Moe asks with a look of abject disgust. "His boss is brutally murdered, and he skips the initial investigation interview to be daddy? That's fucking lame."

Warren uncrosses his legs and stretches toward Moe, cupping his knees with his hands. He's preparing to drop a bomb of his own. "I'm guessing Brinkman told him the interview had been canceled, Lieutenant."

"Why would she do that?" he asks.

"Because he'd know she was lying about Patterson's affair."

"And now I'll bet you're going to tell me why she would lie about that."

Warren describes Sampson's dire need to find a few million dollars. "A company owned by Brinkman's family came to the rescue with a wire transfer into Sampson's checking account. We don't know the underlying terms of the transaction, but it may have violated state campaign laws."

"You're losing me, Lindquist. You're saying Brinkman and her rich daddy came to Sampson's rescue, so why would she claim he and Patterson were having an affair if it weren't true?"

"Leverage, Lieutenant. If Detective Barnes and I are right, Natalie Brinkman and her father have put the mayor in a compromising position, beholden to them. She could be testing their power over him by fabricating this affair. The big question is—what, if anything, does this have to do with Kate Patterson's murder?"

"What you're telling me, then, at least for publication to the mayor's office, is that we don't think this was a random murder. We still believe Councilwoman Patterson knew her killer. We are pursuing legitimate leads, and the investigation continues. Is that vague-enough bullshit to enable you two to proceed?"

"That's perfect," I say.

"Brilliant," Warren adds.

"Good, then get back to work."

Warren and I get up and turn to leave.

"Barnes," summons Moe.

"Yes, Lieutenant."

"I know I sent you an email, but I wanted to tell you in person. Excellent work on the Holloway murder."

"Thank you, sir. A sad end to a tragic case."

Warren and I walk across Fifth Street together. We both parked in the municipal ramp adjacent to the Government Center.

"Barnes," Warren bellows in his best Sherm Moe voice. "Excellent work on the Holloway murder."

"Eat shit and die, Warren."

"Whoa! A little sensitive today. You deserve all the credit on Holloway, but I think Sherm has more than a professional interest in you. He's divorced as of a month ago, and I know you have a thing for the senior circuit."

"You must have swallowed an asshole pill this morning along with your statins and beta blockers. Moe is over sixty, even older than you, I think, and if I so much as looked at his shrunken, wrinkled package, he'd have an infarction."

"So does that verbal barrage mean things aren't going well with the judge?"

His question ends the good-natured banter, mostly because it forces me to decide whether I'm ready to share my growing concerns about the judge with Warren. I'm not. I ignore the question—it's rhetorical anyway, and I'm about to get off the elevator, having parked a floor below Warren. Fortunately, we're the only two riders.

"I'm going to track down Josh Cummins, tomorrow," I say, turning to face Warren while holding the elevator door open. "Want to join me?"

"That's a good idea, but I have a board meeting in the morning and a late lunch with the head of the teachers' union, who's also chairman of Union Bank. Maybe we can double-team Natalie Brinkman later this week." The elevator starts to groan.

"Let's touch base tomorrow. Remember, I leave Thursday afternoon, and I'm off on Friday and Monday for the race in Mexico, so Brinkman might have to wait until next week."

"Oh, Christ, I forgot that was this week. Are you ready?"

"Never for the swim, but otherwise, yeah. We need to talk before I go, okay?"

"Okay, partner."

CHAPTER 18

It's the warmest day of the young year. I decide to take a slower, circuitous route around the lakes to enjoy the scenery and to map out the priorities of the next few days. As I turn west onto Lake of the Isles Parkway, the late-afternoon sun hovers above a stand of birch trees like a ball of fire about to descend like a phoenix to incinerate a most deserving world.

The judge has left two voice messages to go with two texts, all conveying the same message: "I'd like to see you before you go." I'm getting desperate for answers about Robin or Jason or whoever he is. But I'm also desperate to see him, even though I know it's not smart.

Five minutes later, I feel an odd combination of anxiety and joy when I see his distinctive gold Mercedes parked across the street from my building on Forty-Fourth. I park the Jeep in the underground garage and take the stairs to the first-floor lobby. I assume he's in the building even though there's a security system, but I'm wrong. He's sitting on the single wooden bench along the path that leads to the main entrance. Dressed in a hooded Nike sweatshirt with jeans and black sneakers, he's more casual than I've ever seen. His legs are crossed at the ankles, and he's engrossed in a paperback, *Blacktop Wasteland*.

I sidle up to him on the bench. "So, I guess this means you really did want to see me before I go," I say, and can't help caressing his knee while waiting for a reaction.

He slips a bookmark in the paperback as he turns to face me, peering over black-rimmed bifocals I've never seen him wear.

"I know you've been busy, and I should have called first, but something's come up, and I have to leave town tonight." He's caught me off guard. I thought I was the one leaving town.

"Business or pleasure?" I ask.

"Business, I'm sorry to say. Cassie Hansen, the judge who had a stroke and died last week, was scheduled to be the luncheon speaker at a conference in Orlando tomorrow. She presided over the drug court in the district, and I was her backup, so they've asked me to be the speaker in her place. Cassie's presentation notes and slides are great, and I believe in the program. My flight leaves at nine thirty, so I was hoping to convince you to have dinner with me at Ciao Bella and then drop me off at the airport. You can leave my car in the long-term ramp when you head to Mexico and text me the space number. I'll get it on Friday when I return from Florida and then pick you up after you win the triathlon and return a hero."

Even though he keeps a straight face, I have to laugh. "Suit yourself, but remember, I don't get back until Monday afternoon."

"Just tell me what time to show up at the airport. I don't have a court calendar on Monday."

"How long did you spend devising this plan? I'm not crazy about driving your fancy German car, but if you're buying dinner at one of my favorite restaurants and don't mind reading your book in my messy apartment while I change, I'm in."

What am I thinking? Why am I agreeing to this plan with a man who's definitely a stalker and might be worse?

"Great," he says. "But the sun feels so good, and it was totally presumptuous of me to come over here without any notice, so I'll just wait for you right here if that's okay."

Always the gentleman, at least around me. I'm both relieved and disappointed. "Suit yourself," I say. "I'll be back in ten."

Ciao Bella is tucked in the middle of an eclectic suburban neighborhood that includes upscale condos bordering assisted-living facilities, fancy restaurants abutting fast-food joints, enclosed shopping centers adjacent to strip malls, and assorted professional office buildings. It's where the elite of Edina meet middle-class Bloomington just north of the I-494 strip.

Based on my limited means and experience, I think Ciao Bella has one of the best happy hours in the Twin Cities in terms of people watching, which is an important criterion for a divorced, thirty-six-year-old cop from Chicago. Unfortunately, it's also one of the noisiest restaurants in town.

The judge politely requests a table in the intimate sunroom to the east of the main dining area. With a handful of tables surrounded by washed-brick walls and a row of tall, double-paned windows, our corner table for two is perfect. Though not as expensive or authentic, this place reminds me of RPM Italian in the River North neighborhood of Chicago, the place Wanda and I took our dad for his fiftieth more than a decade ago.

Most of the patrons are dressed casually, but the high ceilings, crystal chandeliers, and white linen tablecloths make me feel underdressed in black jeans, a blue denim shirt, and Adidas running shoes. As a mixed-race woman in an ultra-white suburb, I'm sensitive to people staring at me, judging me, especially when I'm with a professional white man in a nice place. I glance across the table at that white man, wearing a faded sweatshirt and straining to read the menu without his cheaters, and I feel better.

We order calamari and roasted cauliflower, and the judge picks a Rombauer Chardonnay to go with the appetizers without even looking at the wine list. Impressive. I know the wine will be perfect but order a local IPA on tap just in case.

The drive to the restaurant was uncomfortable. The judge asked me about the Patterson case—was there anything new on the investigation? I replied by asking him about the memorial service. Why didn't he tell me he'd be attending? Why did he go if he hardly knew her? I thought he'd be defensive. He wasn't. He said the chief judge suggested district judges should go to show respect. He apologized for not telling me. That was followed by five minutes of silence. I don't know if I believe him.

"So, tell me more about this weekend. You're meeting a friend in Houston?"

Suddenly, I've got the dry mouth. I've had nothing to eat or drink since meeting with Oliver, so I gulp half a glass of ice water and try to remember my weekend plans.

"My college roommate was a track star at Illinois State in the five thousand meters," I say. "She's competed in about a dozen triathlons and persuaded me to try one five years ago. Now I'm hooked, and she's married with a two-year-old. She says this will be her last serious race, but we'll see about that. She's a physical therapist in Houston. I fly down there Thursday afternoon and spend the night with Debby and her family. On Friday morning, we fly to Campeche for the big race."

"Have you ever been to Campeche? I've never heard of it."

"I'd never heard of it until Deb did the IRONMAN 70.3 there in 2018. It's a pretty big city, a half million maybe, on the west coast of the Yucatan. I've been to Cancun, but that's the extent of my Mexican travels. How about you?"

"I've been to Europe a few times and Australia once but never to Mexico," he says. "Do you feel ready?"

He lies so easily and then turns the spotlight back on me. With anyone else, I'd cry, "That's bullshit," but I can't—not yet. "I'll never be ready to swim a competitive mile in the Gulf of Mexico, and I didn't get in as much bike work as I wanted because of the weather, but I'm more than ready to run a good half. I'll need to do better than one fifty if I want to break six hours."

"Well, I hope you have great weather and run the race of your life. I'm curious, do you bring your own bike?" So long as the focus is on me, he's animated and engaged.

"I shipped my bike to the Hyatt in Campeche yesterday. It'll arrive before I do, hopefully in good shape. A lot of the participants ride ten-thousand-dollar racers. I invested a hundred bucks in new tires for my titanium Specialized."

Our server brings the appetizers, and I order the house specialty for dinner, Walleye Milanese over buttery mashed potatoes, the perfect meal for a downshift in my training. We eat fast because the judge wants to be at the airport by eight. He asks again about the Patterson case, and I tell him we still don't have any suspects or even a strong working theory of the case, but I don't discuss the mayor's finances or the key card. I'm relieved he doesn't ask any follow-up questions I can't answer.

As we're leaving the restaurant, he hands me the keys to the Mercedes.

"Care for a test drive?"

"Sure," I say. "But what if I prefer a different model?"

"Feel free to trade it in," he says, opening the driver's-side door for me and placing his hand on the small of my back to guide me into the well-worn tan leather seat but much more as his subtle way of showing affection. It's behavior foreign to me, and I shouldn't like it, but I love it.

Terminal one is five short miles from Ciao Bella on the interstate.

"This is the only Mercedes I've ever driven," I admit. It's got better acceleration than I expected. "You said it was old. How old?"

"Almost as old as you. It's a 1988 420SEL. I've owned it for ten years and put only thirty thousand miles on it. Feel free to take it on a joyride or two."

"Really? That's unlikely, but thanks for the offer. I hope it's okay being parked overnight on the street."

"It's fully insured but probably shouldn't be. I don't think it's worth more than fifteen or twenty grand."

We continue the small talk for the few minutes it takes to drive up to the Delta departure doors. Without saying anything, he opens his door, grabs a carry-on bag and a briefcase from the back seat, and deposits them on the sidewalk. Before I can react, he's opening my door. I get one leg out of the car and he literally lifts me out to face him.

"I'm sorry," he says, looking at me with eyes that are trying to express more.

"For what?" I ask, placing a hand on his shoulder. "Patterson's memorial service?"

"No, not that. I have to go. I hope you set a world record in Mexico or at least have a wonderful time with your friend. I'll be in touch." He gives me an extended bear hug like a man heading straight to prison and then a brief kiss on the lips before gathering his bags and rushing into the terminal.

"Safe travels," I say, to a skycap.

"Detective Barnes, it's Rochelle Griffith from the Strib. Can you meet me at the Monte Carlo for a beer around nine? We need to compare notes on Patterson. Off the record, I promise. Text me if you can make it."

I listen to the message while driving the Mercedes back to my apartment. Griffith is a reporter who splits her time between city crime and politics. I met her last summer when we were investigating the Holloway case. I leaked some information she needed for a story, information we wanted out in the community, and she kept my name out of it, as agreed. I text that I'll be there.

It's ten past nine when I finally find a parking space on North First about a block from the river. I worry a bit about parking a vintage Mercedes in this neighborhood, but it's a Tuesday night, so I chance it. You need a reservation at the Monte Carlo on the weekends and most nights in the summer, but not tonight. The restaurant is half empty, but the bar is packed. I spot Griffith sitting at a high-top nursing a tap beer.

"Hey, Rochelle, it's been a while."

She's loud, obnoxious, and hilarious in a beautiful, extra-large package. If Amy Schumer were a journalist, she'd be Rochelle Griffith. The only difference—she's gay. She assumed an athletic, big-boned, biracial cop from Chicago was butch. Why else would she hit on me the first night we met? I like her; I don't want to sleep with her.

"Hi, Lincoln," she says, giving me the once-over, which makes me smirk. "I almost ordered you a Blue Moon." Maybe early forties, she's let her blonde hair grow down to her shoulders and is wearing a Wild jersey over ripped white jeans.

"That would have been perfect," I say, but when our server stops by, I order a double Irish whiskey on the rocks.

"What the fuck, Detective? When did you start drinking the hard stuff? And a double shot?"

"I've kind of acquired a taste for the Irish, and a single shot isn't worth the trouble. What's the buzz in city hall these days?"

"The place is in limbo," she says, washing down a handful of peanuts with her beer. "Everyone's waiting for you to solve the Patterson case."

"Right."

"I don't get it. I mean, I've been around this town for a long time. We've got more than our share of mental cases, crazy bastards, and senseless violence, but from what I've heard, Patterson was executed by someone she knew. She may have been a tight-assed, controlling know-it-all, but that shouldn't get you killed."

"What does the mayor's office have to say about it?"

"As I said, the place is in limbo. Sampson hasn't said a word, except for his little speech at her funeral. His communications staff refers the media to Chief Hawkins, and as you know, Hawkins serves too many masters. How many times can you say, 'the investigation continues, and we'll update you with any significant developments'?"

"That's a pretty good imitation, Rochelle. Unfortunately, for now, it's the truth. We have no suspects or even persons of interest, but off the record, forensic evidence indicates it's more likely than not she knew the killer. When we have an actionable suspect, I promise you'll be the first reporter to know."

"That promise and eight bucks will get me another beer, so I guess I can't complain."

Our server drops off my drink, and Rochelle orders another beer.

"I don't know what it's worth to you," she says philosophically, "but there's a hot rumor that's been simmering around city hall."

"It's worth one beer if you tell me, and two if it's good," I say, enjoying the kick of the whiskey as it warms my insides.

"Marvin Carter, the mayor's chief of staff, resigned about a month ago to accept an appointment by the governor as commissioner of commerce."

"I read about that," I say.

"But what you didn't read is that Sampson offered the job to Natalie Brinkman, Kate Patterson's top aide, and there was going to be a press release announcing her acceptance on the Monday after Patterson's murder, but now it's on hold."

"You're right. I didn't know. I interviewed Brinkman last week, and she didn't mention it." Instead, she claimed her boss was having an affair with the mayor. This is getting interesting.

"I can tell you, Sampson's staff isn't happy about the prospect of a rich, ambitious white girl running the show. You know what they're thinking."

"I can think of a few things, but none of them good. In any event, I'm picking up the tab." I finish my drink and flip a couple of Jacksons on the table as I get ready to leave.

"Nice tip," Griffith says.

"I'm getting rid of all my twenties until they replace Old Hickory with Harriet Tubman. Let's keep in touch on Patterson."

"I'm counting on it."

A biting wind smacks me in the face as I leave the Monte Carlo shortly after ten and start jogging back to the Mercedes to stay warm. The temperature has plummeted. The North Loop neighborhood is eerily dark and quiet. I recall deciding to leave my jacket in the car, even though my badge, gun, and mace are all in it. That uneasy feeling hangs in the air as I reach the Mercedes, dig in the pocket of my jeans for the keys and sense a looming shadow approaching under the streetlamp at the intersection of First and Third.

"Give up your keys and purse, bitch."

Startled, I pivot to the left, toward a muffled, adolescent voice, and see I'm surrounded by four boys, all shorter than me, all wearing leather jackets and dark masks, two holding switchblades. White, Black or some other race I can't tell in the dark, and I don't care. I decide in an instant that telling them I'm a cop will do more harm than good. Instead, I devise a plan and buy precious seconds.

"Okay, just let me get my wallet out of my back pocket," I say with both hands high in the air in a surrender pose. With their undeveloped teenage brains, I'm betting their eyes will be fixed on my hand as it moves slowly, deliberately from above my head toward the nonexistent pocket. I bend slightly at the waist and knees, wait for the starting gun in my head and spring through a small opening between the two hoodlums not brandishing knives. I'm in a dead sprint down Third Avenue toward the river. A quick glance behind reveals two of the delinquents are giving chase, and one is actually closing the gap, so I pick up the pace and veer north on River Road. Note to self—the Walleye Milanese with beer and whiskey is not a good pregame meal.

A stitch in my left side makes me turn my head and see that one of my pursuers has dropped out of the race; the other must be on the track team. I grab my cell phone from a side pocket and clutch it in my left hand as I decelerate slightly to give the remaining masked crusader the impression he's catching me. This motivates him to go all out at the same time I stop abruptly, turn, and rearrange his face when the heel of my right hand collides with his fast-moving nose. He collapses onto the pavement, dropping his knife and crying out in pain. I wish I could find it in my overtaxed heart to feel sorry for the little prick, but I don't have time. I punch in 911, identify myself and the situation to intake, and suggest that two squads meet me at my car.

My assailant sits up and removes his mask to examine his injuries. He either is Hispanic or simply specializes in Spanish profanity. I put his knife in my pocket, snap a few photos of his blood-stained face, and start running back to my car, worried that his three friends could still be in the neighborhood and might come to his aid with more than switchblades.

I get back to the Mercedes without incident, but my right wrist and palm are throbbing. I don't recognize any of the four officers who emerge from two squads that show up to meet me, flashers on but thankfully no sirens. I expect a rash of shit for leaving my badge and weapon in the vehicle but am pleasantly surprised by the empathy and professionalism of my fellow cops. One of them even hands me a chemical cold pack to reduce the swelling in my hand. They ask about the old Mercedes, not a car they associate with a thirty-something female detective, and I lie, telling them it's my dad's and hoping they don't check the plates.

I hand over the knife and describe the attempted carjacking and ensuing chase and knockout punch. I also share my photo of the bloody attacker, who might pass for a youthful Ricky Ricardo with a badly broken nose. I thank my colleagues for the quick response and wish them luck trying to apprehend the four baby gang members, but we all know that's unlikely.

Back at my apartment, I move the Jeep to the street and park the Mercedes in the underground garage. No use tempting fate a second time. It's too late to call Warren, so I text him that I'm meeting Josh Cummins in the morning and will be in touch before I leave for Mexico. For the first time, I feel a sense of dread about my partner's imminent retirement. Do I want to keep doing this job in this city without him?

CHAPTER 19

A short, slight young man with slicked-back brown hair and wire-rimmed glasses, Josh Cummins wears the preppy uniform—tan khakis with a powder-blue dress shirt and navy blazer—and appears to fit the definition of a political wonk. I hand him a Styrofoam cup filled with steaming green tea from a dispenser and sit across from him with my Starbucks dark roast at the round worktable that Warren and I share.

"I'm sure it's awful," I say with conviction. "But I'm not a tea person."

"At least it's hot," he says.

"Thank you for coming down to the precinct to meet with me. I imagine it's difficult to leave the house, with a new baby and all."

"As I explained over the phone, Natalie lied to me and then lied to you. She told me that the meeting with you and your partner had been rescheduled and then she told you I was blowing it off to stay home with my kid. Listen, Detective Barnes, my boss for the past four years, a woman I respected and busted my butt for, was murdered. I'd have to be an uncaring, irresponsible dick not to assist the investigation in any way I could, new baby or not."

"So why didn't Natalie want you at the meeting?"

"What do you know about Natalie Brinkman, Detective?" Another man who doesn't know you never answer a question with a question.

"I know she worked for Kate Patterson longer than you did and was one of the last people to see her alive. I know her father is one of the wealthiest men in America." I gamble on this last one. "And she told us your boss was having an affair with Mayor Sampson, but I have serious doubts about that."

"I'll spill my guts about Natalie if you promise not to use my name in any report or document that might become public."

"I can do my best to protect you, Josh, but I can't promise confidentiality or anonymity. What are you afraid of?"

"Natalie. I'm afraid of Natalie. She's the most conniving person I know. I would even say evil or maybe diabolical is a better word. You mentioned her dad. No one's seen him in weeks because his lung cancer, which has been a well-kept secret for over a year, has metastasized into his liver and brain, and he's in Germany getting some experimental treatments. Natalie's an only child. Her mother signed a prenup and left the marriage with fifty million and a condo in Aspen after fifteen years. He had a live-in girlfriend younger than Natalie, but when the cancer got bad, he paid her a few million to get lost. In other words, Natalie will inherit an empire worth over a billion dollars. It would be several billion but for the devaluation of the Brinkman portfolio during COVID."

"Whoa, whoa, hold on a minute. I appreciate the information and your perspective, but I have to ask, how do you know all this?"

"I'm a professional researcher, Detective. The information on the Brinkman companies is readily available through a number of public sources, but most of what I'm telling you comes directly from Natalie. She's been using me as a sounding board for her schemes and ambitious plans, knowing I would never betray her and, even if I did, I don't know anyone who matters. On the other hand, she'd betray me or anyone else in a nanosecond. She's incredibly bright, but her only moral compass is political expedience. She has a lust for power that would make Machiavelli blush. She has a six-year plan to be a congresswoman, a ten-year plan to be a US senator."

"Wow," I say. "What did Councilwoman Patterson think about these plans?"

"I'm sure she didn't know, at least not the details. She and Natalie worked together on issues and campaign strategies, but they weren't close because no one got close to Kate Patterson. It was a classic mutual use. Patterson exploited Natalie's connections, access to wealthy contributors, and willingness to do anything to get the job done, and Natalie used the councilwoman's position and political connections to learn the system and the players and to position herself to run for office. According to Natalie, Patterson had assured her she would run for mayor last year, which would have vacated the only ward in Minneapolis that can be won by a rich, white woman. But after the upheaval caused by the pandemic, the uptick in violent crime on the north side, and the protests, destruction, and calls for reform that followed George Floyd, Patterson figured she had no chance in a citywide election, so she would continue to push her agenda as president of the council.

"Natalie was livid. She felt betrayed, though I'm sure she never confronted Patterson. Instead, she found a way to convince Marcus Sampson to offer her the top job in his administration. Just like a GPS unit, she recalibrated the route when she encountered a roadblock. Her appointment as chief of staff was going to be announced last Monday, but it got derailed by the murder."

"Do you think Kate Patterson knew about that?" I ask.

"Not from Natalie. No way. And not because she was afraid to tell her. No, Natalie has a cruel, vengeful gene. She wanted Kate to learn about it from a press release."

"Unless the mayor told Patterson when they met on the afternoon before she died," I speculate. I'm beginning to understand why Natalie might have made up the affair between her boss and the mayor.

"I was on leave Friday afternoon. I didn't know they'd met, but if the mayor told her, she would have been royally pissed but would have acted like she already knew. Without question, she would have considered it an act of betrayal."

"I get that," I say, "but I don't get why Mayor Sampson would hire Brinkman away from the president of the city council, someone he might want on his side of an issue from time to time."

"He wouldn't, Detective, unless he didn't have a choice. I don't know what dirt or leverage she has on him, but it must be big."

"You don't think the mayor was having an affair with Kate Patterson, do you?"

"I would be less surprised if Donald Trump were having an affair with Rosie O'Donnell."

"Really?" I say skeptically, cringing but smiling at the unappealing image.

"Seriously, there was no chemistry between them. It was all business—business and politics. There was animosity from time to time but nothing close to attraction. It seems pretty clear that Natalie wanted to hinder your investigation, keep you occupied trying to investigate something that's impossible to disprove. One of the participants is dead, and the other would never admit it even if it were true. And believe me, Natalie doesn't care if you catch her in a lie. She thinks rules and morals that apply to the rest of us mortals don't apply to her."

"Good to know," I say. "Maybe she's the one having an affair with the mayor."

"Possible, but not likely. She's been living with the head of security for her father's corporate empire for about a year. He's a former marine officer and cybersecurity expert. She's brought him to a few events and dinners. He's an impressive physical specimen, the strong, silent type who wouldn't be sanguine about sharing his girlfriend, but like a lot of those types, he has an Achilles' heel, two of them in his case."

"Really? And are you going to tell me what they are?"

Josh cracks a smile for the first time in our conversation. "Sure. Natalie Brinkman is one of them. He is absolutely smitten with her, and she knows it and will use it to her advantage, since I don't think she's capable of loving anyone but her father. The second is vodka. He's hooked on Russian vodka. It nearly got him dishonorably discharged from the service."

"How do you know that? Did Natalie tell you?"

"Are you kidding? She would never disclose a weakness about her perfect boyfriend. Remember, Detective, I'm a researcher. I've always feared Natalie, so I've made it my business to acquire information about her, especially stuff I can use against her if I need it."

Oh my. Josh is beginning to scare me. I take a good look at him and think, maybe not. "Then you must know the name of this gentleman?"

"Sure. It's Andrew Slayton. Major Andrew Slayton."

"Do they live in the city?" I ask, thinking I need to have a follow-up conversation with Natalie at her place.

"She has a luxury condo in Kenwood, overlooking downtown. I've been there once. It must be worth millions. I'm not sure how much time she's spending there though. When her dad's not around, she often stays at his compound out on Lake Minnetonka."

"Thanks, Josh. This has been helpful. What about you? Will you try to catch on with Kate Patterson's successor on the council?"

"No. I've already accepted a position as a researcher with the state senate. I start in two weeks. I love politics, but I need a job with more stability than working for an elected official."

"Well congratulations. If I have more questions, can I reach you on your cell?"

"Sure, but please don't tell Natalie that I told you any of this stuff."

"You're really afraid of her, aren't you?"

"Terrified."

Andrew Robert Slayton. Between icing my purple hand and packing a suitcase for the hot, sticky weather in Campeche, I spend Wednesday night researching the senior vice president and director of security for Brinkman, Jacobs & Company. Now forty-four, Major Slayton retired after a twenty-year career as a Marine Raider. That means he was on a team of highly trained soldiers who conducted covert operations in places like Rwanda, Somalia, Libya, Syria, and Afghanistan. It also means he could be a skilled assassin. Mix that fact with a fifth of vodka and a whiff of Natalie's expensive perfume and who knows what kind of trouble he could get into?

The company's website says he lives in Chicago. I ponder the nature of his relationship with Natalie Brinkman but only for a few moments. I end the insistent buzzing of my phone by taking Warren's call.

"Are you still going to Mexico?" he asks.

Someone has told him about the thwarted carjacking and the injury to my hand. "Of course. Why wouldn't I be?"

"Let's just say I know a few more patrol officers than you do, and one of them said you didn't play nice with some naughty boys last night. I'm glad you're okay. They said four teenagers tried to steal your dad's Mercedes. I know part of that statement isn't true, but I let it slide."

I give Warren a recap of my night in under a minute and then tell him about my conversation with Josh Cummins. He gives me the silent treatment for several seconds. He may be the worst phone conversationalist since Alexander Graham Bell invented the damn thing.

"Are you still there, Warren?"

"Of course," he says. "I was just jotting down a few notes about Slayton. Anyway, all of this together with what I learned yesterday confirms my feeling that, at least until we get some intel on that key card, we should focus our efforts on Natalie Brinkman."

"And what did you learn yesterday?"

"The chair of Union Bank is also the executive director of the Minnesota Education Association, the main teachers' union in the state. Her name is Sally Alworth. She's a former high school principal with a master's in education. She's also a CPA. Several unions, including our police union and the MEA, use a firm called Williams-McBane to administer their health and welfare plans. I met Sally at one of the firm's seminars a few years ago and had lunch with her a few times to discuss the performance of our respective medical and pension plans. When I heard that Mayor Sampson was turned down for a loan, I called her. She's the one who told me about the mayor's financial straits and the bailout from the Brinkman organization. But she declined to tell me any more over the phone, so we met for lunch yesterday at the Capital Grille."

"Ooh, romantic," I interrupt because I can't resist.

"Her choice. It's quiet, and we sat in a corner booth far from any eavesdroppers."

"Of course," I say.

"Wait till you hear what she had to say before being such a smartass."

"Sorry," I say, more sincerely.

"Sally makes good money with the teachers' union, but she's married to a partner at the Boulay accounting firm, and she's inherited a few million from her family. Now here's the rub—her next-door neighbors in Linden Hills are Kate Patterson and Paul Bagley."

"You are kidding me," I say, incredulous. "Were they friends?"

"Acquaintances would be more accurate," he says. "But no one was a bigger champion of teachers and the teachers' unions than Kate Patterson, so she and Sally talked shop frequently and had a close professional relationship.

"After the mayor's loan was denied by the bank's senior credit committee, his dealings with the bank were reviewed at a special board meeting. Sally was concerned that Sampson was violating campaign laws, so the first person she consulted was Patterson. Apparently, the council president didn't appreciate gray areas or nuances when it came to campaign laws. She told Sally she needed to confront the mayor and force him to make a full disclosure. She also threatened to go to the state board. A week later, Patterson was dead."

"And when during all this do you think she started having the affair with Sampson?"

"Precisely. I'll try to schedule something with Natalie Brinkman for the middle of next week."

"Good luck," I say. "She has no incentive to talk to us."

"Good luck to you too. Safe travels and bring back the gold."

"Thanks, Warren. I'll be happy to finish."

Before I can slip my phone in my pocket, I get another call from a number I don't recognize with a 218 area code. It's Northern Minnesota, so I take it. "Lincoln Barnes speaking."

"Hi, Detective Barnes. It's Sheriff MacDonald, Sam MacDonald up in Lake County."

"Sheriff, good to hear your voice. Did I forget a pair of gloves or a notebook in Two Harbors?" I'm sure I didn't, and that means he's got some news about the judge.

"No, nothing like that. Your story about J. R. Campbell piqued my interest. I did some snooping around and discovered a few things I thought you'd like to know."

"Thanks, Sheriff. I appreciate that." Even though it creeps me out when he calls him J. R. Campbell.

"The first thing I did was check out Hilda Gildemeister's cottage on the lake. I had assumed it was boarded up, and the yard was an unsightly tangle of overgrowth and weeds. You can't see the house from Highway 61. When I drove down the gravel driveway, I was amazed. It's apparent that not only has someone been maintaining the place, but they've made some major improvements, including a second-floor loft and a new firepit. The yard was neat, wood for the fireplace stacked in a bin. The half logs on the cottage and the cedar boards on the back deck have been stained recently. I remembered that John Guzzo, a friend of my dad's who had a machine shop and construction business in Finland Township, did some work for Hilda many years ago. The family had a side business taking care of the nicer properties on the lake. They did everything from plowing to painting to roofing. John's long dead, but one of his grandsons who's in his forties has carried on the business. After my visit to Hilda's, I drove up to Finland and dropped in on Jake Guzzo. I learned he's been working for the judge for fifteen years. Says he's a good guy who's paid a lot to upgrade and maintain the place, especially since he started spending a couple weekends a year up here. He said he hasn't seen him for a few years, but the last time he was up, right before the pandemic, he was with a woman."

"I'm not sure how I feel about that. It seems like another part of his life he's concealed from me," I say.

"That may be," he says. "I figured you'd like to know that he's been coming home occasionally. He seemed to be trying to escape his past for many years, but perhaps he changed his mind."

"You're right about that, Sheriff," I say, wondering why I miss the man and am beginning to fret because I haven't heard from him since last night.

"I wouldn't have called you this late if that was all I had," he says. "I have a friend in the U.S. Embassy in Mexico City. He worked for me in the Secret Service, and now he's the lead navy attaché. He confirmed with the state police that the investigation into Sara Hyatt's suspicious death is still very active. He even got his hands on a summary that was prepared by the local police in Playa del Carmen through the consulate general in Mérida. All of the reports are in Spanish, so he's having them translated before forwarding them to me. I should be able to email a PDF to you sometime this weekend."

I decide not to tell him I'll be in the Yucatan this weekend. "That's great, Sheriff. I'll need to do something to return the favor."

"Come visit again, and we'll chat," he says. "As I said, I'm curious about how this mystery will play out, and I might have something else that could intrigue you."

"Now I'm curious," I say.

"By the way, good luck in your big race this weekend."

"I can't believe you remembered. I didn't think I mentioned it." But he's already gone.

CHAPTER 20

Deb picks me up at the George Bush Intercontinental Airport north of Houston at half past three. We'll be back here tomorrow morning at six for the flight to Campeche via Mexico City. She and her husband, David, a security officer at Johnson Space Center, met on the track team at Illinois State, where he threw the shot put and javelin, and she was a distance runner. They moved from a tenth-floor condo to a three-bedroom Colonial with a pool on Copper Canyon Drive in Heritage Park when the baby was born. Their seemingly happy life in urban, middle-class America reminds me of my sister's storybook existence in Saint Paul. Some might say I'm jealous, and maybe I should be, but I'm not. Like my dad, I want to have a positive impact on this world, despite, or perhaps because of, all the racist, self-centered cowards who create barriers for people like me. If I had a family, I would have to make compromises I'm not ready to make.

I'm not a thrill seeker, but I love adventure, especially outdoors amidst the elements, and I have a visceral drive to challenge myself, physically and intellectually. After enduring an abusive partner and bad marriage, I'm prepared to live alone indefinitely. I've been open to dating and vulnerable, on occasion, to short-term hookups for sex or, more accurately, the warmth and complete release of sharing my most personal space and longings with another human being.

The judge is different from anyone who's been close to me—unanticipated but not unwanted. He's smart and thoughtful and kind, and I'm physically, magnetically drawn to him. But he's also a stalker and possibly a murderer. How could I be infatuated with such a man? He's an enigma who's thrown me off my game. My instincts tell me to confront him about the contents of his diary, his evasiveness, and his downright lies. But I'm afraid—not afraid of him but afraid to alienate him forever because I'm making incorrect assumptions with only partial evidence. And he hasn't contacted me since I dropped him off at the airport. Why?

———————————

There's a right turn after the first hundred meters of the 1.2-mile swim in the warm, choppy waters of the Gulf of Mexico near the Campeche Country Club marina. The course is teeming with bodies of all shapes, sizes, skin tones, and strokes. The fastest swimmers break out into a tapered line ahead of the pack. Plodders like me struggle to find open water to maneuver. As I navigate that first turn, I see a course marker a few yards to my right. There's not room for another swimmer to pass me on the inside. A thick, broad-shouldered white woman wearing a gold swim cap and matching one-piece literally shoves me sideways with her left hand while cutting in between me and the marker. She's a splasher and a thrasher. As I struggle to right my body in the water, she kicks me in the temple, drawing blood with her toenail like a razor.

"You fucking bitch!" I scream, choking on salt water and checking the size of the gash with my hand. I notice an ugly skull and crossbones tattoo on the cheater's calf. She's moving too fast for me to catch in the water, but I will catch her.

I settle into a rhythm in the middle of the pack. The adrenaline ignited by my confrontation with the thrasher gives me an extra boost in the tepid water. I make it to the finish with a belly full of salt water, a bloody face, and a swollen right hand that resembles a steamed lobster. Jogging to the transition area, a soccer field a block away, I find my bike and duffel. I don't break fifty minutes in the swim, but I'm close and feeling strong enough to make up time on my bike.

The fifty-six-mile road course is flatter than an Iowa farm field and hugs the picturesque gulf for the first several miles. I'm aided by a westerly wind and a throng of locals cheering wildly for anyone and everyone, including "USA 3425!" which happens to be my bib number. While I'm aware of a montage of colors and shapes—the faces, storefronts, and buildings along the way—I have to focus on the course and the other cyclists or I'll collide with another bike and wipe out, or worse, get disqualified. I want to average better than twenty miles an hour, which takes all the strength, stamina, and concentration I can muster.

The route is a half loop and back, so the last twenty miles will be into a fifteen to twenty-mile-per-hour headwind. With temperatures in the mid-eighties and high humidity, I don't mind some air resistance. Thanks to my diligent training regimen, my legs feel strong, though I know I'll need a reserve tank of energy for the half marathon ahead. My hand is throbbing, despite the four ibuprofen I swallowed after the swim, so gripping the handlebar and applying the right brake is difficult. I have to ignore the pain. Easier said than done. The surplus of salt water in my gut makes me regurgitate the energy bar I ate right before hopping on my bike, much to the disgust of onlookers and cyclists in the vicinity.

After losing time in the water, I gauge my performance on the bike by whether I pass more bikers than bikers pass me. I have a pretty accurate sense of it, and the ratio must be at least four to one in my favor.

According to my Garmin watch, I finish the cycling course in two hours and forty-seven minutes, eight under my goal. I force myself to eat a peanut butter granola bar and wash it down with water after dumping my bike in the second transition area and heading for my best leg of the race. I take a minute to cover the stinging wound on my face with an oversized Band-Aid from my first-aid kit, though I know it's unlikely to adhere for long under the sweltering conditions.

The running course winds through the heart of downtown Campeche. Like the cycling track, it's flat and filled with cheering spectators. Deb said the course was fast, three four-mile loops and then the big finish at the sea gate. My strategy is to start slow, between seven-and-a-half- and eight-minute miles, and quicken my pace to seven minutes or better by mile six or seven. My hand feels numb but better now that I have nothing to grip. It's still hot, but the tall downtown buildings block the afternoon sun, and the prospect of a personal-best triathlon time keeps my spirits up as I start passing other runners at a fast clip, wondering how many of them kicked my ass in the swim.

I'm not a vengeful person, most of the time. Maneuvering to the left side of the road to pass a slower runner, I look up to my right and see a distinctive tattoo on the calf of a burly, pasty-skinned woman directly in my path. She's wearing a lime-green top with black shorts and a white baseball cap. A brown, braided ponytail bounces off her thick neck with each stride. We're nearing the end of the second loop with about five miles to go.

It's the thrasher for sure. I feel a sudden boost of energy as I consider my options, most of which will get me disqualified from the race. I decide to take the "high road" in the spirit of wily old Denny Green, one of my dad's favorite football coaches, who had a stint with Northwestern before making it big with the Vikings.

I speed up to get next to her. We're running stride for stride when I turn and look straight into her dull gray eyes while pointing to the bandage on my temple. Squinting at me and then tossing her head back as if she doesn't know what she's done, the thrasher is laboring in the heat. She speaks haltingly, trying to catch her breath, with a heavy Russian accent.

"I don't know you. What you want from me?"

"You shoved me in the water to get ahead at the first turn of the swim and then kicked me in the face," I say with daggers in my eyes. "You really need to cut your toenails!"

I don't wait for a response and run the next mile in under seven minutes, leaving her in my wake. In fact, I should thank the thrasher for motivating me to finish the run in an hour and forty-five minutes, five minutes faster than my goal.

I cross the finish line exhausted but elated. I spot Deb talking to a couple of women about twenty yards beyond the warm-down area. She's not expecting me for another five to ten minutes. When she sees me, she raises both arms above her head and jumps up and down. Then she sprints over and gives me a bear hug that nearly squeezes the life out of me but feels wonderful.

"Lincoln! You did it! You broke six hours!"

"Thanks, Deb. I got sidetracked a bit during the swim but made it up in the last two legs."

"What happened to your face?" she asks, staring at my half-bandaged temple like a concerned mom.

I tell her about my encounter with the thrasher, and we both have a good laugh. I grab a banana, a few granola bars, and a bottle of water from a kiosk of healthy goodies, and we enjoy a giddy stroll over to the transition area to retrieve our duffel bags. We've already arranged to have the bikes picked up, packed, and shipped home. Our hotel, the Campeche Plaza, is about a mile away, which we happily walk on this gorgeous, sunny day.

The official race results are online by seven thirty. We order room service and champagne to celebrate. Deb finishes second in our age group (thirty-five to thirty-nine) and ninth overall with a time of five hours and fifteen minutes. I finish eighth in our age group and twenty-first overall with a time of five hours and forty-one minutes. In my euphoria, I text my results to the judge. I've told Deb about him but not the whole story, not about the diary or his possible involvement in the death of Sara Hyatt. I downplay my feelings for him, mostly to protect myself until I get some answers, and partly because I'm embarrassed that I'm in this predicament. Our flight to Houston leaves at seven on Sunday morning, so we make final plans to get to the airport, and she catches me off guard with a simple question.

"Hey, Lincoln, I understand why you're flying from Houston to Chicago on United, but why are you going to Milwaukee instead of Minneapolis?"

Thanks to my mom's status at United, I was able to make a last-minute change to my return trip. Instead of flying from Houston to Chicago to Minneapolis, I'll take an earlier flight to Chicago in order to catch a connector to Milwaukee. I'll only have an hour to make the Chicago flight out of Houston. I was originally scheduled to leave Houston late on Sunday afternoon, getting into Minneapolis at ten at night, which would have enabled me to have a leisurely lunch with Deb.

"I'm sorry, Deb," I say, my mind scrambling for a plausible explanation. "There's been a development in one of my cases, and I need to interview a witness in Milwaukee on Monday. I'll be back in the Twin Cities later that night."

"With the pandemic lingering, I figured most long-distance interviews were still done via Zoom."

"Many still are," I agree, "but I'd like to assess this guy and his living situation while conducting the interview."

"Sounds dangerous and a lot more exciting than my life," she says. "Truthfully, I've really enjoyed reconnecting and was looking forward to a few more hours with you before getting back to my little family. Maybe we can set our sights on another race in a few years in a fun place like Napa or Miami Beach. You could be a world-class triathlete by then."

"Whenever you're up for another one, I'm in," I say, ignoring her "world-class triathlete" comment.

CHAPTER 21

Sunday is a long day—longer because I don't get a reply text or phone call from the judge.

My flight from Chicago to Milwaukee's Mitchell International Airport leaves two hours late and lands at six thirty. I rent a Nissan Rogue, grab some unhealthy snacks at a convenience store, and drive to my hotel on Blue Mound Road just north of I-94. I spend most of the evening researching Dr. Timothy Hyatt, celebrity orthopedic surgeon. After graduating from Medical College of Wisconsin, he had residencies in general and orthopedic surgery at St. Luke's Medical Center in Chicago and earned a fellowship in sports medicine at New England Baptist Hospital in Boston. He's been the team physician for the Milwaukee Bucks and Marquette University basketball teams for over a decade and has written three books on reconstructive joint surgery techniques and his successes on competitive athletes. He commands a $20k speaking fee and has given lectures and speeches around the world. Hyatt is a big shot for sure.

Not wanting to give him advance notice of my visit, I call him at eight, explaining that I'm a Minneapolis detective who's come across evidence that might connect someone to his wife's death. I say I want to talk to him before sharing my information with authorities in Mexico and possibly with the FBI. I thought he'd be curious and appreciative, but he's terse and all business, clearly not happy at being disturbed on a Sunday night or reminded of his dead wife's case. He instructs me to be at his home in Brookfield at eight on Monday morning. He'll give me thirty minutes, even though he knows my so-called evidence is "bullshit" because, no matter what anyone claims, his wife was the victim of an accidental drowning in the Gulf of Mexico. I wish I had the Mexican police reports from MacDonald's friend, but I don't.

After a light breakfast and three cups of mud-butt coffee, I leave the Brookfield DoubleTree at seven thirty. Siri leads me into the middle of upper-crust suburbia, past pristine Westmoor Country Club and ultimately to Driftwood Court, where the Hyatts have a sprawling modern mansion of brick, stone, and glass, complete with a manicured front lawn the size of a softball field, a four-car garage, and a fenced-in backyard that I see, through some slats, includes a rectangular swimming pool.

I park the Rogue near the end of the driveway in case one of Dr. Hyatt's adult children, or perhaps a lady friend, needs to exit the garage, though I'm pretty sure both kids are married and don't live at home. I grab my nylon portfolio from the passenger seat, and my cell starts to vibrate. It's Warren. I'm taking a day of vacation, but it's on a need-to-know basis, and I neglected to tell my partner. Truth be told, I intended to text him earlier but forgot.

"Good morning, Detective Lindquist. I'm surprised I didn't hear from you last night."

"You said you wouldn't be back until tonight, so I wanted to let you enjoy your time away." I guess I did tell him. "How was the big race?"

"It was great," I say. Dr. Hyatt must have seen my car. He's standing on his porch, wearing a dark suit and red tie, his arms folded in front of his chest. Not a patient look. "I'll tell you all about it when I get back this afternoon. I gotta go, Warren."

"Okay, but did you read the Metro section of the Strib this morning? You probably already knew."

"No, I haven't read the paper and knew what?" I ask, hurrying down the driveway and making eye contact with Hyatt.

"Your friend, Judge Gildemeister, resigned last week. The article says for personal reasons."

I have to end the call, but I'm in semi-shock. Resigned? He just attended a conference in Orlando. Didn't he?

"Good morning, Dr. Hyatt. I'm Detective Lincoln Barnes," I say, extending my right hand toward this imposing man, who must be at least six and a half feet tall.

"Morning," he replies in a booming bass voice, turning away without shaking my hand and opening one of the glass double doors to his home. "Come in and have a seat on the couch. There's coffee and water on the table. You need anything else?"

"No, sir, I've already eaten, but thank you." I sense the need to be on my best behavior to get any information out of this guy. I pour myself a fourth cup of coffee as we sit across from each other, me on a white leather sofa, and Hyatt, whose full mug of coffee is already waiting for him, on a matching chair. I recall reading that Hyatt played football at Penn, where he was Phi Beta Kappa. He must have been a lineman; he makes Sheriff MacDonald look small. When he turns briefly to cough into his fist and I catch a side profile—a strong, square jaw and receding hairline—it hits me. I've seen this man before. I'm sure of it.

"You have a beautiful home, Dr. Hyatt," I say, trying to break the ice. The two-story great room is stylish but not ostentatious. The focal point is a stone fireplace with a large, framed watercolor of sailboats on Lake Mendota hanging above the mantel.

"Thanks," he replies, and then wistfully says, "It's all Sara. So, tell me what someone in Minneapolis knows about what happened to my wife in Mexico two years ago. I have to be at my clinic at nine, so you've got about thirty minutes." Snap.

"Let me say how very sorry I am for your loss, Doctor," I make a point of saying before getting to the real point. He doesn't respond or react in any way. "Did your wife ever mention the name Robin Gildemeister?"

"Not that I recall, but she knew a lot of people in the publishing business, her tennis leagues, and the kids' schools, so she might have."

"What about Jason or J. R. Campbell?"

"You mean Sara's hometown boyfriend? I haven't heard that name in twenty-five years."

"You know him?"

"Only of him. We've never met."

Now I remember where I've seen Hyatt. But how could that be? "Were you at Councilwoman Patterson's funeral in Minneapolis last week, sitting with her family?"

"Why, yes I was. Paul Bagley has been one of my closest friends since med school. You were there too?"

"I was. I'm investigating Patterson's murder."

"That was a terrible tragedy, but what does it have to do with Sara?" He's not making this easy.

"Probably nothing," I admit. "But since you're only giving me thirty minutes, I ask that you give me some latitude. Fair enough?"

"Sure. You've got about fifteen minutes left."

"So, you knew Kate Patterson?"

"Kate and Sara were roommates at Ripon College, about an hour north of here. Paul met Kate during the summer before her senior year when they worked in the same office building in downtown Milwaukee. Paul and I were in our last year at Wisconsin Medical College. We had an apartment near the school, which Kate visited every weekend. She kept telling me her roommate and I would be perfect together, if only she could convince her to expand her horizons and spend a weekend with us in Milwaukee. It took two weekends with me and Kate's powers of persuasion for Sara to dump the hometown boyfriend. The rest is history, Detective."

"Did the four of you remain close?"

"We'd get together maybe two or three times a year as couples. Sometimes for a destination vacation or just a weekend here or in the Twin Cities. Recently, we've seen each other at our kids' weddings. To be honest, Paul and I have been so busy with our practices that we probably wouldn't have gotten together if Sara and Kate hadn't planned things. Neither of us texts or has a presence on social media. On the other hand, Sara and Kate would communicate in some fashion at least once a week. They were like sisters. But again, what does this have to do with Sara's accident?"

I recall Paul Bagley saying that Kate's best friend had died recently, but it never would have occurred to me that her best friend was the judge's high school crush. Why would it? In the "Dear John" letter in the diary, Sara refers to her roommate as "Patty."

"I'll get to that in a minute, Dr. Hyatt, but did your wife ever refer to Kate Patterson as Patty?"

"She did back in college because there were two Kates living in their four-person suite when they were freshmen. She called her Patty throughout college and maybe for a few years beyond, but not after Kate married Paul. How would you know about that? Did Jason Campbell tell you?"

"No. I think Dr. Bagley might have mentioned it. Anyway, it's not important. What is important is that I've seen evidence that someone was stalking your wife during your trip to Mexico."

"Who and what evidence?" he asks, setting his coffee mug on the table. Lowering his bifocals to the edge of his patrician nose, he gives me a look intended to make me feel small and inferior. It's a look I've seen many times from overbearing white men.

"I can't disclose all of it at this time, but I can say it's likely the man you know as Jason Campbell was in Playa del Carmen when you and your wife were there in March of 2020. We have evidence that he made the trip to surveil and photograph his former girlfriend, Sara Wheaton Hyatt. I assume you never saw him. Did you?"

He looks like he swallowed a beehive. "That's hard to believe, but no, no, absolutely not. As I said, I've never met the man."

"I know this might be difficult, but can you tell me everything you remember about the night your wife died? Starting with the dinner in your honor. What was that about?" Flattery could get me somewhere with this guy.

"I guess you've done your homework," he says, leaning back in his chair. "I was the featured speaker at the annual meeting of the Academy of Orthopedic Surgeons, a four-day conference for fellows of the academy and guests. On Friday night, they honored a handful of doctors at the awards dinner. I was the recipient of the Tipton Leadership Award. Sara and I sat at the head table, and I gave the usual two-minute gratitude speech. She's had her fill of these conferences and dinners in recent years, so I wasn't surprised when she begged off attending the poolside reception after dinner. I spent time with colleagues and vendors, and she did her own thing. It's been that way for years. She said she was going to take a stroll on the beach, maybe go for a swim, and be back before midnight. At some point, she must have returned to our suite to change into a swimsuit.

"I went from the reception to the bar to talk shop with a couple surgeons and completely lost track of the time. When I returned to our room, it was one in the morning and no Sara. When she didn't answer her cell, I got worried and walked down to the beach to look for her. I walked over a mile, passing the major resort properties and swimming beaches. I saw a few couples making out or strolling in the sand, but no Sara. I tried her cell several more times, sent her a text, and then called the front desk at our resort at about two thirty. They contacted the local cops and state police. I sat in my room for over an hour before a resort manager called me to come to the lobby and meet with the police. They said some British tourists found a woman matching Sara's description floating in shallow water about a half-mile from the Fairmont. Apparently, one of them tried to revive her, as did the paramedics. They transported her to the nearest hospital in Playa and continued to work on her. The officer with the best English drove me to the hospital to identify her. Needless to say, it was the worst night of my life."

Shoulders slumped, head bowed, but no tears, Hyatt is a convincing storyteller, though I can't tell whether he's an honest one.

"So, you're satisfied that it was an accidental drowning?" I ask.

"I'm sure of it," he says.

"But from what I've read, the authorities in Mexico aren't so sure."

"Where'd you read that?" he asks, giving me that look again.

"An Associated Press article in the *Journal*. I haven't seen anything recent though," I say, which is true. Where are those reports from MacDonald's friend?

"Look, Miss Barnes, I appreciate your interest and efforts, but I am tired of going over this nightmare again and again. Whether some jilted boyfriend was following her or taking her picture, though sick, is irrelevant to Sara's death. She attempted to go for a swim and had a tragic accident. She had a deep puncture wound in her head. Her body was found near a long pier between two resorts. There are a series of old pilings next to the pier, and the speculation is that she slipped on the wet surface of the pier at high tide, fell over the side, and became impaled on one of the pilings. She was able somehow to extricate herself but then lost consciousness and fell into the gulf, where she died. No one stabbed her or shot her or drowned her. Now, if there's nothing else, I need to get to my clinic." He stands and waits for me to do likewise.

"Do you have an official report that says all that?" I ask as I stuff my pen in the portfolio and follow him to the spacious foyer near the main entrance. He opens the door and stands in the entryway, waiting for me to walk out before responding to my question.

"Not yet, but I understand the investigation is wrapping up, so there should be one soon. The local police are completely inept, and the state police are understaffed."

I turn to shake his hand and thank him for his time, but he's already closed the double doors and moved on to more important matters.

The interview leaves me with more questions than answers. As I drive to the airport for a noon flight back to the Cities, I can't help but ask myself, why would Sara Wheaton choose an obnoxious, self-important prick like Hyatt over J. R. Campbell? Rich family? MD? Less baggage? He never even asked me about the bandage on my face. And he's a doctor.

Of course, I haven't heard a thing from the judge since I dropped him off at the airport last Thursday, and apparently he's no longer a judge and probably never went to a conference in Orlando, if there even was a conference.

I drop off the rental, buy a sandwich and the *Star Tribune* at a shop near my gate, and board the plane. I read the article about the judge's resignation. It's as uninformative as he is. He's leaving "for personal reasons." No family, few close friends. What personal reasons?

I open my laptop and connect to the internet. Warren, the anti-texter, has sent one of his typical, staccato emails.

Your place at 3. Info on key card. Getting closer.

There's also an encrypted email from someone at the US Embassy in Mexico—MacDonald's friend. There's a second email with a password. It's a chronology and summary of the evidence and findings in the Sara Hyatt case, complete with photos. I wish I'd read it before my meeting with Hyatt, but maybe there's nothing in it. I lean back, pull my laptop close, and start reading. My eyes grow as wide as silver dollars as the mystery of the man from Two Harbors grows even more intriguing.

CHAPTER 22

A short, stout yet handsome woman in her sixties lightly grips my forearm and looks into my eyes with strained familiarity. "Detective Barnes?"

"Yes," I reply, still waiting for my second bag on carousel six at Twin Cities international.

"I thought you'd be on the United flight from Chicago. That's what Judge Gildemeister told me."

"Excuse me for just a moment," I say, seeing my oversized duffel slide by and hustling to keep it from making a second lap on the merry-go-round. She follows close behind.

"I'll relieve you of one of those," she says, holding out her hand.

"Really? Where are we going?"

"I'm sorry. I'm Drostyn Anderberg. I've been Judge Gildemeister's assistant since before he was a judge. He asked me to pick you up and take you wherever you want to go."

"And where is he?" I ask, somewhere between snidely and snottily.

"He said you'd be upset, at least until you'd heard the whole story. I'm in short-term parking. Please let me give you a ride."

I doubt she knows what I now know or that she's got the whole story, but none of this is her fault, so I decide not to be a bitch.

"Okay," I say and give her the handle to my rolling case while lifting the duffel strap over my shoulder. "I'll follow you, Drostyn. Then we can chat on the ride to my house."

It takes about five minutes to get to her late-model Honda sedan. It's funny how so many cars fit their owners, and this one definitely does.

The trunk is immaculate—big surprise. So is the interior.

"I have the directions to your apartment in Linden Hills, if that's where we're going," she says, paying the parking fee with a credit card and driving toward the Bloomington/Minneapolis exit. She's wearing a white blouse under a navy business suit, very professional. Her short, permed black hair is transitioning to white. It doesn't matter, but she must be married, based on the expensive-looking diamond-studded wedding band on her ring finger. She's also wearing large-but-tasteful diamond earrings.

"That's right. Thank you for picking me up, by the way. I'm sure I have more questions than you have answers, but for starters, why don't you tell me what you know about the judge's conference in Orlando, recent resignation, and failure to communicate with me over the past six days?"

"I'm afraid I don't know much about two of those three, but I'll gladly tell you what I know. The judge told me he'd decided to leave the bench and move to the North Shore about a month ago. We've been working with the chief judge to reassign some cases and complete others by settlement or trial. The chief agreed not to make a public announcement until Saturday, but the other judges in the district have known for a few weeks. As for why he resigned, the only thing he told me, and not in confidence, is that he'd been a judge for ten years and that was enough— that he wanted to accomplish other things and to move back to the North Shore."

"Do you happen to know why he never told me any of that, including that he was retiring?"

Drostyn stares out at Interstate 494, pondering the best way to respond to a question dripping with sarcasm. "The judge is the most private person I've ever met. He's thoughtful and generous, but I know next to nothing about his personal life, and I've been with him for nearly twenty years. In fact, yesterday was the first time I heard your name.

"I don't know anything about a conference in Orlando. He arranges his own travel, always has. He said he had some personal business to attend to out of town. Where, I don't know. He also said he lost his phone and needed to buy a new one. That may have something to do with why he hasn't contacted you. I saw him briefly yesterday, but otherwise we've been communicating via email."

None of this is a surprise to me. There's a hint of frustration in this clearly loyal, professional woman's voice, and she's known him for twenty years. If he's moving away from the Cities, maybe he wants me out of his life as well.

"Okay," I say, "but can you tell me whether he's still living in his condo by the river?"

"He isn't," she says. "He sold it about a month ago and had a remote closing yesterday. His realtor arranged for a sale of some of the furnishings at an estate sale last Saturday. The rest has been shipped to his place on the North Shore.

"Look, I know this might feel like the *Twilight Zone,* but he assured me he'd contact you today or tomorrow and asked that you be patient and give him a chance to explain everything."

The irony is I know much, much more than he thinks I know, though I'm far from putting all the pieces of the puzzle together. Just who are you, really, Jason Robin Campbell Gildemeister? Who are you?

"I'm not a very patient person," I say, "but what choice do I have other than to wait or just forget about him?"

Drostyn stops in front of my building and pops the trunk of the Honda. She turns toward me with weary eyes and a forced smile.

"He was an easy man to work for," she says, "but if I were you, Ms. Barnes, I'd run."

Funny, she's not the first person who's told me that. An incoming call from Warren prevents me from asking why; instead, I thank her for the ride, grab my bags from the trunk, and take the call.

"What is it, Detective Lindquist?"

"Are you home?"

"Barely. Walking up the sidewalk to my building. Are you changing our meeting, or do you miss my voice?"

"Both. Moe has summoned us. I guess the mayor wants to play nice. Freddie Tyler is releasing his phone records. I'm just leaving the BCA. We can placate Sherm and have our meeting at MPD central. Can you meet me there at three?"

"I'll be there," I say without enthusiasm.

"Is something wrong?"

"I'll be there."

CHAPTER 23

"Robert Brinkman died last night on an operating table at the Cleveland Clinic. The press release says he had a fatal heart attack while undergoing an experimental procedure to treat his cancer." Lieutenant Moe dispenses with any small talk and gets right to the headline.

"I suppose that has something to do with the mayor's change of heart," Warren says, giving me a quick wink because we both know Moe will ignore his stupid pun.

"Of course it does," says Moe. "Freddie Tyler called Chief Hawkins this morning. Warned that nothing he disclosed was for public consumption. Said his client wanted to assist with the investigation to find Patterson's killer but needed to protect the confidentiality of some text and email conversations with Natalie Brinkman. Apparently, Brinkman had accepted an offer from Sampson to be his new chief of staff before Patterson was murdered."

"We've heard about the job offer, Sherm, but there's more to it—a potentially illegal campaign contribution from a firm controlled by the Brinkman family could have been the quid pro quo for the offer," Warren adds.

"Whatever it was, it's off the table now, according to Tyler. He says Natalie will be taking over the Brinkman corporate empire, where she'll have a lot more power and influence than Sampson's chief of staff. I'm betting there's nothing incriminating in Sampson's phone records. Tyler and the mayor want to look like they're cooperating, but it's really just a diversion."

Having been out of the loop for four days makes me feel like an outsider in the conversation, especially when Warren has important new information.

"I've tracked down the available data on the key card we discussed last week. According to the BCA's expert, it's an active proximity card, also called a vicinity card, that opens the security gates at the Hennepin County municipal ramp and was issued by Dalton Management Group to all approved monthly parkers. The monthly parkers are mostly city and county employees who work at city hall and the Hennepin County Government Center.

"I talked to Doug Epstein, the Hennepin County facilities operations manager. Dalton Management gives his department an allotment of these cards, and then he distributes them to both city and county employees from a master list. They have a record of all employees who have cards but don't match a particular card or card number with an employee. The lithium batteries in the cards run down after five or six years, and then the cards need to be replaced. This particular card is three years old. Although they can't identify the card user, they do have a record of when and how many times this card accessed the ramp. There used to be CCTV cameras at ramp entrances and exits, but when the ramp became fully automated, they removed those and installed more-sophisticated cameras on each floor of the parking garage."

"You're such a nerd, Lindquist," Moe interrupts and takes a few gulps from a plastic tumbler filled with either water or gin. "This is all very interesting, but how does it narrow the field of inquiry?"

This is one of the reasons I love Warren. In his shoes, close to retirement, I would have told Moe to fuck himself at this point but not patient Professor Lindquist.

"According to Epstein's records, this particular card has rarely been used during the past three years. However, it was used several times during the past month and entered the garage at five forty-five on the night before Patterson was killed, exiting at eight thirty. Natalie Brinkman owns a 2018 Bentley Continental, which, according to both

Josh Cummins and Patterson's executive assistant, she never drove to work. She has a driver. Doesn't everybody? Anyway, her boyfriend has been living with her for the past few months, and apparently, he prefers the Bentley over his F-150 pickup. Natalie told us she had dinner with someone at six thirty on that Friday night. I did some professional sleuthing, as I do from time to time, and learned that she and a man who fits Slayton's description had dinner at Manny's Steakhouse on Marquette. They paid using her Amex card. Epstein got me a shot of the second floor of the parking garage on that Friday night at five after seven. Parked two spaces from the skyway entrance to the ramp is a gold Bentley Continental. Natalie will no doubt resign from her job with the city in the next week or so. I'm betting she won't be able to find her key card."

"Okay," says Moe. "I'm still a little confused."

I feel the need to contribute to the conversation. "Natalie knew her boss was meeting with the mayor when she went to dinner with Slayton, and she probably knew Patterson intended to blow the whistle on her deal with Sampson, which means they both had a lot to lose unless the mayor could convince her to back off."

Thinking we were on the trail of something big, Moe begins to salivate. "So, Sampson's unsuccessful, and you think Brinkman convinces her boyfriend at dinner to ambush and kill Kate Patterson?"

"I don't think that," says Warren.

"Neither do I," I say. "I think Natalie was incredibly pissed at Patterson. First, for not giving up her seat on the council, so Natalie could run. Second, for threatening to thwart her opportunity to gain power and status through the mayor's office. We don't know what transpired at the meeting between Sampson and Patterson or whether Natalie even knew the outcome when she had dinner with her boyfriend, but my theory is that she made it very clear to Major Slayton that Patterson was making her life miserable and things could get worse before they got any better. I believe if Slayton killed Patterson, it was his idea, fueled by passion, mixed with vodka. And it wouldn't surprise me if he still hasn't told her."

"I agree with Barnes, Lieutenant. Brinkman got an urgent text from Patterson around midnight, saying they needed to talk. If Slayton were with her at the time, Brinkman's response to this text could have motivated him to act, to be the hero. Stalking an unsuspecting fifty-year-old woman and then moving in for the kill would have been an easy day at the office for someone with his skills, even under the influence. What's more, Patterson knew him and would have at least stopped to talk if she recognized him at the lake."

"If Slayton gets wind that we're onto him, he'll disappear," says Moe. "Given his girlfriend's resources and his background, he might be gone for good."

Warren flashes a look my way that's a combination eye roll and signal that he's had enough of straight-shootin' Sherm. Now he'll find a way to end the meeting and get what he wants.

"I have messages into Brinkman's work phone and city-issued cell that we want a follow-up interview," Warren says, "but no response. I assume they're flying her dad back from Cleveland for some kind of memorial service this week, so I doubt she's left the state. I'm betting that she and Slayton are out at the family compound on Lake Minnetonka. Maybe Barnes and I should head out there tonight. At the very least, we can ask her to produce her key card to the city ramp. After talking to her, we can decide whether Slayton graduates from a person of interest to a suspect."

Moe's eyes light up. He might have a hard-on. "And if she refuses to talk or lawyers up, why don't you just bring him in for questioning?"

"Congratulations, by the way," Warren says as we sit at a four-person table in a tiny conference room at MPD headquarters after escaping Moe's office and stealing a couple Diet Cokes from a twelve-pack someone foolishly left in the break-room fridge.

"For what?" I ask.

"Eighth place in the big race in Mexico and a time under six hours. I found the results online by googling recent triathlons not near me."

"Thanks, Warren. I really enjoyed it, even though I picked up a battle scar." I took the bandage off after a quick shower at home.

"I wasn't going to ask where you got that nasty scrape. I was afraid maybe you and the judge were playing a little rough."

"Good one, but not even close. I haven't even heard from him since I gave him a ride to the airport last Tuesday." That's not entirely true if you count the ride from Drostyn as a message from the judge.

"Really? And you honestly didn't know he was resigning from the bench?"

"Not a clue, Warren." It's time to put more cards on the table with respect to now-former Judge Gildemeister. I tell Warren about the diary I stumbled upon in his chambers and the strange and disturbing contents of the sections I was able to read and copy before hastily returning it to avoid getting caught. I also recount my trip to Two Harbors and some of the background information I learned from Sheriff MacDonald.

Warren's wide eyes nearly pop out of their sockets when I tell him about Sara Hyatt's death in Playa del Carmen and my impromptu and highly unofficial visit to Milwaukee to question pompous Dr. Hyatt. But the real stunner for Warren is the connection between Sara Hyatt and Kate Patterson, roommates who married roommates.

"So, what you're telling me is that your boyfriend is a stalker and maybe a murderer, but you're still interested, right?"

I take the summary of the Mexican state police reports out of my folio and hand it to him. "Read this and you can tell me whether I'm crazy or stupid or both."

"But you're going to give me the Lincoln Barnes unexpurgated version, right?"

"Whatever that means, but of course I am. Dr. Hyatt gave basically the same—in my opinion, rehearsed—story to both me and the Mexican authorities. He walked along the beach looking for Sara at about one in the morning. He didn't see her and couldn't reach her on her cell, which has never been recovered, by the way. He returned to the resort around two and reported that his wife was missing to the concierge, who, in turn, notified local police.

"Unbeknownst to Hyatt, someone on a second-floor balcony witnessed him approaching his casita while in the act of removing a dress shirt that was dripping with water. She said it was between two and two thirty. Five minutes later, this same woman observed him leaving his villa wearing a clean, dry dress shirt and different dress pants."

"Why didn't he change into something more comfortable at three in the morning?" Warren asks, tongue in cheek, though I can tell he's into the story.

"This witness didn't come forward right away, only after there were articles in the local paper and in places like *USA Today* and the *Milwaukee Journal*, calling it a mysterious death. In any event, a server at a restaurant at the Viceroy Riviera Maya, about a mile from the Fairmont, told her manager that she'd seated a woman matching Sara's description and a tall, dark American man at about eleven that night. She said they shared a bottle of wine and ordered some food to go. The man charged the food to a two-room villa at the resort. Turns out his name is J. R. Campbell from Two Harbors, Minnesota."

"Ooh, I like the double-life stuff," Warren says, "but I don't get why it's necessary."

"Remember that this trip to Mexico occurred right before the pandemic struck with a vengeance in the US and Mexico, and the hospitality industry went into hibernation for over a year. It took the Mexican state police months to make the connection between J. R. Campbell and Robin Gildemeister. At one time, they believed he was the last person to see Sara Hyatt alive and was definitely a person of interest in her death."

"I'm surprised they didn't just accept Hyatt's version of the facts and close the case. Why should they care about the death of a rich gringo?"

"Because rich, white gringos are the lifeblood of the tourist economy in Cancun. Anyway, the judge, not J. R. Campbell, responded to a confidential diplomatic inquiry that made its way through the system to him a few months ago via the state department and admitted he might have important information relating to the case. He said he didn't want to reveal anything over the phone or on a video conference but would arrange to visit Playa del Carmen when it was safe to travel. That trip occurred last week, shortly before he announced his retirement from the bench.

"According to the state police, the judge revealed he and Sara had been having a long-distance affair for over twenty years. They'd get together three or four times a year, often when Dr. Hyatt was busy with a conference or out-of-town speaking engagement. He said they'd had a relationship in high school and college before she became involved with Hyatt and that she broke it off. Now I know the part about their past relationship is true, at least according to Sheriff MacDonald. Here's where it starts to stretch the bounds of believability. The judge told the police that Sara sent him an impassioned letter five years into her marriage, admitting she'd made a terrible mistake. She thought about him often and wished things had turned out differently, but she wasn't willing to disrupt her family's life in Milwaukee. She didn't love Hyatt but wouldn't leave him. Mostly, she wanted J. R. to know she was sorry for hurting him, for listening to her roommate, and for not following her instincts. He drove to Milwaukee the next weekend and the affair began, which, in my opinion, is what she really wanted."

"All this crap is in the police reports?" Warren asks. "Sounds like he's trying a little too hard to sell a story he's concocted in his dreams."

"You could be right. It could be an elaborate ruse to distract them from focusing on him as a suspect. But I don't think so."

"You don't want to think so."

"You'll see in the police notes that he actually gave them Sara's apology letter and a few emails that reflect her strong feelings for him. He also gave them his cell phone that has hundreds of texts substantiating their relationship. But here's the kicker—with both kids married and on their own, Sara had decided to leave Hyatt and move back to the North Shore with the man she knew as J. R. According to his statement to the police, she planned to tell Hyatt she was leaving him during this trip because she suspected he knew about the affair. Though he'd never been physically abusive, Hyatt had a volatile temper, especially when his ego was bruised."

"So, if you believe the judge's story, how do you think Sara died?" Warren asks. "Was it an accident?"

"After reading the police reports and meeting Hyatt, I vote for manslaughter. Here's how it went down. Sara leaves J. R.'s villa at one thirty, later than she'd planned, and suspecting that her spouse might be looking for her, insists on walking back alone. Hyatt sees her on the beach and they get into an argument somewhere near the pier. He gets agitated. No one's going to leave him. He pushes her. He's about the size of a grizzly bear. She loses her balance and falls backward onto the pilings, becoming impaled, and probably dying instantly. In a panic, Hyatt carries her lifeless body into deeper water and hopes the sharks, attracted by her blood, keep her from washing ashore."

"Very nice," says Warren, "but I prefer this alternative ending. It's simpler and follows the rules of human nature that I've observed over my nearly sixty years. Your boyfriend was obsessed with this Sara and stalked her and her family for years. Like most sociopaths, he's able to separate his professional life from the darker side, and he's clearly a very capable guy. On the evening in question, he decides to confront Sara after all these years. He's fantasized about this meeting hundreds of times, but when he professes his unending love for her, she's shocked and maybe even horrified. Think about twenty-five years of pent-up emotions met with total rejection. He, not Dr. Hyatt, pushes her off the pier and then dumps her body into the gulf and runs. After escaping from Cancun, he has plenty of time to create the letters and texts and whatever else he needs to substantiate his fictional affair with Sara."

"Murder or manslaughter?" I ask, not believing the judge did either.

"Does it matter? I'll let the Mexican lawyers figure that one out."

"You might have to give them some instruction. While I think your scenario could have happened, here's why the local police and I don't think it did. If your theory is correct, why is Hyatt so adamant that his wife's death was an accidental drowning? If there was any possibility that someone else had caused her death, intentionally or not, don't you think he'd want to know? Unless he knew that he'd caused it. In that case, the more the authorities probe, the more likely they are to find some evidence implicating him."

"Let me think about that while I digest this report," Warren says, guzzling the last dregs of his Diet Coke. "You said Sara suspected her husband knew about the affair. After deceiving him for twenty years, what happened around the time of the trip to Mexico to make him suspicious?"

"You'll love this. Apparently when Sara decided to leave Hyatt, she confided in one person other than the judge."

"Kate Patterson."

"Yeah, her best friend. But Sara was careful not to disclose the name of her current love interest to the woman who had persuaded her to dump J. R. She said she'd met someone and her marriage to Hyatt was over. Given the condition of her own marriage, I don't think Patterson was in any position to try to convince her otherwise."

"Why would Patterson betray her best friend by telling Hyatt about the affair?" Warren asks with more than his usual skepticism. "You'll call me sexist again, but tell me why women have this compulsion to tell their deepest secrets to their so-called friends? It always boomerangs. Men are better at being deceitful."

"You're an incurable sexist, Warren. Apparently Sara believed Patterson told her husband that the Hyatts' marriage was in trouble. I'm guessing Paul Bagley said something to his old roommate that made Hyatt suspicious, unless, as you say, the judge has fabricated everything."

"Do you know what the Mexican cops plan to do now?" Warren asks.

"The report says they've sent interrogatories to Hyatt's lawyer because he's refused to return to Cancun for further questioning. They haven't decided whether they have enough to seek extradition."

"And what about you? Will you be trying to contact Gildemeister, or whoever your mystery man is, to get more answers and maybe resume some kind of relationship? I'm serious, Lincoln. I think you'd be better off just forgetting about the whole thing. It's not your case, and it sounds like this guy is moving to the north country."

I need to be honest with someone about the judge, and I trust Warren. "I hope he'll reach out to me soon, or I will contact him. I appreciate your concern, but I might be in love with this guy, so I need to know the truth. You're right, of course. I should run. He's obviously been obsessed with another woman and, even though she's dead, he may be incapable of loving anyone else."

"I can't help you with that, but I keep wondering whether your first encounter with the judge at the health club was totally random."

"What do you mean?" I ask, never having given that a second thought.

"Not sure." He's lying, so he'll change the subject. "I see it's starting to snow outside. Why don't I pick you up in the Explorer at seven, and we'll take a ride out to one-percenterville. I'm betting Natalie Brinkman and her beau are scheming about their future with all of daddy's money. I think we need to get to her before the memorial service. She and Slayton could be on the move after that."

"Do we ask her to produce the key card today?"

"I think so, especially if Slayton is in the room. His reaction will tell us a lot."

I grab my folio and open the conference room door.

"See you at seven."

CHAPTER 24

Wanda and I always looked forward to weekends with our dad in his two-bedroom, third-floor apartment on Maple Avenue in Evanston. Mom made sure we finished our homework, ate our vegetables, developed good manners, and went to church. Dad pontificated from time to time on everything from city politics to jazz pianists, and he always had stacks of good books for us to read, but mostly, he was about fun. We might spend ten weekends a year with the man, but on those precious days, he'd take us to Wrigley to see the hapless Cubs or to Soldier Field for Sunday with da Bears. I remember hot summer afternoons at the beach on Lake Michigan and the extraordinary wild animal exhibits at Lincoln Park Zoo.

The man wasn't perfect by a long shot, but he was special to us, despite the fact that he loved McDonald's cheeseburgers. Every time we had lunch or dinner at McDonald's, and it was way too many times, he would order the same thing, the number-two special-value meal—two cheeseburgers with a large order of fries and a Diet Coke, as if a Diet Coke would somehow make it a healthy value meal at about two thousand calories. Wanda and I would invariably order McNuggets with fries and a shake, and though it all tasted good going down, at least one of us would regret it later in the day.

As I drive home from city hall, it's still snowing, and the roads are getting slick; someone said March is the snowiest month in Minnesota. All I can think of is, I'm starving. I have no food in my apartment and less than ninety minutes to get home, eat, and prepare for a confrontation with Natalie Brinkman. That's why, when I see the familiar golden arches on South Hennepin, I make a split-second decision to turn into the lot and follow a green minivan filled with kids to the drive-thru lane. It's been nearly ten years, so I'm a little surprised that the number-two value meal is still on the menu. I order my very first one with a Diet Coke. Between the big race and the fear of Montezuma's revenge, I lost close to ten pounds in Mexico, so a little saturated fat won't hurt.

"Here's to you, Dad," I say to myself before devouring the first cheeseburger in four or five monster bites and then unwrapping and eating half of the second before aiding the digestive process with a sip of Diet Coke, all while one-hand driving through rush-hour traffic in south Minneapolis.

I believe McDonald's adds a secret addictive ingredient to their most-popular menu items that creates unnatural cravings. Even though processed cheese food and pickles dominate the razor-thin beef patty in these cheeseburgers, I have to admit, I like them. I'll have to tell Wanda what we've been missing all these years.

I park the Jeep in my underground space, glad that Warren will be driving tonight. Back in my apartment, I toss the bag containing evidence of my gluttony and see I have a new text on my cell. It's from an unfamiliar number with a 218 area code.

Saw your results from Campeche—impressive, but not surprising. You know now I wasn't in Orlando and have abandoned my life in Minneapolis. Couldn't tell you the truth. I will now but understand if you're not interested. Call me if you want to talk.

I don't know whether to laugh or scream. I start to call him but decide to wait until later tonight or tomorrow. I already know more than he'll ever tell me, and if he knew how I know, we'd be through for sure. I'm a fool, but I miss him.

It's not a blizzard yet, but blowing snow and temps in the teens make the drive out to Wayzata challenging, even for a veteran of Minnesota winters like Warren. When I suggest postponing the trip until tomorrow, he laughs and says it's all the more likely that Natalie and her boyfriend will be laying low at the Brinkman mansion.

More than seven years in the Twin Cities and I've never been on Lake Minnetonka, a sprawling lake in the western suburbs with over twenty bays and ten cities that touch its shores. I've seen it from a lakeside bar in downtown Excelsior, but I can't say I know anyone with a home on the lake that's synonymous with wealth and status in Minnesota. Warren says that over the past decade, many of the middle-class homes built on Minnetonka in the last century—some still in good condition—have been purchased at wildly inflated prices only to be torn down and replaced by mega-mansions.

About five years ago, Robert Brinkman did much more than that. He paid a prominent CEO in the consumer electronics business ten million dollars for a five-bedroom Tudor that had been built in 1995 on one of the few five-acre lots on the lake. Warren claims that, at best, the place was worth five million and that it's probably the most expensive tear-down in the history of Minnesota. What he built in its place isn't visible from Ferndale Road West, but according to Zillow and Realtor.com, it's over twenty thousand square feet with eight bedrooms, seven bathrooms, indoor and outdoor pools, a home theater, a golf simulator, and four tennis courts. There's a ten-foot-high brick, stone, and iron fence on three sides of the property and a locked iron gate at the main entrance. There are parking spaces at the service entrance a half-block down the road, which is where we park the Explorer. We're both wearing department-issued navy parkas with "MPLS DETECTIVE" sewn in white lettering over the heart and black leather gloves. I'm carrying a black folio with a notebook and my iPad inside.

Blowing snow reduces visibility and stings my face. A milder-than-normal March had melted most of the snow in the Cities, but today's storm has already left accumulations of at least four inches, and plows won't make it out to side streets in the suburbs for hours.

"There must be some kind of intercom system," says Warren as we trudge our way from the service entrance to the gate. I see several CCTV cameras covering the property and surrounding area. There's a simple, silver call box with a white button, above which is a sign that reads, "Push here once and wait." Warren pushes it, and we wait. A couple minutes later, I recognize Natalie Brinkman's voice.

"Hello, detectives," she says, obviously recognizing us on some expensive screen. "I can't believe you're out on a night like this." It seems stranger to me that she's in the monstrous stone-and-granite mansion at the top of the hill because the front of the place is completely dark.

"We seek justice in all kinds of weather," Warren says. He's getting crazier the closer he gets to retirement.

"Sure you do," she says. " Against my better judgment, I'm opening the gate. Come up to the black double doors on the main porch. I've only got about a half hour to give you."

"Is Major Slayton with you?" Warren asks.

"He won't be." We hear a click, and then there's a low humming sound near the gate as it slowly opens.

"That was way too easy," I say. "I was sure she'd tell us to go to hell."

"Maybe she still will," Warren says as we start walking up the long driveway, its expensive pavers partially covered by fluffy snow, which oddly seems to be melting in below-freezing temps.

"What's that?" Warren asks. I hear the roar of a powerful engine and then see the headlights and fog lights of a vehicle pierce the snowy darkness at the top of the driveway.

"It looks like a truck or van is heading our way!" I yell at Warren but don't think he hears. It's a truck, and it's barreling down the driveway right for us. Instinctively, we split away from each other, Warren to the left, me to the right, abandoning the driveway and seeking the relative safety of Brinkman's yard. And then, though at first I don't believe my eyes, the horror of what I witness makes me gasp and then scream.

The truck veers to the right near the end of the driveway and smashes into my partner. Warren's at least ten feet into the yard and moving away from the driveway when he's hit in the back and becomes airborne, like a human missile, traversing twenty feet in the air and then bouncing on the driveway near the open gate and sliding across Ferndale headfirst into the trunk of an old maple on the other side of the road.

"Stop, you son of a bitch!" I scream at the silver pickup as it slides sideways across the snow-covered lawn and through the entrance after catapulting Warren.

After hesitating for an instant on Ferndale, the truck spins its tires, throwing snow in my direction, and then heads east toward downtown

Wayzata. As I sprint toward Warren, I unsnap the holster at my hip and pull out my Glock 9mm. I stop in the middle of Ferndale, whip off my gloves, and try to maintain a wide, stable stance while firing four or five rounds at the cab as the back end fishtails left and right, and the pickup disappears into the night.

I slip the Glock into my parka and grab my phone. I should call for help first, but I need to check on Warren's condition.

He's not moving, sprawled facedown at the base of the tree.

"Warren, Warren, can you hear me?" I ask, not expecting an answer. I kneel down in the snow and press my freezing fingers against the side of his neck, relieved to feel a weak-but-steady pulse from his carotid artery. He's unconscious, and blood is oozing from his nostrils and trickling down his face, staining the snow from abrasions on his forehead and chin. These injuries are minor, but I fear he's got serious internal bleeding and some broken bones. The slippery conditions make it easy to maneuver him slightly to ensure he can breathe. I call for an ambulance and some backup from the Wayzata PD and Hennepin County, indicating Warren's injuries might require a trauma facility. Then I remove my parka and gently tilt Warren onto the quilted fabric to make it easier for the EMTs to check his vitals before moving him. I sit next to him, leaning against the maple tree. I remove one of his gloves and hold his hand.

Within five minutes, I hear sirens. I look across at the Brinkman property. Someone has flipped a major switch, illuminating the front of the house. But where's Natalie? Doesn't she wonder where we went? Did Slayton tell her what happened? Or was she driving the truck? I try to call her government-issued cell but go straight to a voicemail message saying she's no longer employed by the City of Minneapolis.

A Wayzata squad arrives, closely followed by an ambulance from North Memorial. I introduce myself and describe how the driver of the pickup attempted to murder my partner. The paramedics check Warren's vitals and carefully transfer him onto a fancy electric stretcher. They say he's in shock, with shallow breathing and a weak, rapid pulse. Once they hook him up in the cabin, they'll call the trauma center at North Memorial Hospital and help the ER prepare for his arrival. I want to cry but don't and remember to take the key fob for the Explorer out of Warren's parka before I kiss the top of his head.

Too upset to think, I try to give the two Wayzata cops a better explanation of why two MPD detectives are in the billionaire district on a stormy Tuesday night. Officers Goldstein and Sanchez are aware of the Kate Patterson murder, but they're surprised someone from this neighborhood might have been involved. I assure them that if we'd suspected any violence, we would have alerted their department of our business in their city, which is standard practice.

"Detective Barnes, we should have said something earlier," Goldstein says, "but our priority was to get your partner into that ambulance. There was a Hennepin County Sheriff's squad ahead of us when we turned up Ferndale South from Wayzata Boulevard. Before getting to you, we came upon a silver F-150 that plowed into a stucco fence at the corner of Ferndale South and Ferndale West—I think it's the Holmes property. The deputies said they'd check out that crash while we came over here." Goldstein is a fiftyish white man with a square build accentuated by a black leather jacket. He's sporting a manicured black beard, sprinkled with strands of silver and white, and wearing a black wool cap.

"That's got to be the truck that hit Warren," I say, starting to feel the harsh wind on my face and struggling to shove my stiff, frozen fingers back into wet gloves.

"I don't think there's much doubt about that," says Sanchez. She's under thirty and taller than her partner, with dark eyes and black hair stuffed under her Wayzata PD winter trooper hat, its furry flaps covering her ears. "The deputies have radioed for assistance. The driver is unresponsive. He's been tentatively identified as Andrew Slayton, and he's got a gunshot wound in the back of his head. You didn't mention that you shot him." Sanchez and Goldstein glance at each other and then stare at me.

"I wasn't sure who the driver was," I say, the overwhelming concern for my partner now compounded by the guilt of possibly killing another human being, even a total asshole, "but when the truck veered into Warren and then wouldn't stop, I fired three or four rounds at the back of the cab with my Glock. I never thought I'd hit him. I was just hoping to scare some sense into the idiot, but I guess it was a lucky shot."

Goldstein gazed up at the Brinkman estate, now lit up like the White House. "Or a very unlucky one."

CHAPTER 25

My mind is spinning out of control as I speed across the western suburbs, heading to North Memorial in Robbinsdale. It's nine thirty, not too late to call Lieutenant Moe at home. He answers before the first ring.

"Barnes, I've heard about Detective Lindquist and the aftermath. How are you holding up, and where are you?"

"I can't lie, Lieutenant, I'm upset, and I'm on my way to North Memorial to check on Warren. After talking to you, I'm going to call Diane, unless someone else has already informed her."

"Normally, that's my responsibility, but if you're up to it and going to the hospital, I'll defer to you." His voice is much softer and kinder than usual.

"I'd like to do that, so thanks," I say. "Who told you so fast? The sheriff's office?"

"No. I got a call from the chief. Apparently, Natalie Brinkman called the mayor and was hysterical, claiming her boyfriend had been drinking and didn't want to be around for your meeting. She used the word 'interrogation.' Anyway, she said if he hit your partner in the middle of a blizzard, it was an accident. He probably didn't even know he hit someone and then you shot him in cold blood. Her language was much more colorful than that, but that's the gist of it. The mayor called the chief, who called me. I knew you'd call me when you were ready, so I contacted Wayzata PD and Hennepin County to get whatever information I could. Officer Goldstein said you were shaken up but gave them a rational explanation of what happened. When he and his partner reported the incident to Brinkman after you left, she was not as rational."

"So, what now?" I ask, knowing the answer won't be good.

"Let's meet at your precinct tomorrow morning. It's actually closer to my house than city hall. I'll be there at eight o'clock. You'll be suspended with pay pending an administrative review of the whole incident by the BCA. But, Lincoln, based on what I know so far, I don't think you should worry too much about that." It's the first time he's called me by my first name.

"I'm much more worried about Warren," I say. "If shooting at that prick wasn't the right thing to do, then I don't think I want to be a cop anymore, sir."

"Unfortunately, that prick was also a decorated soldier and in deep with a powerful family." But nothing to worry about, Lincoln.

"And also a murder suspect."

"Give Diane a hug for me, Barnes." It's back to Barnes.

"Yes, sir. See you tomorrow."

Diane starts crying even before I can explain the little I know about Warren's condition. She's on the way to the hospital before I end the call. With the possible exception of Wanda and Craig, I don't know anyone with a better marriage than Warren and Diane Lindquist. They raised three exceptional daughters together, both working full time in stressful jobs, and they still adore each other.

It's another busy night at North Memorial, a place where my police badge only gets me so much information, especially given today's medical privacy laws like HIPAA, which medical professionals are quick to cite when they don't feel like providing details to nonfamily members. After much prodding and begging, I learn that Warren is in the intensive care unit in an induced coma. I tell the ICU nurse that his wife is on her way, and he politely explains that one of the two hospitalists on duty will update her, not me, on Warren's condition after she checks in at the night desk. I contemplate telling him I'm Warren's daughter or sister, but it's too late for that. This is what you get at a big-city, level-one trauma facility with a reputation for treating the worst of the worst in terms of gunshot and stab wounds, severed limbs, traumatic brain injuries, and severe burns.

Diane was an emergency room nurse for twenty years and then a physician's assistant at a women's clinic for ten more before retiring three years ago. She returned to the ER during the pandemic and often worked twenty-hour days trying to comfort patients she knew wouldn't make it. She wanted to enjoy more time with Warren and their daughters and her ninety-year-old mother, who lives in Bonita Springs. She had begged him to join her in retirement, but he wanted one more year on the force, one more year as my mentor and confidante. If Warren survives, he'll be joining Diane a little sooner than planned.

I find a vacant chair in a small area designated for family members just as Diane bursts through the double doors from the elevator lobby to the ICU. She's tall and rail thin with perfect white teeth that sparkle under a button nose and round, friendly hazel eyes. She's cute, if not beautiful, with an angular face filled with tiny freckles. Her strawberry-blonde hair turned white in her forties, and it's cut super short, like mine, giving her what I call the athletic-chic look. But tonight, she looks disheveled, wearing a Saints baseball cap and one of Warren's down ski vests over a gray sweatsuit and Converse All-Stars. She practically tackles me with a hug before I make it to a standing position.

"Oh my god, Lincoln, why, why, why did this have to happen to Warren!" Her cap is dripping with melting snow, and her tears have destroyed her hurried attempt to apply some makeup. "What do you know?" she asks, digging her fingers into my forearms.

"Not much more than I told you over the phone. They'd only tell me that he's in an induced coma—I assume because of a brain bleed, but the head duty nurse over there said the docs would give you an update on his condition after you check in."

She grabs my wrist and hustles over to the reception desk. "I've been through this drill with others too many times. You're family tonight. I can't call the girls until I know more."

"Thank you," I say, happy to be part of the family and hungry for information about my partner.

I fetch two cups of vending-machine coffee to sip while we wait for answers. Waiting isn't a good state for me right now. I imagine sitting in a packed courtroom, on trial for manslaughter. Fortunately, the wait is short. We're escorted into a special meeting lounge for the families of ICU patients. There's a long couch and three upholstered chairs surrounding a rectangular coffee table. We sit next to each other on the couch. I decide not to finish the wretched coffee and lean over to toss the cup into a wastebasket as two white coats enter the room.

"Hello, Lindquist family. I'm Dr. Larsen, an internist, and this is Dr. Gau. She's a neurologist on staff here at North Memorial. We've also consulted with an orthopedist, who's in emergency surgery right now."

We stand and give them each a fist bump, which has become the standard greeting protocol since the pandemic, though I sometimes wonder why we even bother. They each sit, Dr. Gau with an iPad, Dr. Larsen with a clipboard.

Larsen must be seventy. He has a friendly, outgoing demeanor and a warm smile. Wearing blue scrubs beneath a white lab coat, he fits my image of the classic family doctor. About six feet tall, hunched shoulders and a permanent slouch make him appear shorter, but more approachable. He's got thinning gray hair and gray-blue eyes behind thick, black-rimmed glasses, but his most prominent feature by far is a bushy gray mustache reminiscent of Wilford Brimley.

"I'll let Dr. Gau discuss the head trauma and what we're doing to remediate it, and then I'll review the fractures and other injuries. But first and foremost, Warren is in serious-but-stable condition. Dr. Gau?"

Wearing a buttoned-up white coat over her scrubs, Dr. Gau is petite, a foot shorter than Larsen, with black hair pulled back and fastened with a hair clip, fine facial features, and large, intelligent-looking brown eyes.

"Your husband and colleague presented with a subdural hematoma, or bleeding in the brain, as a result of blunt force trauma to the right side of his head, presumably when he hit the pavement after being struck by a vehicle. It is small and should heal on its own, but we'll monitor it. The more serious problem is some swelling of brain tissue, which can cause permanent damage. That is why we've used a drug called thiopental to induce a coma state to allow the brain to heal. That is the hope, and I believe it will work in this case, given Mr. Lindquist's vitals and overall health. We'll also monitor his brain activity with an EEG and his heart rate, blood pressure, and respiration. If all goes well, we'll begin to reverse this comatose condition within the next forty-eight hours. You can certainly see him if you wish, but he will not be responsive. Any questions?"

Diane is squeezing my hand so hard I need to pull away before she breaks a bone or I piss myself. "Thank you so much, Doctor," she says, trembling from head to toe. "I've been an emergency room nurse and a PA, so I'm familiar with induced comas. I also know that some patients don't survive the swelling in the brain."

"That is true," Dr. Gau agrees. "We'll know a lot more in the next twenty-four hours, but I'm optimistic your husband will improve."

"Thank you, Doctor," Larsen says. "As soon as we finish here, you're welcome to see your husband and to sit in his room as long as you'd like, Ms. Lindquist. Detective Lindquist has multiple bone fractures, most of which will not require any special surgery. He cracked his pelvis and suffered clean breaks of the main bones in his right forearm and bicep, the radius and humerus, but the worst break occurred to his right tibia, the main bone just below the knee. Once he's out of the coma, we'll need to operate on the compound crush injury there to ensure better circulation and, potentially, to insert a titanium rod in the area. We think he must have hit that area first when he landed on the pavement.

"He was fortunate in two respects. First, that he was moving away from the truck when he was struck, and second, based on a large contusion in his lower buttock and upper hamstring area, it appears the vehicle's lower bumper made first contact with him and, on a slippery surface, lifted him off his feet and catapulted him forward like a projectile, instead of hitting him in the back and running him over, which would probably have killed him. There's nothing fortunate about this terrible accident, but it could have been worse."

"And I'd call it attempted murder, not an accident," I add, not suppressing my righteous indignation.

After the docs leave, Diane and I walk down the hall of the ICU to Warren's room. He's unrecognizable under a maze of bandages and tubes, with only a patch of his gray hair and about a third of his face visible. Diane kisses his cheek and moves a chair sideways next to the bed so she can sit and touch him. I grab the other functional chair and sit next to her, and we begin a vigil that family members will maintain until Warren wakes up, which, for the good of the world as I know it, he must.

High-tech machines and monitors whir, beep, and blink as a man we love in different ways appears to be in a state of suspended animation while his broken body slowly heals.

"Have you called the girls?" I ask, knowing she intended to but understanding she might be in a state of emotional shock.

"Oh, Christ, Lincoln, I was in a daze for a few minutes." She fishes her phone out of a pocket in her sweatpants. It's almost midnight, a good time for my exit.

"I'm going to let you have those conversations in private, Diane. I'll check in with you tomorrow morning."

"Thanks for everything, Lincoln. And I mean everything."

"We'll see how that works out," I say, referring to my shot in the dark. "All I care about right now is getting my partner back to health. And you need to take care of yourself and get some rest." She nods as I lift my parka from the back of the chair, touch Warren's hand, and walk out of the room, out of the hospital, and into the cold, lonely night.

CHAPTER 26

My exhausted body doesn't react well when the alarm on my phone starts chiming at six o'clock. I stretch for ten minutes before taking a hot shower and selecting my most professional-looking ensemble for a day of reckoning. I can't eat anything, but I brew a pot of Sumatra and pour most of it in a twenty-ounce YETI tumbler. I intentionally avoid turning on a TV or getting on the internet. I don't want to know—not yet. The only thing I listen to on my way to the precinct house is a voicemail message from Officer Goldstein. Lieutenant Moe already told me that Goldstein and Sanchez visited Natalie after I left to deliver the tragic news about her boyfriend. Goldstein uses the words "inconsolable" and "hostile" to describe her reaction. He wanted to give me a heads-up that she might try to influence people in power to hurt me. Great. Warren was right about her and so was Josh Cummins.

My meeting with Moe is at eight but, anxious to be done with it, I knock on the door of the conference room he's selected at seven thirty.

"Barnes, is that you?" he growls. "I knew you'd be early, so I'm ready for you now. Sit down and grab one of these low-fat delicacies."

There's an open box of pastries in the middle of the conference table from Denny's 5th Avenue Bakery. I set my coffee tumbler and notebook down and, against my better judgment, pick out a custard-filled

Bismarck. Moe hands me a paper napkin as I take a few deep breaths to calm my nerves and slow my racing heart.

"Have you seen this?" he asks, handing me the front section of today's *Star Tribune*. The headline reads, "MINNEAPOLIS COP KILLS WAR HERO IN WAYZATA."

"Oh my god," I sigh. "No, I haven't seen it. Is the article as misleading as the headline?"

"It's not good," he says, gently taking the paper from me and setting it on the chair next to him. "You can have that to read when we're through. The reporter talked to Ms. Brinkman and Chief Hawkins late last night. He also talked to a Wayzata cop and somebody from the sheriff's office. Brinkman admits that Slayton had been drinking. She says they had just finished eating dinner and were discussing her father's memorial service this weekend when you and Detective Lindquist arrived at the gated entrance and requested an interview. Apparently, Slayton wanted to tell you to get lost, but Brinkman preferred to get the meeting over with before she had to deal with family and friends later this week. She and Slayton argued briefly, and then he stormed off, indicating he didn't want to be around for the interview. Brinkman says he would never have intentionally hit Warren with the truck, that he simply lost control on the slippery driveway and probably didn't even know he hit someone, given the poor visibility in the storm. She's the only one really quoted in the article. The Wayzata officer, Greenberg, I think—"

"Goldstein?"

"Right. Goldstein. He indicated that neither he nor his partner witnessed the incident but that you were distraught and preoccupied with Warren's condition. That's not a bad thing, Barnes. You're human and you care about your partner in the best possible way. I get it. The spokesperson from the sheriff's office said Slayton was dead at the scene but it wasn't clear whether he died from the bullet wound or subsequent crash."

"What about the chief?"

"He withheld any comments about your actions, saying the BCA would investigate the matter, but added that the department's greatest concern and thoughts and prayers were with Detective Lindquist and his family."

Kirby Hawkins has been the chief of the reconstituted MPD for three months, having been a professor of criminology and sociology at the

University of Michigan for over twenty years. Though he'd written several books on policing and the best methods to reduce violent crime, he'd never been a peace officer of any kind until his former college roommate, Marcus Sampson, convinced him to apply for the job and persuaded a majority of the city council, not including Kate Patterson, to approve his appointment.

"Other than the headline, that doesn't sound so bad," I say, taking a healthy bite of the unhealthy but incredibly good pastry.

"Here's what's bad. Brinkman says you should be charged with manslaughter for shooting a defenseless driver who didn't pose a threat to you and wasn't a danger to anyone else."

"Manslaughter? Are you kidding me? That's crazy! What do you think about that?"

"Knowing everything I know, I think it's beyond crazy, but the article doesn't mention that Slayton was a person of interest in the Kate Patterson murder. In fact, it doesn't mention Patterson at all. It says you and Warren were at the Brinkman mansion to talk to Natalie about a pending police matter, so it's hard for the reader to divine a motive for Slayton's actions, if he did intentionally hit Warren. Obviously, if you had thought it was an accident, you wouldn't have shot at the fleeing truck. Unfortunately, the article, specifically Natalie, tries to create the impression that the only intentional act was your shooting Slayton, and no one even tries to refutes it."

"I'm shocked, Lieutenant, shocked that no one in the department is publicly backing me up on this or at least providing an alternative explanation for my actions. That truck was a deadly weapon that Slayton aimed directly at my partner—that's attempted murder, and I'm entirely within my rights as an officer to meet deadly force with deadly force. I screamed at that asshole to stop, sir. And given his history, it's likely he was intoxicated and could have killed someone else. And what about Warren? What does this article say about him? Does it mention that he's in the ICU, fighting for his life?"

"Hey, I'm on your side here. I think the chief could have said more, but he's a pretty deliberative guy. I'm sure he wants to wait for more evidence to come in before committing the department to a position on this. For now, I'll need your badge and service revolver, and you'll be suspended with pay pending a review of the incident and your actions by the Bureau of Criminal Affairs."

"What about the Patterson case?" I ask, knowing what the answer will be but needing to hear him say it.

"We'll reassign the case today or tomorrow. At this point, after filing your report on the shit show last night, you should prepare to be interviewed by the BCA in the next day or two, but I'm hoping to have you back within the next two to three weeks.

"Listen, Detective, the next week could get pretty brutal. Given Brinkman's wealth and influence and the fact that Slayton was a decorated marine, this incident will make the national media—it probably already has. I wouldn't be surprised if Slayton's widowed mother shows up on Anderson Cooper tonight to rip you and our department a new one. And now Natalie Brinkman has lost both her father and her boyfriend in the same week, so there'll be a sympathy factor for sure. You need to keep a level head. As you know, Brinkman also has some leverage over the mayor, and the mayor and the chief are tight, so I'm not sure how much public support you're going to get from the city's senior leadership or how diligently they'll want to follow up on Slayton as a suspect in Patterson's death."

I feel like crying, but I'm too angry to produce any tears. "I appreciate your support, Lieutenant." That is a heartfelt statement. "I've already given my badge and Glock to Marlys. Have you received any updates on Warren's condition?"

"Marlys tells me he's still not awake but stable. That was as of six o'clock this morning. I'll be heading over to North Memorial this afternoon."

"Maybe I'll see you there," I say. "I'm still hoping he'll be coming back to work."

"I'd just worry about yourself for now, Detective. Warren will be lucky to come out of this alive and in one piece." Moe takes a huge bite out of a jelly donut, and most of the jelly ends up on the front of his powder-blue dress shirt. He grabs a napkin to wipe it off, only smearing it into a Jackson Pollock-like design. It's time for me to go.

"Thanks again, Lieutenant," I say, taking my coffee and half-eaten Bismarck and dashing out of his office before he says something else to upset me.

It's eight fifteen in the morning, and I'm already having one of the worst days of my life. I drive to the Speedway on Thirty-Eighth and Chicago, fill up with gas, and buy copies of today's *Star Tribune* and *Pioneer Press*. I read the full Strib article while devouring the rest of my donut in the Jeep. It makes me want to throw up—the article, not the donut. After washing the remnants down with the dregs of my coffee, I exit the parking lot and head for downtown Minneapolis, hoping to spend my first day as a suspended cop salvaging my reputation.

I've never felt as conflicted as I do at this moment. For the first time in my ten years as a police officer, I have killed another human being. I know the hollow, burning feeling in the pit of my gut will be recurring, regardless of the number of times people tell me the shots I fired at Andrew Slayton were justified. Even with a couple of Xanax, I hardly slept last night, waking up several times, thinking about Warren and Slayton, replaying yesterday's events in my mind, and sobbing. I probably need professional help, but except for my boss, no one at the new and improved Minneapolis Police Department has even asked me how I'm doing. Brinkman has them all running for cover.

"Oh, God, Lincoln, how are you doing?" I figured she'd be too embarrassed to pick up, but Rochelle Griffith answers after the first ring.

"Are you home?" I ask.

"I am right now. Why?"

"I'm five minutes away, and we need to talk."

"I didn't have anything to do with that article, Lincoln."

"I'm three minutes away."

"Okay. I'm in 611. Come to the front entrance, and call me on the intercom."

Griffith lives in a downtown condo overlooking the Mississippi in a building called Bridgewater Lofts. She rents a two-bedroom unit from the owner, her editor at the Strib and a former lover. She buzzes me into the building, but when I knock on 611, a petite Middle Eastern-looking woman wearing a hijab and a tan winter coat opens the door.

"Hello," she says with a distinctive British accent. "I'm Laila. You must be Lincoln."

"Yes I am," I say, surprised to see someone other than Rochelle. "Good to meet you, Laila."

"You as well. Come in and have a seat. Rochelle will be out shortly. If you'll excuse me, I have to run." And with that, she slips by me and out the door.

Before I get comfortable on a crushed-velvet sofa, Rochelle emerges from the bedroom in a blue terry-cloth robe, her hair wrapped in a white towel, a bundle of clothes tucked under her arm.

"So sorry," she says, half out of breath, her bare legs striding past me into the kitchen. She returns a few minutes later dressed in black jeans and a navy wool sweater, carrying a small wooden tray with two coffee mugs and a plate of vanilla-bean scones. "I hopped in the shower right after you called. I have a meeting at the paper at nine thirty." She sets the tray on a modern metal coffee table and sits next to me on the sofa.

"You met Laila." It's a statement, not a question. She places a mug in front of me.

"Very briefly," I reply. I've had enough coffee already, but this morning, another cup can only help.

"You like it black, just like me, right?"

"Yes, thanks. So, Laila?"

"Laila and I have been together for about six months, but we're keeping our relationship quiet for now."

"Why? She's young but not that young."

"No, nothing like that. She's a recent grad of the U of M journalism school. She's a copy editor at the competitor paper across the river for now, but she was a reporter for the *Daily* at the University and eventually wants to write about national and world affairs for a publication like the *New Yorker* or *Atlantic*."

"What's she doing in Minneapolis?"

"She was born in the States, but her parents met and married in Turkey and immigrated to the US in the late 1980s. They are highly educated Sunni Muslims. Her father's the editor of a monthly newsletter published by the Turkish American Association in Washington D.C., and her mom is his assistant. Since early middle school, she's been attracted to women, but that's not allowed or even recognized according to her dad's version of Islam. She chose the U of M and Minneapolis to get an education far away from home so she could be herself without having to reveal her orientation to her parents. After graduation, she went home for the summer and told them she was gay. Her dad reacted worse than she had imagined, telling her so long as that was true, she wasn't his daughter. She returned to Minneapolis for grad school. I met her at a lecture at the Humphrey Institute a year ago."

"What about her mom?" I ask, thinking about Billie's short, lonely life.

"She's conflicted, neither approving of same-sex relationships nor wanting to cross her partner of thirty years but needing to have a relationship with her only child. She actually sends Laila handwritten letters and calls her from a friend's cell phone, assuring her daughter of her love but also beseeching her to give up her way of life to preserve her relationship with her father. Laila's also conflicted because, believe it or not, she remains a practicing Muslim even though her faith won't accept or even accommodate her orientation and lifestyle."

"How difficult and sad," I say, shaking my head, but not in disbelief. "Good people can be poisoned by religion, not by God but by man-made religion."

"That's for sure, and I don't have the heart to tell her I'm a committed atheist. But enough about me. You didn't drive down here to discuss my girlfriend."

"You know what I came to discuss," I say, getting a buzz from the strong Turkish coffee.

"Tony Hilger is a dick. What can I say?"

"I saw his name on the byline, but I have no idea who he is or why he's out to get me."

"He's not out to get you, Lincoln, but he's the most sensationalist reporter on the staff. Think about it. Normally, when a cop is involved in a fatality, we get nothing but stonewalling bullshit for the first few days, unless there's clear body-cam or video footage that forces the police chief, mayor, or even the governor in high-profile cases to talk specifics about cop behavior.

"So, what happened here? Except to express concern about your partner's condition, Hawkins and the mayor had nothing to say, nothing about Slayton or you, except that the sheriff and Wayzata police had jurisdiction, and the BCA would be investigating your actions. That's standard operating procedure, Detective, and you know it. What's different this time is Natalie Brinkman. She's clearly trying to influence the investigation and the outcome. The real question is, why? Revenge against you? I'm sure that's part of it. She may actually have been in love with Slayton. For political purposes? Perhaps. She's got plenty of money, but that doesn't get your name in the news. Why not get some free publicity supporting the anti-policing sentiment in the city?"

"How about distracting the press and police from solving Kate Patterson's murder?"

"What does Kate Patterson's murder have to do with Andrew Slayton?"

"Why do you think Warren and I were in Wayzata last night? Andrew Slayton is a person of interest in Patterson's execution."

"What?"

"If you want a good story, look into why our crusading Black mayor chose a rich, white millennial like Brinkman to be his chief of staff." Maybe I have had too much coffee.

"So, are you saying that Brinkman and Slayton conspired to kill Patterson? Based on what?"

"Remember my promise at the Monte Carlo—that you'd be the first reporter I'd tell once we had a viable suspect?"

"I do, but I dismissed it as rhetorical cop talk."

I tell her about my conversation with Ollie Burns, the key card the old man found in the street, and the likelihood that the card was issued to Natalie Brinkman, who rarely drove herself to work.

"According to Josh Cummins, Natalie's boyfriend liked to drive her Bentley. We have video footage of the Bentley in the Hennepin ramp on the night of the murder."

"That's all very interesting," Griffith acknowledges, "but why would Brinkman want to kill her boss?"

"That's where it gets tricky. Cummins says Brinkman has ambitions to run for office—city council, then maybe Congress or governor. He claims Patterson reneged on a promise not to run for reelection last year. That's why Natalie sought the chief-of-staff position. And the reason she was going to get it is she put Sampson in an incredibly difficult position. It has to do with paying off a huge campaign debt, another lead you should be following."

"Okay, she's got dirt on Sampson. That could be a good story, and thanks for that. But that's no reason to kill Patterson."

"Not unless someone tells Patterson about the illegal contribution, and Patterson demands that Sampson disclose it or she will."

"And of course, disclosing the bribe exposes Brinkman and explains why Sampson has made her chief of staff," Griffith says, proud that she beats me to the punch line. "That gives both the mayor and Brinkman motive, but I don't see either one of them willing to go that far to stop Patterson."

"I totally agree. Brinkman and Slayton had dinner together downtown on the Friday night before the murder. It was right after Patterson told the mayor she knew about the payoff. That's my theory—well it's actually Warren's theory—but it makes perfect sense. Brinkman complains to Slayton that the woman who's already screwed up her plans is now going to ruin the backup plan by blowing the whistle on Sampson. Slayton may have been a good soldier, but he has a serious drinking problem, which, as we know, can impair your judgment. He wants to be Natalie's hero and a senior, respected member of the Brinkman organization. Surveilling, stalking, and murdering a fifty-year-old, unsuspecting woman and making it look like a random killing in a park should be no problem for an experienced Marine Raider, right?"

"I get it, and I'm certainly going to pursue all of this, but I'm not a hundred percent convinced of your theory. If Slayton's so good, why didn't you and your colleagues believe it was a random killing and not, as you call it, an execution?"

"Probably the vodka," I say. "The man's got a documented drinking problem. I'll be very interested to see the blood-alcohol results in the post-accident tox report."

"If you're right about all this, it should exonerate you, Lincoln."

"Attempting to mow down my defenseless partner with a pickup truck is no different than whacking him with a machete. In either case, I'm justified to use deadly force to stop him from fleeing the scene. Don't you agree?" Maybe I'm too sensitive about this issue, but I can't help it.

"Actually, I do agree, if that's what happened." I'm about to interrupt, but she cuts me off by standing and staring down on me from nearly six feet of uncompromising womanhood. "Listen, I gotta go, but with the involvement of Kate Patterson and the mayor in this mess, it falls directly under my beat. I can make sure Tony backs off, and I'll write any follow-up stories. You know I'll get to the truth or bust my ass trying."

I get up and we're eye to eye. "That's all I ask, Rochelle, just no quotes or attributions from me, okay?"

"Our usual rules apply. How do you want to communicate on this?"

"I'll give you a personal email that's encrypted through Proton. You can use it to set up a face-to-face meeting, but not for anything substantive. You can also text me on my cell."

"Thanks for trusting me, Detective," she says, grabbing a parka from the hall tree and covering her messy, wet hair with a Lynx cap as we head for the elevator.

You know you're in trouble when a reporter is the only person you can trust.

CHAPTER 27

At home on a forced vacation in the middle of the week, I check in with Diane. She and one of her daughters continue the vigil in Warren's room. He's still in a coma, but his vitals are improving, and the doctors are hopeful they can ease him back into consciousness later today. I say a short prayer for him because I don't know what else I can do to help.

It's sunny and above freezing, so I change into sweats and head out to run around Harriet and Lake of the Isles, about seven miles total. It's my first workout since Campeche, and it helps clear my head of a boatload of negative thoughts. It also helps counter the effects of this morning's custard donut and scone. At least that's what I tell myself.

After a hot shower and a yogurt smoothie, I check my messages: phone, text, and email. My mom and Wanda have read the Strib article; they're worried about me, and Wanda invites me over tomorrow night for pizza and beer and to watch first-round NCAA basketball tournament games. Craig has sent me a bracket to fill out for a high school coaches' pool. It's ten bucks an entry, and the winner gets a couple grand.

A Paige Winters from the Bureau of Criminal Apprehension wants to interview me tomorrow or Friday at ten in the morning at her office in Saint Paul. She doesn't answer when I return her call, so I leave a message saying I'll be there at ten. BCA agents are all business, so I need to be prepared.

The only two men I know from Two Harbors leave voicemail messages three minutes apart. Sheriff MacDonald says he has some important news and asks me to call him back. The former judge has read the nasty Strib article and thinks it's "disgraceful" but adds, "Maybe that's because I know what kind of person you are." I wish I knew what kind of person he is. He, too, asks me to call but suggests that I come up north for the weekend "to talk."

I'm not mentally prepared to talk to the judge, so I call Sheriff MacDonald. I'm surprised when he answers after one ring.

"Hello, Detective Barnes. I didn't expect a call back so soon, given what you've been through this week. I read a blurb in the Duluth paper this morning about an altercation in Wayzata and a fatal shooting but didn't know you were involved until I read the *Star Tribune* article online this afternoon. How is your partner doing?"

"Still in a coma, Sheriff, but improving. His vitals are good, and they expect to wake him up in the next twenty-four hours. Thanks for asking."

"And how are you doing?"

I know from his history that MacDonald has endured some tragic and difficult situations in his career, so I feel comfortable sharing my feelings with him. "Feeling a bit persecuted and unappreciated. And to be honest, Sheriff, I feel horrible, just horrible about the loss of a life. I've replayed that thirty seconds over and over in my mind, and I can't see myself doing anything different."

"That's a good thing, Detective, on both counts. If you need to talk through anything, I'm always available for a chat."

"Thanks, Sheriff. I appreciate that."

"I have some news for you and an invitation. My friend with the Mexican embassy says the state police are trying to extradite Sara Hyatt's husband on a manslaughter charge. It's in the Milwaukee paper this morning and, because Sara's from here, the story made the local news on public radio. Apparently, the doctor is fighting extradition."

"After interviewing him for an hour, I can't say I'm surprised by any of it, but it's certainly not what I expected after reading that diary and hearing your account of the relationship and breakup of J. R. Campbell and Sara Wheaton."

"You were afraid the judge was involved in Sara's death. I was as well."

I didn't want to believe it, but I couldn't shake it. "So have you seen the man formerly known as Judge Gildemeister haunting the streets of Two Harbors?"

"I haven't, but he's the talk of the town. He's buying the old First National Bank Building downtown that's owned by Wells Fargo. He's filed plans to rip off the aluminum façade and restore the old stone-and-granite structure as a small office building. If he opens a law office up here, he'll have all the business he can handle. By the way, apparently folks are calling him J. R., and he's not correcting or discouraging them."

"That's all very interesting, Sheriff. I assume he's living in his grandmother's house on the lake?"

"As far as I know. One of my deputies is good friends with Jake Guzzo, the local carpenter and builder. I think I mentioned that Jake and his grandfather have done a ton of work maintaining and remodeling the Gildemeister property. My deputy has been inside and claims Jake has transformed the place into a beautiful and functional cottage. It's one of the best lots in the county in terms of privacy and access to the lake."

"Maybe I'll get to see it someday," I say, half-heartedly.

"That brings me to the invitation. As much as I love it up here, it's not an easy place to recruit and retain skilled peace officers. I sensed you really enjoyed your trip up here and also might be ready for a change, whether or not that change involves your friend J. R. Like a lot of places, Lake County has had an increase in violent crime over the past few years, and I've been fortunate to have Gail Klewacki, a wonderful person and one of the best detectives I've ever known, as the only designated detective on my staff. Gail gave her notice two weeks ago. Her husband's family owns hotels and recreational properties in several states, and they want her spouse to manage a new acquisition in Big Sky, Montana. The Bozeman police chief has already offered her a job out there, and I don't have anyone internally who can replace her. I'd like you to send me a resume if you have any interest in living and working up here. I can promise you a collegial, supportive staff and a community that values and respects what we do as much as any today."

"Wow, thanks for thinking of me, Sheriff. I've had a lot of negative thoughts about my job and the MPD over the past twenty-four hours, but I haven't gone so far as to consider quitting." That's not true if I'm totally honest. "For now, I'll send you a resume and promise to have a candid discussion with you about me and the position sometime soon."

"That's great. Call me when you're ready to set something up. In person would be best. I hope your partner recovers soon, and Natalie Brinkman finds someone else to torture."

"Thanks, Sheriff. You don't know Brinkman, do you?"

"I don't, but in another life in the Secret Service, I was very familiar with her father. He was mean and ruthless and wasn't afraid to break the rules to gain an advantage in business or politics. He and George Soros, two very powerful, unscrupulous men who supported the president it was my job to protect, had a common enemy, the man who followed my boss into the White House and became maybe the worst president ever and, most definitely, the worst human being ever to be president in the history of this country. So, while I may have agreed with their objectives, I never condoned their methods. I have no doubt that Robert Brinkman's only child, even in her twenties, is capable of destroying lives to get what she wants."

"We agree on that point, for sure. I'll be in touch."

———————

It's the conversation I've been dreading, only because I fear I'll be disappointed by the outcome. I picked up a bottle of Green Spot at France 44 on my way home from Rochelle's, so I pour myself a shorty and get comfortable on the overstuffed rocker in my living room. Why not have a drink at three in the afternoon? I'm on vacation, after all.

Before I muster the courage to call the judge, I answer a call from a number I recognize as Helen McCrary, my police union rep and one of Warren's best friends. She's a zealous advocate for the average street cop, but her support doesn't extend to racists or downright criminals, meaning she's different from some of her colleagues.

"Hi, Helen. I wish I had more news about Warren. Last I heard, he was still in a coma, but his vitals were improving."

"That's the same report I got from Diane an hour ago," she says. "I'm calling to see how you're doing and to let you know your union is behind you a hundred percent."

"Thanks," I say, "good to know someone is behind me. What have you heard about my case?"

"You need more friends in high places, girlfriend. That's what I think. Until last week, I thought Natalie Brinkman was an aide to Kate Patterson—an up-and-comer, for sure, but not a major player. I had no idea the mayor wanted to make her chief of staff or that she was the only child of that billionaire who just died. The scuttlebutt downtown is that Sampson and Chief Hawkins have already talked to the attorney general about reviewing the case for possible criminal prosecution."

"Prosecution? Of me? What's going on, Helen?"

"It makes no sense," she says, trying to keep me from going ballistic over the phone. "Especially since the BCA hasn't completed their investigation."

"Oh, it makes sense," I say. "It makes sense if Brinkman has something big on the mayor. The chief will do whatever Sampson tells him to do." I don't think it's wise to tell Helen about the illegal campaign contribution. I need to let Rochelle's investigation expose that part of the case. I'll divulge something else to give her some insight into Natalie Brinkman. "When Warren and I interviewed Brinkman the Monday after Patterson's murder, she claimed Patterson and Mayor Sampson were having a secret affair, and that they had a two-hour meeting in Patterson's office on the Friday afternoon before she died."

"I would never have put those two together. Any evidence to corroborate that?"

"None. It's a lie. The meeting occurred, but not the affair. It's probable that Sampson was the last person Patterson met with, and Brinkman was the last person she tried to contact before she died."

"So that's why you were out at the Brinkman compound the other night. You were going to do a follow-up interview with Natalie. Right?"

"There's more to it than that, Helen, but I'd rather not get into it until I talk to the BCA tomorrow."

"Fair enough. Would you like counsel present for that meeting? You're entitled to representation from here on out."

"I appreciate the offer, but I think I'm better off not lawyering up unless they charge me with a crime."

"I can't argue with that logic, Detective, but many of your colleagues want representation when being interviewed by the BCA. We can talk again after tomorrow. Give Warren my best if you visit him before I do."

"Of course, I will."

If Sampson and Hawkins are taking orders from a twenty-eight-year-old white heiress, and those orders include charging me with a crime to divert attention from the mayor's financial mess, I will hand in my badge, regardless of the outcome. I might be through anyway because, without Warren as my partner, being a cop in this town has more downside than up.

I take another gulp of whiskey and call the judge. It rings four or five times before a familiar voice sounds oddly comforting.

"Hi, Lincoln. How's your partner doing?"

"Still in a coma, but I think improving. And that's the good news. I'm having a really bad day."

"I assume you're on administrative leave, but that's standard police protocol, so there must be something else."

I tell him everything I know about Brinkman, Sampson, and Slayton, the key card, and the campaign contribution. As usual, he's a patient listener. He offers to come down and invites me to come up. And then, I turn the tables.

"Enough about me. How was Orlando?" My sarcasm is fittingly brutal.

"Good one," he has to admit. "What can I say but I'm sorry? I don't want to get too deep into this over the phone, but I've had my reasons for being evasive and not telling the truth. You have to decide whether they're good enough."

"Well, for starters, where were you?" It doesn't feel right knowing the answer to my question.

"Actually, I wasn't far from Campeche, just across the Yucatan south of Cancun. I was providing evidence to the Mexican state police in a murder investigation."

"What? Mexico? Were you trying to extradite someone who committed a crime in Minnesota?" It's much easier to feign surprise and make stuff up over the phone than it would be in person, where he could see my face.

"Oh, no," he says. "I wasn't there in an official capacity. I'd been there as a tourist right before the pandemic hit in March of 2020. I was meeting a woman who'd been the love of my life. Unfortunately, she was married to someone else. She died in a bizarre accident that the state police have been investigating for over two years, though COVID has made it much more difficult."

"Did you witness the accident?" I ask, thinking he actually sounds human and vulnerable.

"No, but I believe her husband did more than that. He'd found out she intended to leave him and wasn't happy about it." Now he's getting pretty "deep" after saying he didn't want to.

"Was she leaving him to be with you?" I ask. Again, I feel sheepish knowing the answer, but I need to do this or forget about him.

"She was." Long pause. "Lincoln, I understand if you don't want to see me again. But if you're willing to give me another chance, I'd love to see you. I can come down there, or even better, I'd love to show you my place on the North Shore. I promise to tell you as much about me and my past as you want to know."

I want to be with him, but I won't tolerate any more lies. "I need to get away from here for a while, so I'll come up there. How about I meet you on Saturday night for dinner? Let's try your favorite place in Two Harbors. I have some business up that way that I can accomplish during the day."

"You know you're welcome to stay at my place in Castle Danger."

"Castle Danger? I love that name, but I think I'd prefer to find my own accommodations on this trip. I'd like to see your place though."

"Sure, I understand," he says. "I'll make a reservation at the Grand Superior Grill for seven on Saturday night if that works for you. We can have a nightcap at my place if you're up for it."

"We'll see," I say.

"It's great to hear your voice, Lincoln."

It doesn't feel great to hear the judge refer to another woman as "the love of my life," though between the diary and Sheriff MacDonald, I already knew it. Does that mean I can never be the love of his life? Second place? She knew him for thirty years; I've known him for three weeks. Besides, I've got enough to deal with right now without trying to build a relationship with someone I don't trust.

What really bothers me is his obsession over a woman. Or maybe that makes him more attractive to me. I've been attracted to several men over the years but have only had long-term relationships with two: my ex-husband, a Black detective ten years my senior, who, though he looked like Idris Elba, was an abusive, high-functioning drunk who will never get the help he needs; and Darnell Taylor, a boy I met in sixth grade, who was the cutest and fastest kid in my high school and a track star at the University of Kansas.

I've learned to repress thoughts of my ex-husband, but I often think about the life I would have had with Darnell. We started dating as sophomores, and by the time we graduated high school, both with Dī scholarships, we were tight and pledged to continue our relationship from a distance—he in Lawrence, Kansas, and me in Normal, Illinois. After my first two weeks at a large, diverse university, I knew that wouldn't work. I wanted to try new experiences, including new relationships. I wasn't ready to commit to one person, the only person I'd ever dated, for the rest of my life. When I tried to explain this to Darnell over the phone, he became upset and started yelling at me and crying. Then he hung up. I thought he'd come to Normal to talk in person, to work out a compromise, a nonexclusive relationship, but he never did. I haven't talked to him since that call.

There's a reason I've thought about Darnell lately. Last month, I read he's been promoted to head coach of the men's track team at the University of Minnesota Duluth. The article mentioned that he has two kids and is married to the women's softball coach, which irks me just a bit. I had no idea he was living three hours away.

A call from my mom interrupts my little reverie. She's home after spending five days in the sky on flights from Chicago to Paris to Rome to New York and back to Chicago. Wanda told her about the incident in Wayzata and the article in the Strib. She's "worried sick" about both Warren and me and says she'll see me tomorrow night at Wanda's to "catch up." I'm not in the mood to be grilled by my family, but I tell her I'll be there.

After a light dinner, I send Sheriff MacDonald a short email thanking him for his help and attaching my resume. Anticipating another sleepless night, I find a horror movie to watch on Netflix and take a Xanax. Shortly before midnight, I get a text from Diane.

Warren is awake and talking. He wants to see you. Tests & therapy in the morning. Can you stop by hospital around noon?

I can't reply fast enough.

Best news, Diane. See you tomorrow.

CHAPTER 28

The Bureau of Criminal Apprehension, or BCA, is a state agency that provides investigative and forensic services to help local law enforcement solve serious crimes. Paige Winters is a special agent with the BCA's Force Investigations Unit, a separate division that investigates incidents where the use of deadly force by a cop results in the death of a civilian. I sit across from her at an oval table in a sterile conference room at the BCA's main office in Saint Paul. Professionally attired in a light-gray jacket and skirt with a red blouse, Winters is a stocky white woman with permed brown hair, a ruddy complexion, and the stained teeth and gravelly voice that come from years of smoking two packs a day. She's probably in her late forties but looks older. After working her way from neighborhood patrol to sergeant in the Bloomington Police Department, she made a lateral move to the BCA and eventually became the chief investigator of peace officer shootings. I'd never heard of her before she called to set up this meeting. Now my future is in her hands. She opens a manila file folder, removes a few typewritten pages, and starts scribbling on a yellow legal pad.

"Thanks for coming in this morning, Detective." I didn't think I had a choice. "You won't be surprised to hear I'm very concerned about the politicizing of your case. For some reason, Freddie Tyler, the mayor's lawyer, has been in contact with the AG at this early stage of the investigation, trying to convince him to consider criminal charges against you."

"Excuse my language, Special Agent Winters, but that is total bullshit. Someone tried to kill my partner using a pickup truck as a battering ram and then, like a coward or a paid executioner, fled the scene. I admit using deadly force to stop him. If that's a crime, then I'm guilty, and I need to find a new career." I'd rehearsed that little speech for hours yesterday, but I didn't think I'd get to use it so early in our meeting. Should I also mention that I hit the target about five percent of the time under those conditions?

"That's your interpretation of what happened. Apparently, the mayor is circulating a different story. My contact in the attorney general's office says Mr. Tyler claims you and your partner had no business disturbing Ms. Brinkman at her father's home while she was grieving his death. She'd already spent over an hour answering your questions and was concerned her boyfriend would interfere with your visit, so she asked him to leave, not realizing there was a blizzard outside. Tyler's position is that Major Slayton lost control of his truck on an icy driveway and didn't know he hit Detective Lindquist. In fact, he probably didn't see either one of you in the blinding storm and certainly never heard you yelling for him to stop. And then he was gone. Dead gone."

Really? Can she seriously believe that? A blizzard?

"My interpretation is the only one based on the facts," I reply. "I'm sure you've read my report. Detective Lindquist and I were following a lead in a murder case. We weren't going to wait until after Robert Brinkman's funeral to do that. I have no doubt that Slayton saw both of us and intentionally targeted one of the best cops ever to wear a badge."

Suddenly, Winters's demeanor softens. "You're a lucky cop," she says, giving me a half smile and pulling a two-page typewritten report from her notebook. "Three pieces of evidence found their way to me last night that I believe exonerate you. Officers Goldstein and Sanchez took some photos of Brinkman's property after you left. They reveal a couple of things. First, there are heating coils that melt the snow on contact on that driveway, so it was wet but definitely not icy. Second, several photos show clear tire tracks leaving the driveway and continuing well into the yard. That truck didn't skid on the snow until it was twenty feet from the stone wall, well after it smashed into Detective Lindquist. Third, and probably most important, Slayton's blood-alcohol level was .25, over three times the legal limit. At that level, his judgment was seriously compromised no matter how skilled a soldier he was. We'll never know what he was thinking, but he definitely pursued your partner with his truck and could have been considered a danger to others that night. I still think whether or not to shoot in that situation is a close call, Detective Barnes, and I'm guessing you let emotions control your actions, but my report will indicate that it was within the bounds of proper policing. I will not be recommending any discipline or further action against you."

"I'm grateful for that, Agent Winters. Do you think this will end any inquiry by the attorney general?"

"It should, but I have no authority to intervene or even comment if the AG wants to pursue criminal charges against you. My report won't be issued for a couple of days, so I'd appreciate it if you wouldn't discuss it with anyone except your attorney, if you've got one, until then. And given the high-profile of this case, you'd be wise to retain counsel."

"I haven't," I say, "but you're not the first person who's suggested it."

"Do it," she says emphatically. "That's all I have for you, Detective. I'll pray for your partner and stick to the facts, law, and sound policing practices in my report. It's challenging being a peace officer these days. I wouldn't want the job, especially in Minneapolis."

"I appreciate your honesty," I say as I grab my stuff and stand to leave. I don't tell her I've been questioning whether I want to continue risking my life for Hawkins and Sampson, two powerful Black men who have forsaken their sister.

I get to North Memorial a few minutes before noon. I consider stopping at Wuollet Bakery for Warren's favorite raised donuts but decide not to incur Diane's wrath. There'll be a time and place for pastries in our future. It's a good sign that the door to his room is open. The TV is on, but Warren is engrossed in the *Star Tribune* and doesn't look up until he feels me sit on the edge of his bed and wrap my hands around his wrist.

"Where is everyone?" I ask.

Warren drops the paper and envelops my hand in his big mitt. "The girls were here all morning, and the older two are coming back after dinner," he says in a weak, raspy voice. "Diane went out to pick up some lunch for the three of us. How are you holding up?"

How am I holding up? The man nearly died and looks like a mummy. His head is shaved and heavily bandaged, and his right arm and both legs are in temporary casts.

"I'm doing fine. I just left the BCA torture chamber, and I survived."

"It shouldn't be a difficult case for them," he says, lifting the front section and sticking it under my nose. "I just finished this article in yesterday's Strib, and I'd like to meet the fuckwit who wrote it. We were literally running for our lives from a crazy man who would probably kill his own mother to impress his girlfriend. Brinkman cries police brutality and manslaughter, and neither Sampson nor Hawkins defends your actions to stop a fleeing felon. Hey, I, for one, appreciate what you did. I'd have tried to do the same—only I would have missed."

We both laugh a little, and then I start to cry.

"I know you, Lincoln. I know you're hurting inside for ending a life regardless of the circumstances. I'm sure you've researched this guy's family and history because that's what you do."

"He comes from a long line of soldiers. Father was a colonel in the army who fought in Viet Nam, and his grandfather was one of Eisenhower's executive officers in Europe. His parents are alive and live in Columbus, Ohio. A married sister who's a prosecuting attorney lives in Pennsylvania. So, yes, I've done some research, and it doesn't make me feel any better. But Special Agent Winters just informed me that Slayton's blood-alcohol was over .20. We knew the guy had a serious drinking problem, Warren, and I have no doubt it affected his judgment."

Warren tosses the paper to the floor in disgust. "That's the understatement of the year," he says. "I believe Brinkman weaponized this guy, probably intentionally, with a combination of sex, booze, maybe drugs, and a lavish lifestyle that few people ever experience. That's a partial explanation, not an excuse, for murder and attempted murder. By the way, do you know who's taking our place on the Patterson case? I left a message for Sherm this morning, but he hasn't called me back."

"I'm completely out of the loop," I reply. "But I'm betting that Sherm steps in and takes it on himself. Caseloads are overflowing, and it's too high profile to give to somebody new."

"You could be right. He's done it before, and he used to be the best on the force. Warren clears his throat a couple of times and envelops both of my hands in his.

"Lincoln, I asked Diane to give us some time alone. I know you've figured this out already, but I won't be coming back to work at the MPD."

I assumed that was the case, but I decide not to respond until my partner,mentor, and best friend says everything that's on his mind.

"I'm scheduled for two surgeries over the next three weeks, and then I'll probably need a cane or maybe even a walker to get around. I thought seriously about retiring when the pandemic hit, but I decided to stick around for two reasons. First, the aftermath of the Floyd killing gave all of us a bad name, and I couldn't leave under that cloud. Second, you're the best partner I've ever had—or better said, the best person I've ever had as a partner. It's been an adventure, an honor, and a joy to work with you, and I wanted to keep it going for a couple more years. But I'll be fine. Diane and I have planned for this for years." I start to cry and my head drops into his hands which a grab with mine.

"I'm worried about you though," he says. Not about your suspension. I'm confident the BCA will clear your name, and I can't imagine the political hacks in the AG's office would charge you under these facts just to appease the mayor and that conniving bitch.

"The city and its police department are dysfunctional right now, and it's only going to get worse. Hawkins isn't a bad guy, but he's a puppet for the mayor, a man who's lost his moral compass. The public perception of the department is as low as it's ever been. If it turns out Patterson was murdered by the boyfriend of her chief aide, an aide who orchestrated an illegal contribution to the mayor in order to extort a political appointment, there will be zero confidence in Minneapolis city government. That's the big picture. Think about—" Warren starts coughing uncontrollably. He's way too worked up for a man who was in a coma eighteen hours ago.

I find a pitcher of water on his side table and pour him a glass. "I don't disagree with anything you're saying, Warren, but maybe you should rest a bit before Diane gets back."

"I'm okay," he says, trying to sit up straight but quickly losing strength and sliding onto his back. "Bear with me. I'm almost done pontificating. You need to think about the roster of potential new partners, Lincoln. A handful of rednecks, racists, and Trumpers. This is your chance to take a well-earned hiatus from the MPD. Get a master's or a law degree or submit an application to the FBI or BCA."

None of those suggestions is bad or something I haven't considered during the past few days. I tell Warren about the job in Lake County, working for Sheriff MacDonald, thinking he'll discourage me from leaving the big city for the northern tundra. But I'm wrong.

"Duluth is a great town," he says. "One of the most progressive places in the state. MacDonald has become kind of a legend up there. You know he's a former Secret Service guy."

"I heard that," I say.

"George Redman, an old friend from Saint Paul Homicide and the BCA, told me MacDonald saved his life more than once when they were investigating the Lauren Fallon murder a few years back."

This is evidence that Warren isn't a hundred percent. He's told me the Redman story at least three times in the past two years, even though every cop in the state knows about George Redman, a legendary detective who was gunned down by thugs from the Chilean mafia on the shores of Lake Superior. The ongoing battle between proponents of copper mining and environmentalists is one of the many things that intrigue me about northern Minnesota.

"I really haven't made up my mind, Warren. Maybe Sherm will want to leave the desk and go back out in the field with me." I'm relieved Warren hasn't brought up the judge's name. After all, Warren's the one who told me about the judge's retirement and move back to the North Shore. For some reason, he's not a fan of our relationship. Maybe it's the age difference.

"Well, if that happens, then you should definitely stay," he says, just as Diane rushes in carrying a Fat Mike's Delight from Pig Ate My Pizza and a pitcher of root beer.

"Hey, Lincoln," she says, nearly out of breath. "Someone had a hankering for the best pizza in Robbinsdale, and it wasn't me."

"Let me help you," I say, relieving her of the pitcher and a stack of paper plates and napkins resting on the top of the pizza box. "I've heard of that place but never had their pizza."

Diane sets the pizza on a side table near the window. When she opens the box, a waft of a delicious combination of aromas fills my nostrils.

"Did you hear?" Diane asks. "They just recovered the body of a guy who got accosted on his bike and thrown into the Mississippi this morning. They haven't identified him yet, but who would do such a thing?"

Warren and I give each other the "a lot of people would" look but don't say anything except that neither one of us has heard about it.

Lieutenant Moe has called my cell three times in the last two minutes. I'm wondering if there's a connection. It's too early for the BCA's report to be out. Perhaps there's been a breakthrough in the Kate Patterson case. Maybe Natalie Brinkman has confessed to aiding and abetting the murder. The possibilities make me edgy.

"Are you going to the service tomorrow?" Warren asks while Diane feeds him pizza with a plastic fork.

It takes me a few seconds to regain my bearings. "What service?"

"The Robert Brinkman memorial service at the Lafayette Club."

"Not in a church?" I ask sarcastically, knowing the service is at eleven. "His mother was a devout Catholic, and his father was a ruthless developer whose only visit to a church was probably on the day of his funeral. Is this thing by invitation only?"

"You always do your homework, Detective Barnes. The paper didn't say, but I'm sure it's open to the public. You need to try a slice of this stuff."

"I'm sorry, Lincoln," says Diane. "I should have made a plate for you too. Please help yourself."

I get a text from Moe, a guy who texts even less than Warren.

Please call me NOW!

"Thanks, Diane. I've got to make a few calls, but I'll be back tomorrow to see our feisty patient." I give Warren a peck on the top of the head, wrap a piece of pizza in a napkin, and head for the parking lot.

"It's about time."

"I just left Warren's hospital room."

"Oh, shit. I haven't called him back. I need to get over there and see him now that he's awake."

"He'd appreciate that, I'm sure."

"How's he doing?"

"For someone who's been through what he has, he's doing great. He can't shut up. He's happy to be alive. He might not be as chipper when reality sets in."

"I'll get up there tonight. Right now, I need you to meet me in the middle of the Stone Arch Bridge. Park on Nicollet Island and walk from there. I'm at city hall. I can be there in ten minutes. How about you?"

"I'm in the parking lot at North Memorial. I can be there in twenty. What's this about, Lieutenant?"

"See you in twenty minutes."

A sunny Thursday afternoon with temperatures in the fifties attracts a crowd to Nicollet Island, some starting the weekend early and others seeking an antidote for spring fever after a long Minnesota winter. I find a parking spot near the artist lofts at the corner of Sixth and Main and leave my parka in the Jeep. Unfortunately, I'm still dressed in the suit I wore to the BCA meeting, with black leather pumps that have hardly ever, or maybe even never, been worn. Blisters are forming on both feet.

The Stone Arch Bridge is an impressive limestone and granite structure with multiple arches that span the Mississippi just below St. Anthony Falls. The plaque on the historic landmark says it was built by James J. Hill in the 1880s as a railroad bridge and functioned as such for over a hundred years. A few decades before I moved here, the bridge was converted to be exclusively for pedestrian and bike use with designated lanes for each. Dozens of runners and bikers zip past as I walk onto the bridge. It's exhilarating. A pack of rollerbladers glide by, a few shirtless with milky-white torsos adorned with colorful tattoos.

In the middle of the throng, I spot a burly man in a dark suit and tie, both hands gripping a brown metal railing, head bowed at a forty-five degree angle, eyes fixed on the fast-moving water below. He's in a daze, so much so he doesn't move a muscle as I approach but flinches at the sound of my voice.

"Lose something down there, Lieutenant?" I ask.

As he turns to face me, his squinting slate-blue eyes and gravelly baritone remind me of Clint Eastwood, one of my dad's favorites, until you look at his physique.

"You got here fast," he says.

"That's because I thought you were going to return me to duty."

"Not yet," he says, turning back toward the river. "I thought having you come down here might help you recall more specifics."

"Specifics about what?"

"Do you remember the conversation in my office on Monday? About Brinkman and her boyfriend?"

"Of course."

"You and Lindquist mentioned a Josh Cummins."

"Yes. One of Kate Patterson's aides."

"Three deputies from a sheriff's rescue squadron fished Cummins out of the river this morning."

"Not suicide?" It's more of a statement than a question.

"No, not with a lacerated face and broken neck," he says. "It was murder. A murder caught on closed-circuit TV and witnessed by at least a half dozen people, but we have no suspects and minimal clues to find the bastards."

"Tell me more."

"According to Cummins' wife, Beth—who's absolutely hysterical, by the way—Josh was a big-time biker, as in bicycle, not motorcycle. During the winter months, he rode a fancy Peloton in their bedroom, but he preferred early-morning rides outside. So as soon as the snow melted, he'd hit the road before sunrise and ride fifteen to twenty miles along the river and around the lakes.

"They live in an apartment on University Avenue near the river, so Cummins was just starting out on his first outdoor ride of the year. He rides down Main and onto the bridge at the same time this massive guy in gray sweats wearing a black COVID mask jogs onto the bridge from the other side. When Cummins and this guy are about twenty feet from each other, the perp pulls a two-foot pipe from his sweats and swats Cummins across the face and neck, knocking him off his bike. Without missing a beat, the guy lifts Cummins off the pavement like a Raggedy Andy doll and flings him over the railing and into the river. Then he sprints across to Nicollet Island, where he's picked up by a black Suburban with out-of-state plates. Two women on an early-morning stroll call it in within seconds of the crime, and a half dozen bystanders witness it, but no one pursues the perpetrator. I'm sure they were all stunned. By the time anyone can react, the guy is off the bridge and off the streets."

"Did anyone report any identifying marks or features on either the suspect or the getaway car?" I ask.

"Nothing. Just a lot of black. So, we need to approach this investigation from the victim's side. Did he have a girlfriend? Did he owe money to anyone? Did he have enemies? His wife says no to all three of those questions. The poor woman needs time to process everything. Maybe she'll think of something helpful in a day or two.

"You're the only cop who interviewed Cummins in connection with his boss's murder. That's one of the reasons I called you down here. Now I'm worried about your safety too. What else did you learn from Mr. Cummins?"

"He's the guy who first told us about Brinkman's boyfriend, the now-dead Major Slayton. For some reason, Natalie confided many of her ambitions and schemes to meek, mild-mannered Josh—her foiled plan to run for office, her feud with Kate Patterson, and her deal with Sampson. Lieutenant, he used the words 'evil' and 'diabolical' to describe her. And he made me swear we'd never tell her that he was our source."

Moe gives me his patented look, squinting his left eye and cocking his head to the right. "His wife claims he never talked about Brinkman, that he described Patterson as a cold fish who was all business."

"That doesn't surprise me. He was your typical smart, nerdy, wonky research guy. He didn't want trouble, but he clearly resented Brinkman on a number of levels. I exploited that resentment to get information."

"Barnes, are you tearing up?"

"Maybe I am," I say, with a trace of hostility. I wipe my eyes with the back of my hand. "It's getting harder and harder to separate the good guys from the bad. But Josh Cummins was definitely a good guy who didn't deserve this, and I feel partially responsible."

"You were just doing your job, Barnes, but I get it. I've taken over the Patterson investigation and now Cummins, too, because I believe they're related. I'll get one of the newbies from downtown homicide to be my gopher, but I'll take all the heat. Paige Winters and I used to be partners back when you were in diapers. She may have let it slip that, by the middle of next week, the BCA will issue a report clearing you from any misconduct. Until then, why don't you take a well-earned vacation somewhere far away from Minneapolis?"

"If you insist, Lieutenant, but what about Robert Brinkman's memorial service tomorrow? Wouldn't it be good to be a fly on the wall, so to speak?"

"I intend to be a big ugly bear in a seat at the fancy Lafayette Club, so don't get any ideas about showing up. Early next week, I'll conduct that follow-up interview with Brinkman that you and Lindquist had intended before you got derailed, so to speak. She'll probably lawyer up by then. I've already determined that the City's HR department never received her parking garage PROX card. Of course, she hasn't turned in her laptop or cell phone either. That's probably a good thing. Yesterday, they sent her an email request for everything, which I'm sure she'll ignore.

"Keep this in mind, however. When the mayor and Hawkins learned about Slayton's blood-alcohol results, they shifted gears. Hawkins claims he's reviewed all the evidence in the Patterson case and it was clearly a random act by someone who didn't know the victim—either a frustrated robber looking for drug money or one of the many homeless nomads suffering from mental illness. Either way, he says we need to get the word out to the media and 'change the dynamic' so we can stop wasting resources on a dead-end investigation."

"Was that before or after he found out about Josh Cummins?"

"I'm not sure about that."

I step back from the railing and look up at a cloudless sky occupied only by a large passenger jet headed out of the Cities. "It's hard to know what's motivating someone with the wealth and resources of Natalie Brinkman. Is it the loss of her father, the killing of her boyfriend, or her thwarted lust for power? Regardless, she can't be in a good mood, so if she discovered that Josh betrayed her confidences in any way, she may have sentenced him to death without giving it much thought."

"That's pretty heartless," Moe says.

"Yes it is, Lieutenant. Just plain heartless. Do you need anything else from me?"

"Not right now, but please take my advice and get out of town for a while. Just make sure it's someplace with good cell service. I'll be in touch."

"Sure thing, sir. See you around."

CHAPTER 29

'm not a gambler. Never played the slots or cards for money. But for four of the last five years, I've been part of a group that's placed parlay bets at Bellagio's Sportsbook in Las Vegas during the first and second rounds of the NCAA men's basketball tournament, better known as March Madness.

Six years ago, my brother-in-law, Craig, flew to Vegas with three of his high school coaching buddies during the first week of the tournament. Of course, this meant that none of their respective high school teams had advanced to the regional finals, but that's another story.

All in their early thirties at the time, they played golf in the morning and placed bets and watched games in the afternoon and evening. A white-haired bartender at Caesar's Palace overheard the four lamenting that they were winning more than losing on their bets but still not doing much better than breaking even. He offered some unsolicited, but sage, advice, suggesting that if they picked the three games of which they were most confident about the spread and placed one bet on the combination, called a parlay, they could increase their winnings exponentially.

Now, these four guys are not stupid. They knew their odds of winning a parlay were not good, but the possibility of making more on one bet than they'd been winning on ten was intoxicating. As a group, they made one $200 parlay bet on each of the next three days and rang the bell on one of them, winning $2,500. More than the money, the total rush they experienced watching the last game of the three-game parlay was epic.

With growing families and coaching responsibilities, these four guys haven't been back to Vegas for March Madness since that first parlay, but they've continued to place bets through a friend, their "mule," who moved from Saint Paul to Vegas to take a job as an assistant coach for the UNLV Runnin' Rebels. When one of the four bettors dropped out of the group at the request (i.e., demand) of his spouse, Craig turned to me as a potential source of $200 for four parlay bets at the best sporting event in the history of the world—a small price to pay, in my opinion. I've been in ever since. We've won two parlay bets in four years, more than covering all of our losses.

Today, we've picked two slightly favored nine seeds to beat eights and one mid-major fifteen seed, with the best three-point shooter in the country but no defense, to beat a twelve-and-a-half-point spread against a hated two seed from the ACC. Our games air at one fifteen and five o'clock in the afternoon and five after nine at night. When I arrive at Wanda's at seven, the kids have eaten and Craig is ordering pizza and salads from Davanni's for the adults. I spend the first fifteen minutes assuring my mom Warren is very much alive, I'm not in imminent danger, and—the best news she's heard in years—my tenure as a Minneapolis cop may be coming to an end. She gives me her patented response to all of life's uncertainties.

"All you can do is pray, Lincoln. Even your dad believed that God has a plan for us."

Even my dad. Nice. I wish I could get a sneak preview of whatever that plan is. I'm not against religion. I just don't believe in it at present. I give my mom credit for surviving forty-three years as a United flight attendant. When your job is to serve people in a metal tube thirty thousand feet in the air, an unwavering belief in God might be your best insurance policy.

I build Lego airplanes and pilots with Henry and Theo for about an hour, and then we read their favorite picture books until Wanda the Enforcer puts them to bed.

The four of us spread out on the sectional in the Decker great room to eat pizza, drink wine and beer, and watch a college basketball game. Wanda played basketball in high school and has coached some girls'

AAU teams. Mom pretends to care because we do, and that's great.

The game is tied at the half, but Craig and I know better than to count our winnings. With ten seconds to go and Duke up by nine, Valpo has the ball and calls a time out to clear the end of their bench, a nice gesture by the coach. They pass the ball around the perimeter for five seconds and then miss a three hard off the front rim and into the hands of a Duke forward who hasn't scored.

The right play here is to hold the ball for three seconds or dribble it in place and then flip it to a referee. But no, he dribbles to half-court and, a nanosecond before he flings the ball toward the hoop, he's pushed in the back by a frustrated Beacon. A whistle blows just as the buzzer ending the game goes off. The ball caroms off the backboard, rattles inside the rim, and falls through the net: eighty-eight to seventy-six. Our fate (i.e., our 12.5 point spread) is now in the hands of a six-foot-nine graduate student named Bates. He shoots one free throw and, as fate would have it, scores four points in the final second of the game. Eighty-nine to seventy-six. Thank you, Master Bates.

It's well after midnight. Wanda went to bed at the half. Mom is lightly snoring on the sofa, where she'll spend the night. Craig and I commiserate for five minutes. We both hate Coach K but still love to parlay.

I drive from Wanda's Highland Park neighborhood to the corner of Fairview and Jefferson without seeing another vehicle on the road, except for one truck or SUV, based on the position of its headlights, that I sense is following my Jeep. I take a circuitous route through the Mac-Groveland neighborhood, winding through Tangletown, until I get to Grand Avenue, one of the main east-west thoroughfares in Saint Paul. Grand has a mix of retail shops and apartment buildings and, because of its proximity to the University of St. Thomas, is always well lit by streetlamps. Checking my rearview mirror as I approach Cretin Avenue, I see I'm being tailed by a dark-colored Suburban or Escalade, which reminds me of the description of the getaway vehicle in the Josh Cummins incident.

Heading up Cretin toward I-94, I accelerate to see whether I can lose my pursuer before getting on the freeway. I zip past the highway entrance and through an industrial park to University Avenue, doing about fifty miles per hour. I drive east to Prior and then double back to the I-94 West access ramp. There's traffic on the four-lane freeway but not enough to confuse an experienced car chaser, cop or otherwise. I move to the far-left lane and hit eighty-five on the speedometer, leaving the traffic behind as I cruise past Augsburg College and the Cedar-Riverside neighborhoods, and then slow to seventy-five after crossing the river near downtown Minneapolis. Moving to the center lane to avoid the I-35 South turnoff, I look to my right and see a white BMW SUV blowing past. Then I'm startled when I look to the left. Not only do I see a black Suburban with smoke-tinted windows, but the front passenger-side window is down and someone wearing a vivid Donald Trump mask with a red MAGA hat is pointing what looks like a Ruger with a long suppressor in my direction. I glance in my rearview mirror for a split-second before I duck and hit the brakes simultaneously, but the Ruger doesn't fire and the Suburban heads south on I-35 while I continue west on I-94. Activating my Bluetooth, I call 911, identify myself, describe the incident, and recommend that squads from the MPD, state highway patrol, and Hennepin County Sheriff's office converge on the Suburban.

I decide to get involved but, given my status, only as an observer. I exit on Penn and return to I-94, heading east to I-35 South. I flip on my police radio and check in with the MPD dispatch and highway patrol, only to learn that no one was able to spot the Suburban. They'll all keep an eye out, but it's one fifteen, and I'm beat, too much adrenaline for one day. The Trump mask could have killed me but decided to scare me instead. Mission accomplished, but why?

CHAPTER 30

After the early-morning excitement, I don't get to sleep until after three and keep my Glock on the nightstand. I finally get up at eight-thirty, late in the day for me, and feel like somebody tossed me in the river. That's not funny.

I pack two large duffels with enough clothes and gear to spend a week on the North Shore. I've reserved a room at Cove Point Lodge in Beaver Bay for three nights. My morning plan is to make myself a thermos of strong coffee, grab a smeared everything bagel from my favorite place in Linden Hills, and drive out to Shoreline Drive on Lake Minnetonka with my best binoculars and a lot of camouflage. Sherm will not be happy if he sees me.

Dressed in a black down vest over dark-green sweats, I park on Lake Road by Minnetonka Beach City Hall and jog over to the Lafayette Club with nothing but my phone and compact but pricey Upland binoculars. One of the many things Warren has taught me—don't scrimp on essential equipment. The three-story, Spanish-style white edifice that is the private club's main facility is surrounded by a golf course and sport courts as well as a private beach and boat launch on Lake Minnetonka. I think the place used to be a fancy hotel for the leisure class.

It's ten fifteen. The service begins in forty-five minutes, and the main parking lot is scattered with limousines and assorted luxury vehicles.

The staff must park in the back lot. I'm only interested in the attendees. Robert Brinkman was a rich, ruthless prick, a narcissistic tyrant. Anyone attending his memorial service, with the possible exception of a few close family members, must have an ulterior motive.

I note the placement of local police and private security and pick out the perfect spot for my surveillance perch: a deep sand trap near the ninth green. The sand isn't visible from the parking lot or the clubhouse. All the snow has melted for now, but the course is wet and muddy. I get as comfortable as I can in the sand. Most of the traps have been covered with tarp, which would have been even better, but I'm not complaining. If the security company flies a drone overhead, I'm screwed, but no sense in looking for trouble.

Brinkman has already been cremated, so there won't be a hearse or a casket. I focus the binoculars on the expansive front porch of the club, where several men are milling around in dark suits and sunglasses— hired security masquerading as Secret Service agents. Natalie Brinkman opens the double doors and steps out onto the porch with a black-haired woman in her thirties, who I speculate is Brinkman's exiled former girlfriend. They're braving forty-degree temperatures to greet some of the distinguished guests. Both women look like they came straight out of Hollywood casting with designer sunglasses and the perfect mourning attire. Natalie is stuffed into a lacy black dress, of course, with a black mink or lambskin stole wrapped around her alabaster shoulders to warm her cold heart. I wonder whether she'll wear the same outfit to Andrew Slayton's funeral in Ohio next week. The label "black widow" may well apply, at least indirectly, to young Natalie, as she could be responsible for the deaths of three people, maybe more. Daddy would be proud.

Twenty to eleven and a crowd begins to gather. The mayor and police chief emerge from the back seat of the mayor's official Tahoe. CEOs from several major companies arrive, a few with spouses but most alone. They weren't Robert's friends, but it's the right corporate thing to do.

One of Minnesota's two US senators is in a large group of politicians that includes three US House members and assorted staff and minions. Even the governor, lieutenant governor, and their state patrol security team have come, meaning that Brinkman contributed large sums to all of their campaigns and, maybe more important, they hope Natalie will continue the tradition.

I'm hoping to spy someone suspicious among the stragglers, the people who slip into the service at the last minute, hoping not to be noticed but having a more sinister affiliation with the deceased or his family than the big shots.

Lieutenant Moe arrives in an unmarked squad. As he walks toward the club entrance, Rochelle Griffith jogs to catch up, and the two face each other and have an animated conversation. It's a good sign. A beautiful friendship and mutual use in the making. I have no doubt that Rochelle has connected the dots in Josh Cummins' murder.

It's now a few minutes after eleven. A black Suburban with tinted windows bypasses the visitor lot and parks in the back row of the employee lot. Three tall men, one dark-skinned and two white, wearing long, unbuttoned overcoats that reveal white shirts and dark ties but probably conceal assorted weapons, engage in an in-depth discussion as they open the closed doors to the club and likely await further instructions from someone.

Assorted state cops, local police, and security personnel are scattered on the veranda and the grounds, but the employee lot is empty. I take a circuitous route near the beach to the back of that lot, aiming to take a few photos of the inside of the Suburban from the untinted front windshield. All of the doors are locked, EXCEPT the driver's door. What an incompetent idiot—I mean, thank you, thank you, thank you.

The interior smells like stale beer, farts, and cigars. There's a locked briefcase on the floor of the front passenger seat and an iPad in the middle of the back seat. The third seat is folded down, and the cargo area contains assorted pieces of luggage, food wrappers, and empty beer and soda cans—oh, and a terrifying mask and MAGA hat that I think I've seen before. And poorly concealed beneath a white towel is a two-foot black metal pipe. I snap a few photos on my phone. These boys are not from around here. A license plate celebrating "The Birthplace of Aviation" gives me a good idea of their origin and affiliation.

"Hey, lady, is that your vehicle?" One of the private security dolts has spotted me taking photos inside the Suburban. He's walking at a brisk pace toward the employee lot. Given his girth, I don't think I'll need to run all out. I press the lock button as a favor to these felons, close the driver's door and jog across the club grounds to Shoreline Drive. I glance back to check on my pursuer. He's still looking for clues in the Suburban, giving me time to retrieve the Jeep and send a text to Rochelle, hoping she sees it before the end of the service.

Guess who. Is there a dry eye in the house? These are photos of black Suburban w/Ohio front plate in staff lot at Lafayette. Three dark trench coats tried to scare me last night wearing Trump mask and pointing handgun at my Jeep on I-94. Could be Cummins killers as well. (See black pipe.) Might be working for Brinkman and/or friends of the Major. I'm not supposed to be here, so don't disclose your source to Lt. Moe. Go get 'em.

LB

I stop at North Memorial to see Warren before embarking on my adventure to the North Shore. Both he and Diane are sleeping, Warren in his hospital bed and Diane in a contortionist's pose in a folding chair leaning against the bed. She opens one eye, sees me, and motions toward the hallway with her hand. I help her up and follow her out of the room to the small ICU lobby near the elevator, where we sit facing each other on the only two chairs not occupied by other concerned family members.

"He's scheduled for surgery at two," she says, bending toward me and speaking in a half-whisper. "They gave him a mild sedative an hour ago, and it put us both to sleep. I think it's best not to wake him at this point, especially since he's worried about you."

"When he wakes up after surgery, tell him I'm meeting with Sheriff MacDonald tomorrow, and I'll call him soon. How's he doing otherwise?"

"Much better than expected as far as the head injuries. No more bleeding or swelling, and no deficits found on a DTI scan or in the neuropsych exam. And that's great, but the operation on his left tibia today will determine whether he'll ever be able to put weight on that leg. It's also possible they'll have to amputate the leg below the knee." Diane's a nurse, so I get why she can talk in clinical terms about the procedures, but she's also a lot stronger than I'd be under similar circumstances.

"Let's hope his leg heals as fast and well as his brain," I say, trying to hold back tears. "He's a tough guy, Diane. A tough-but-lovable guy." And then we both lose it.

I'm getting familiar with the drive up I-35 to Duluth and the North Shore. But this time, more than any other, it feels like an escape. I'm excited and nervous with anticipation about dinner with the judge tomorrow night, but I can't let that interfere with the prep for my interview with MacDonald at nine tomorrow morning.

Driving from the Lafayette Club to North Memorial, I did something totally out of character. I called Darnell Taylor. He was surprised but very cool. When I told him I'd be driving through Duluth this afternoon, he insisted that I stop by his office at the university for a visit. I accepted.

About halfway to Duluth, I get a text from Sherm.

Strange service. Usual political suspects and corporate big shots. Natalie spoke and didn't shed a tear. Said her father rebuilt this country and paved the way for her to do great things for women in America. I threw up in my mouth. She's a high-functioning sociopath. Unless you say otherwise, I'm going to give your friend some ammo to blow up a few things.

I smile and reply with a thumbs-up emoji. About a half hour later, I get a text from Rochelle, my "friend," that almost makes me drive off the road.

The Suburban's a rental from Ohio. Three scary dudes may be from Slayton's hometown. They sat alone in back but did converse with Brinkman.

Sat in the park for two hours after service. Rewarded with this photo of a couple stragglers. OMG, Barnes. WTF! I am on it.

The photo is of an empty parking lot with the exception of Brinkman's Bentley and an older Mazda sedan in a back corner, partially hidden by fir trees. I'm guessing the Mazda belongs to a city employee who got a ride back to Minneapolis in the mayor's Tahoe along with Chief Hawkins. The mayor and Brinkman are in the throes of a passionate embrace, with Brinkman's legs wrapped around the mayor's waist while her hands grab onto the back of his suitcoat. The mayor appears to be cupping her lower cheeks with his hands, resting her back on the trunk of the Bentley and pressing his manhood against (or in) her. I'm not sure, but I think they're saying some kind of a prayer for Major Slayton.

I arrive at the entrance to UMD at ten minutes after four and locate the parking lot for the Sports and Health Center. Once inside the building, I pass the athletic administration department, looking for room 119, the office of Darnell Taylor, head coach of the university's track-and-field and cross-country teams and my high school boyfriend.

The door is partially open, so I knock. A slim black hand grabs the door from the inside and opens it the rest of the way, revealing a cramped, but tastefully decorated, office. Darnell is sitting behind a gray-and-white modular desk with a matching credenza. With close-cropped black hair and a neatly trimmed beard, he is as buff and handsome as ever. A long, lean Black woman, the one who opened the door, sits on one of two side chairs. They both stand before anyone speaks.

"Oh my goodness, Lincoln Barnes, you have become a beautiful woman!" Darnell declares as he deftly slides by his smiling wife and gives me a bear hug and a kiss on the cheek. "This is my wife, Mandy, UMD's head softball coach and the mother of Zach and Lindsey, our two kids."

"Good to meet you, Mandy," I say, extending my hand but responding in kind to her offered fist bump.

"So glad to meet you, Lincoln. Darnell speaks very highly of you, as an athlete and a person." I can't tell if that's sincere or obligatory. Looking at Mandy is like looking in a mirror, except she's shorter and has bigger, more beautiful brown eyes and much bigger breasts, which I'm sure Darnell appreciates.

"Are these two yours?" I ask, pointing not to her breasts but to a photograph of two cuties wearing winter garb and miniature downhill skis.

"That was taken last winter up at Lutsen, one of the few activities that didn't require them to wear masks," Mandy says.

Darnell suggests that we relocate our meeting to Tavern on the Hill, a bar about a block from the university, and I can't argue with him.

We sit in a booth—Darnell and Mandy on one side and me, the third wheel, on the other. Darnell orders a pitcher of Bent Paddle IPA, a local craft beer. They're animated when describing life in Duluth, where they've lived for the past four years. In short, they love the city, claiming it has the perfect mix of recreation and culture. The schools are good, the politics progressive, and the variety of activities incredible. Darnell has run in Grandma's Marathon twice, and they're both training for the race this year. The whole family took downhill skiing lessons last year, and Mandy has taken up cross-country. They should do a commercial for the chamber of commerce. Living and working around the university, they probably aren't exposed to many rednecks or racists, but because of my line of work, I know they exist up here and everywhere.

When I mention I might be moving to Two Harbors, Mandy instinctively places one of Darnell's hands in her lap and starts caressing it. She's communicating with me, protecting her territory. On the other hand, she invites me to train with them for Grandma's if I relocate north and, shockingly, even asks if I'd be interested in working with her softball team this spring, either as a volunteer or a part-time assistant. I thank her for the offer but wonder if it's sincere or simply an effort to show me she's confident and assured in her relationship. Either way, I'm impressed, despite the fact that I'm envious of her relationship with a man I once loved. Or maybe I'm just horny. If I'm being honest, I have to admit I like her and like what I'm hearing about Duluth.

CHAPTER 31

The drive south from Cove Point Lodge along Highway 61 is enlightening in more ways than one. The big lake sparkles, reflecting the rays of the early-morning sun. I spy two bald eagles making wide, swooping dives at something near the surface of the water and smile when one of them soars triumphantly with a wriggling fish tethered between its beak and talons. Passing the sign for Castle Danger (unincorporated), I wonder which gravel driveway winds down to the judge's place—later.

I arrive at the Lake County Courthouse, an official-looking granite structure with multiple pillars and a central dome, at eight forty-five and park on Third Avenue. MacDonald sits on the courthouse steps, sipping coffee from a tall paper cup in his right hand while holding a similar one in his left. He's accompanied by an oversized black-and-white dog that sits by his side like a statue.

A light southerly breeze off the lake has already pushed temps into the forties. The sheriff wears a navy windbreaker over a hooded sweatshirt that I'd wager says "Lake County Sheriff" somewhere. Not sure how casual I should be for a Saturday-morning job interview, I wear an olive cashmere sweater over a white button-down dress shirt and black wool slacks. As I exit the Jeep with nothing but a notepad, I unzip my down vest. I'm already starting to sweat.

"Good morning, Sheriff," I say cheerily. "Who's your friend?"

"This is Fred," he says, getting to an upright position without spilling a drop of coffee and opening the door for me and Fred. "He's just a big baby. I inherited him a few years ago from a good friend who unfortunately was gunned down in the line of duty."

"George Redman?" I ask.

He doesn't appear to hear me. "Black coffee?" he asks, offering me the extra cup.

"You remembered," I say, gratefully accepting the still-steaming joe and making another notation in my brain in favor of this thoughtful man.

He leads me past a vestibule with an information desk staffed by a tiny, white-haired woman who smiles and winks at the sheriff as he nods and continues down the main hallway to his suite of offices. There's a reception desk with an electronic sign overhead:

SAM MacDONALD
LAKE COUNTY SHERIFF

A few of a dozen cubicles are occupied on a Saturday. A chorus of "Morning, Sam" is followed by "Morning, everybody. It's a beautiful day in paradise." He lifts a ring of keys from a jacket pocket and unlocks the door to his office, offering me one of the two upholstered guest chairs facing an old mahogany double-pedestal desk. He gingerly lowers his big frame onto a worn leather office chair, another sign he's probably suffered some serious injuries over his years of public service. Fred finds a comfy spot under the desk and curls up to take a nap.

"You're right, by the way" MacDonald says. "Fred was George's dog. How did you know?"

"It was a wild guess," I admit. "My partner, Warren Lindquist, knew Special Agent Redman. When I told him I might be meeting with you, he mentioned that Redman had lost his life on a case up here."

"A terrible tragedy, Detective. George was a wonderful guy and quite a character, but like the best cops I know, a little too selfless. "How is your partner doing?"

"Better. His brain swelling subsided, so they brought him out of the coma, but his legs are a mess. He had a major procedure yesterday afternoon to place a metal rod in his leg and repair blood vessels. I guess that's the key—to get oxygenated blood to his extremities. His wife promised to give me an update later today."

"I hope it's good news, but I'm glad his brain is functioning well because, yesterday morning, he gave you one of the most glowing recommendations I've ever heard." I knew Warren was serious when he advised me to take a hiatus from the MPD, but this is a surprise. I smile sheepishly and blush.

"We've got a lot of ground to cover, Lincoln, so let's get started."

MacDonald spends the next fifteen minutes telling me about life and crime in Lake County, the personnel in his office, including Gail Klewacki, the lead detective I'd be replacing, the role of the Two Harbors police department, and the fact that Hallie Bell, the Lake County attorney, is his wife. I ask a few questions about resources and crime statistics, and he's quick with answers.

Tensions have developed up here between factions that favor copper and nickel mining, new pipelines to carry gas and oil, and the jobs that accompany those things, and factions that oppose these activities because of their adverse impact on the environment and Native American lands. MacDonald admits he has opinions on all these issues, but no one knows what they are because his job is to maintain the peace and keep everyone safe regardless of their politics and opinions. I can appreciate that approach.

Then he asks me about a few of my cleared cases at the MPD, and we discuss victims' rights, tactics, surveillance, and the use of deadly force. He's not as philosophical as Warren but just as smart. Near the end of the interview, he hands me a two-page letter.

"I think I mentioned earlier that Gail is moving to Montana. Her husband's family owns ski resorts and hotels all over the country. They're moving him from Cascade Mountain to Big Sky to manage a property there. Gail starts a new position with the Bozeman PD on May first. They know they're lucky to have her. She'll be with us until the third week of April.

"This is an offer letter. You're worth more than I can pay, but I'm stretching my budget as it is, and I'm offering you a month of paid time off so you can get acclimated to life up here. Take a week to think about it, and then give me your answer. I've given your resume and other information to Gail. You're welcome to contact her to talk about the job, the staff, me, or anything else on your mind. I'll be disappointed if you decide not to make the move, but I'll understand."

"I really appreciate this opportunity, Sheriff. I promise to give it serious consideration. You know I haven't been cleared yet by the BCA."

"I'd be surprised if you had so soon, but I'm not concerned about that based on what you've told me and what I've read and learned from your partner. By the way, have you heard the latest on the Sara Hyatt case?"

"I know Dr. Hyatt's been charged with manslaughter down in Playa del Carmen, and you told me he's fighting extradition."

"I just got an update from my contact down there that I thought might interest you. Hyatt's so-called best friend, a Dr. Bagley, gave the feds a statement indicating his wife, the city councilwoman whose murder you were investigating, told him Sara was having an affair with an old boyfriend and was about to make a terrible mistake. She asked Bagley to tell Dr. Hyatt he needed to do something to end it." I wasn't aware of that. Kate Patterson must have been a real piece of work. On the other hand, I wouldn't want to be best friends with either doctor.

"Have you run into Sara Hyatt's old boyfriend, Sheriff?" I ask out of curiosity.

"No, but if you drive down Third Avenue toward downtown, you'll see some new construction at the site of an old bank building. I saw Jake Guzzo putting in new windows and signage, and I asked him what kind of business was moving in. He confirmed the judge bought the building and said the name of the new business is Law Office of J. R. Gildemeister, PA. That's what the fancy new sign says.

"A few of my deputies have run into him around town. They say he's very friendly and introduces himself as J. R. Gildemeister. You probably already knew that."

"I still don't know enough about him, Sheriff, but it's good to know he's comfortable enough to reclaim part of his old name."

"It's good to have him back home. It's good for the town."

Fred emerges from under the desk and stretches his long legs. A protracted yawn reveals some impressive teeth. He must be part Husky. He nudges his master's knee with his nose, prompting MacDonald to stand and scratch him behind the ears.

"He needs to go out," the sheriff says. "We'll walk you to your car."

Thanks, Fred. I'm too ambivalent about the judge to talk any more about him.

CHAPTER 32

He's sitting on a wooden bench in the lobby of the Grand Superior Lodge, reminding me of Paul Bunyan in jeans, hiking boots, and a red-and-black-plaid flannel shirt. He's reading the front page of the *Duluth News Tribune* but looks up at the squeaking of my SORELs on the wood floor as I advance toward the warmth of a raging fire in the stone lobby fireplace. He smiles when his eyes meet mine, and I abandon my plan to keep my distance until we can have an open and honest discussion. He stands, and I wrap my arms around his tanned neck and kiss him, tentatively at first but harder in response to how tightly he hugs me. He smells so good, a mix of an oaky, musky cologne and his natural manhood. Now I wish we weren't in a public place, but I regain my senses, slowly disengage, and take a step back.

"I've missed you," he says. "You look great and feel even better."

I smile, sheepishly, grateful for the compliment but ashamed of my lack of resolve. I'm definitely not dressed to kill in brushed-denim blue jeans and a black cashmere sweater, but all I can think of is, I haven't felt this good, this alive, since the last time I was with him.

We move from the lobby to the Grill, where a fifty-something white-haired hostess, heavy but not unattractive in black jeans and a zip-up fleece top brandishing the Grand Superior logo, recognizes the judge.

"Hello, J. R. I heard you were back in town and then saw you'd made a reservation for tonight. It's wonderful to see you."

"Thank you. It's great to be back. Ellen, this is my good friend, Lincoln Barnes. Lincoln, this is Ellen Magnuson, a friend and classmate of my sister's."

"And a lifelong resident of the North Shore," Ellen adds. "A pleasure to meet you, Lincoln. I hope I'll see you again."

"Glad to meet you too, Ellen," I say, my mind working hard to make and retain the connections.

Ellen seats us at a table for four next to a picture window overlooking the lake and lights a white candle before departing. The wood-paneled dining room has a row of booths near the bar and about a dozen simple wooden tables scattered about the dimly lit space.

We order drinks and appetizers, and he asks me about Warren and the status of the BCA investigation. I tell him everything I know about both in under three minutes.

"She called you J. R.," I say. "I thought your name was Robin."

"Really?" he says with a wry smile. "You are one of the most inquisitive and resourceful people I know. Do you expect me to believe that you haven't researched my background enough to know that my birth name was not Robin Gildemeister?" It's a good comeback. However, it's difficult to know how much I would have figured out without the diary and Sheriff MacDonald.

"You're giving me too much credit. I admit I have googled the shit out of you and couldn't find anything about Robin Gildemeister that predates your law-school days. I'm sure I could find out more by interviewing some local folks like Ellen, but I've been pretty busy and distracted lately and, most importantly, I might be in love with you, so I'd like to hear about you from you, unless you'd prefer that I go back to Minneapolis and leave you alone." I can't believe I said the "L" word.

"I'm sorry," he says softly. "My birth name was Jason Robin Campbell, but because my father was also Jason, my family and friends started calling me J. R. when I was a little boy, and the name stuck."

Over the course of the next hour, interrupted three or four times by our server to take our dinner order and deliver food and drinks, he tells a story I doubt he's ever told anyone. Others lived through it with him, but he created a new persona and left the place he loved so he wouldn't be reminded of a father who was a psychopath and likely murdered both his wives and of the girl with whom he bonded in the aftermath of tragedy. He can't hold back tears when discussing the three women he's loved deeply: his mother, whose name he even has trouble saying; his Grandma Gildemeister, who he claims saved him more than once; and Sara, who he believed was lost forever when she married Hyatt.

I thought I'd be uncomfortable hearing him talk about Sara, but I'm not. It's a fascinating story about love, influence, manipulation, and deceit. He claims he was devastated and bewildered by Sara's sudden change of heart because it had nothing to do with him or with her love for somebody else. Ending their relationship was simply the smart, rational, common-sense move at that stage of her life. But that wasn't Sara Wheaton. It was her roommate. How picture perfect and convenient—roommates marrying roommates, physician roommates at that. And there was nothing he could do about it.

We pass on dessert, as he's nearing the end of the narrative.

"I had changed my name, graduated law school, and taken a position with a Minneapolis law firm when Sara reached out to me, and we began a twenty-plus-year affair. I only saw her a couple times a year, but restoring that connection meant the world to me. I gave up having a family of my own and sharing my day-to-day life with a partner. Lincoln, I can't tell you how excited I was for Sara and me to be together up here. She could work from anywhere, and I was going to open a small firm in my hometown. You know the rest of the story. About a year ago, I made the decision to follow through on my plan to move back up here and open a law practice. Ten years on the district court bench is long enough."

"And what about me?" I ask. "Was I just a diversion while you settled the score in Mexico and packed up your life in the Twin Cities?" That came out of my mouth before it was properly phrased in my brain.

"That's not fair, Lincoln. You're the only person who's heard the whole, unvarnished story of my life. Sara's been dead for two years, and I'm more than ready to move on. If you can't tell that I'm crazy about you, then you're not as perceptive as I thought. I'm fifteen years older, so I admit I'm not a hundred percent comfortable with our relationship, but I'm totally committed to giving it a chance. Are you?"

"Let's get out of here," I say. "I'll follow you to your place, if you're still interested in a nightcap."

―――――――――

I drive behind the judge's Mercedes up Highway 61. We pass Gooseberry Falls State Park and the Rustic Inn. It's nine fifteen on a Saturday night, and I see more deer on the side of the road than cars on it. The judge signals a right turn between mileposts thirty-eight and thirty-nine, and we take a narrow gravel driveway lined with Norway pines and birch down to a well-lit blacktop parking area with room for four or five vehicles. He parks next to a detached garage and exits the Mercedes. There's a large dumpster filled with old furniture and building materials between the garage and a log cottage that's partially hidden by a stand of firs. The eerie darkness of a cloudy night on the North Shore shrouds the rest of the property that must lead to the lake below.

Before I can decide whether to get my overnight bag from the back seat, the judge opens my door and, without speaking, takes my hand and leads me down a cobblestone walkway and up wooden steps to a small porch. He pinches a key from his jacket pocket but, before unlocking the front door, kisses me gently on the lips, which stimulates some neglected parts of my anatomy.

He's left a few lights on in the cottage, and I recognize some of the furniture from his condo in Minneapolis—the baby grand piano, the leather sofa, the kitchen table. It's a simple layout—a great room that opens to a small kitchen, a wall of mostly windows on the lake side with a sliding glass door opening to a deck, a hallway leading to a bedroom or two.

"Let me take your vest," he says and hangs it on a hall tree in the entryway. "Why don't you make yourself comfortable on the couch while I light a fire and get us something to drink. I'll give you a tour of the place later." After he spilled his guts at the restaurant, a relaxing drink by the fire sounds perfect.

"I've got red and white wine, bourbon, Irish whiskey, and cognac for sure."

"A glass of red wine if you've got an open bottle."

"I'll open a Malbec and join you," he says.

Sitting on the couch, I have a better view of this place. Half the great room is two stories with a whirring ceiling fan attached to an oak beam about fifteen feet overhead. There's a second-floor loft over the other half that's open to the great room. It's dark up there, but it appears to be a bedroom, with a rolltop desk the only piece of furniture visible behind a wooden railing.

The judge lights a fire in a wood-burning brick fireplace that looks much older than the rest of the room. Moving to the kitchen, he flips a switch that lights up the deck as well as a walkway to the rocky shore of Lake Superior. I can make out a semicircular arrangement of Adirondack chairs facing the lake, close to the shoreline, probably bordering a firepit.

As I'm taking it all in, the judge hands me a glass of red wine and sets his own glass on a rectangular coffee table in front of us.

"What do you think of the place?" he asks.

"It's perfect," I say, taking a sip of wine, which, not surprisingly, is also perfect.

"So, this place was your grandmother's?"

"The original log home was built during Prohibition in the 1920s, apparently by some gangsters or bootleggers from Saint Paul. There are actually a few bullet holes in the original logs in the front of the house. It's one of the few properties between Two Harbors and Beaver Bay that slopes gently to the lake instead of being on more of a precipice or cliff. I guess the gangsters wanted an escape route by boat, so this lot was ideal. The original cabin was two stories with two bedrooms up and one down and didn't have a garage.

"When Grandma Gildemeister bought it in the eighties, it had shag carpet throughout, and the kitchen and bathrooms had been remodeled in mid-seventies DIY by the couple who lived here. The place was a pit, but I loved living here on the lake.

"No one has really lived here since the mid-nineties, but until my grandma died, she paid a discreet old handyman from the area to maintain the yard and driveway and keep the pipes from freezing and any critters from getting inside. Essentially, though, the place was boarded up.

"After she died, I thought about selling it or razing it and building a new place for Sara and me. John Guzzo, Grandma's handyman, was also a building contractor. He said the structure of the old log cabin was solid and worth keeping, so he and his grandson Jake and I devised a plan to refurbish it. John died ten years ago, but Jake continued to work on this place on weekends for years. He needed help to move the roofline and do some framing, but he's done most of it by himself."

"That's incredible," I say. "I love the fireplace and the light wood on the kitchen cabinets and floors."

"The fireplace is from the 1920s, and all of the wood is northern birch from Canada," he says. "There's no basement, just a crawl space. It only has two bedrooms and 1,600 square feet, but as far as I'm concerned, it's perfect."

"I can't disagree," I say. "The dumpster outside. Where did all that junk come from?"

"Jake finished the kitchen last week. I helped him put in new appliances and a granite countertop. It's also filled with a lot of the old furniture that's been replaced with pieces from my place in the Cities."

"This Jake seems like a special guy. Is he also helping you with your new office?" I need to stop asking questions to which I know the answers, and maybe I should tell him about MacDonald's job offer.

"He's happily married, by the way," he says. "And yes, he's an incredibly talented carpenter, but more than that, he's a good man."

We share a couple glasses of wine, and I tell him about the incident with the black Suburban and my surveillance activities at Robert Brinkman's memorial service.

"Do you think this Natalie Brinkman is behind the murders of Kate Patterson and Josh Cummins?" he asks.

"She's too smart to be directly involved, but I think she's capable of manipulating men to do her bidding."

"A seductress, like Cleopatra."

"If you say so," I say. "Though, she has a lot more than sex appeal to offer men like Marcus Sampson and Andrew Slayton."

"How disappointed are you that you're not still involved in the case? I mean, I assume your surveillance work was not exactly approved by your boss."

"Hey, how about that tour?" I've had too much to drink to talk rationally about Natalie Brinkman and my feelings about the MPD.

He fills our glasses, and we head out to the deck. It must be below freezing, but the wine and the moment give me a buzz that overrides the cold. He asks if I want to go down to the lake.

"Of course," I say, walking ahead of him to the water's edge. The wind off the lake has picked up. Five- to seven-foot waves slap against the rocky outcroppings near the shore and create a rhythmic thrum that speaks to my core and makes me abandon any waning inhibitions.

"You won't find anything like this in the Twin Cities," he says, taking my hand in his. We stand on one of several flat boulders at the shoreline and feel the icy, invigorating spray from the thrashing lake.

"That's true," I say. "There's something both haunting and beckoning about this lake."

"Yes," he says. "And deadly."

I see something in his eyes that reminds me his mother is out there somewhere, along with hundreds of other souls entombed in the dark, unforgiving waters.

We finish our wine and return to the warmth of the cottage. The tour ends a few minutes later on the king bed in the loft.

I'm awake at six thirty with a mild headache and no clothes. Light from the early-morning sun fills the cottage, and there's no escaping it in the loft. Looking around, I see twin nightstands, one with a digital clock, the other, next to me, with a lamp. There's a walk-in closet on one side of the room and a bathroom on the other. Someone has set my iPhone on the nightstand and connected it to a charger. That same person has also retrieved my overnight bag from the Jeep and set it on a chair next to the rolltop desk. I can smell coffee and bacon, so someone has been very busy this morning. Grabbing my phone, I see several text messages but focus on two. The first, from Lieutenant Moe, was sent at four this morning.

The shit is about to hit the fan in a big way. Call me.

Moe

The second is from Rochelle, sent an hour later. I'm betting they're related.

You'll want to read the Strib this morning. And thanks, unnamed, anonymous source, for all your help. Your boss was a sweetheart too.

RG

The article and call will have to wait. I quickly shower and throw on sweats from my bag. I gather my short, frizzing hair in a mini-ponytail and cover it with a Chicago PD cap I haven't worn in years.

"Good morning, J. R.," I say with a sly grin as I descend the stairs from the loft. "Thanks for plugging in my phone and getting my bag."

He's sitting on the couch, holding a Wisconsin Badgers mug, with his laptop open on the coffee table. I plop down next to him.

"Good morning, anonymous source. You need to read this." He turns his laptop toward me. "But first, there's an egg-and-bacon sandwich with your name on it warming in the oven, freshly squeezed OJ in the fridge, and a pot of French roast on the counter."

"Thanks," I say, kissing the top of his head before getting myself a hot cup of coffee and a very messy, but I'm sure delicious, combination of fried eggs, bacon, cheese, tomatoes, onions, and green chiles on a wheat bagel.

"This is incredible, but I'll need a knife and fork to eat it," I say, sitting next to him and getting wide-eyed at the headline in the Strib: "THREE ARRESTED IN MURDER OF PATTERSON AIDE: Heiress, Mayor may be implicated in wrongdoing."

Rochelle is amazing, but Sherm must have helped her even more than I did. The first sentence is a mouthful but doesn't shock me.

> Three men in a black SUV with Ohio plates were detained by the Minnesota highway patrol on I-94 a mile west of the Wisconsin border to execute a warrant to search their vehicle for a weapon that may have been used in the abduction and murder of Josh Cummins, a former aide to slain city council president Kate Patterson.

I'm not sure the warrant will hold up, but at least they're on the right track. The article says these men were contractors who worked for Andrew Slayton and, indirectly, for several Brinkman enterprises. Rochelle somehow obtained detailed information about millions funneled from Brinkman entities to Mayor Sampson's campaign and personal accounts. Apparently, the account Warren discovered was just the tip of the iceberg.

Rochelle quotes a director from Union Bank saying she told Patterson, who was her city councilwoman, about some suspicious transactions and that Patterson promised to confront the mayor. The article notes that, at Patterson's request, the mayor met with her for two hours late in the afternoon on the day before her murder.

Rochelle portrays Natalie Brinkman as a driven young woman with access to millions and an insatiable lust for power, noting she was upset with Patterson for breaking a promise not to run for reelection and had convinced Mayor Sampson to make her, a twenty-eight-year-old with no leadership experience, his chief of staff.

Apparently, Natalie was not a favorite of other staff in the city council and mayor's offices. A few came forward with stories of Brinkman's demanding, manipulative, and even threatening tactics and strange hold over the mayor.

The article refers to an anonymous-but-reliable source that claimed Natalie told her that Patterson and the mayor were having a torrid love affair and then contrasts that juicy allegation with the recent account of an eyewitness who claims to have photos of Natalie and the mayor in a passionate embrace. I'm surprised her editors let that go to press, even though Rochelle herself was the eyewitness.

The bottom line: both Brinkman and Sampson had ample reason to want Patterson out of the picture. Rochelle speculates that it's unlikely Brinkman ordered Andrew Slayton to kill Patterson or run over Detective Lindquist or that she commanded Slayton's brawny henchmen to eliminate Josh Cummins. Instead, she complained loudly and often about how they each had wronged her, and then the worker bees simply acted to please their queen. Rochelle deftly throws in collateral evidence like the missing key card and Slayton's blood-alcohol level.

Of course, Rochelle's editors submitted the article to Sampson and Brinkman for comment before releasing it. Freddie Tyler responded for the mayor, indicating his client would be completely vindicated from any allegations of wrongdoing and would sue the paper for slander if they published the article.

Brinkman's Chicago lawyer said her client had never met Slayton's friends, wasn't aware that Josh Cummins had been murdered, and had nothing to do with any financial transactions with the mayor, though she fully supported him otherwise. She said her client would be spending the next few months at the family vacation home in Nassau Paradise Island in the Bahamas and regrets that she will not be able to attend Major Slayton's memorial. Interestingly, she added that someone on behalf of her client would be returning any city property in her possession, including her laptop, cell phone, and parking-ramp key card.

I'm not sure what's better, Rochelle's four-column article or my egg sandwich. They're both awesome.

"What do you think of the article?" I ask the judge, turning the laptop back in his direction.

"It's well researched, and it's quite a story if it's all true. What's your reaction?"

"You make a fantastic egg sandwich," I say, punching him in the shoulder. "Seriously, Rochelle's done a masterful job with this, but I don't think it'll have much impact on Brinkman or Sampson, though if someone can prove the financial misdeeds, his political career is over."

"What about his marriage?"

"He'll probably get what he deserves," I say.

I take my dishes into the kitchen, feeling the need to do something to earn my keep. The judge follows, and I rinse while he loads the dishwasher. He asks if I'm up for a run. I am, but someone's at the front door.

"It's Jake Guzzo," he says. "He's here to pick up the dumpster." He opens the door and asks Jake if he'd like a cup of coffee.

"I've already had a few cups, but you make the best damn coffee, so yeah, I'll have a cup if it's made." Guzzo is attractive if you like the lumberjack look. In his early forties, he has thick, wavy black hair and an even-thicker black beard. About six feet tall and in good shape, he's all business in a tan Carhartt jacket over faded Levi's and work boots.

"Lincoln, this is Jake Guzzo, the man responsible for everything you like about this cabin. Jake, this is Lincoln Barnes, a friend and very special guest of mine."

"So nice to meet you, Jake. You've done an incredible job with this place."

"Thank you, Lincoln. It's been a labor of love over many years. I'm happy someone will finally enjoy it."

The wistful expression on the judge's face makes me wonder if he's thinking about Sara and the fact she won't be enjoying it. But he snaps out of it quickly and grabs a jacket from the hall closet.

"Most of the junk in the dumpster is rotting wood and broken furniture that's been sitting around here for years," he says. "Jake has a controlled bonfire in the spring and fall every year up at his property in Finland Township."

"I'm planning it for next Friday," says Jake, before taking a healthy gulp of coffee. "We'll have a little party with the kids and their friends. Everyone is a pyromaniac at heart." He sets his empty cup on the kitchen counter and heads for the front door.

"I'm going out to help Jake load the dumpster," says the judge. "It should only take fifteen or twenty minutes."

"As much as I'd like to watch, I have a few calls to make. Hope I see you again, Jake."

"You bet, Lincoln."

I see I've missed a couple of calls from Diane, but she hasn't left a message. I decide to call Sherm first so I can pass on any hot scoops to Warren. I don't know whether Sherm attends church on Sundays, but I assume he won't answer if he's singing a hymn, taking communion, or listening to the Gospel.

He answers after one ring. "Did you read it?"

"I did."

"I don't know about Chief Hawkins," he says, "but Sampson will make a deal to resign within the week and never be prosecuted for anything. Don't be surprised if he ends up as the Brinkman organization's chief counsel."

"You don't think she'll end up in jail?"

"You're kidding, right?"

"I wish I weren't."

"More importantly, you'll be cleared by the BCA tomorrow, and the AG's unofficial response to the revelations in Griffith's piece is to open an investigation into Sampson's campaign practices and close their file on you. So why don't we meet on Tuesday? I've got a new assignment for you, and we can discuss partner candidates."

"Not sure I'm coming back, Lieutenant. I need a week to recharge, recalibrate, and think hard about my future."

"I don't blame you for feeling forsaken, Barnes, but we need you. I need you. Go ahead and take a week. You've earned it. And thanks for hooking me up with Griffith. She should have been a cop."

"She's relentless and fearless but doesn't like to take orders. Thanks for being a solid guy, Lieutenant. You don't know how much I appreciate it."

"Sure," he says. "I'll be here."

I call Diane. The news isn't good. Warren's left leg is dying, and his doctors have concluded it can't be saved. It will be amputated below the knee tomorrow morning. She says Warren wants to talk to me and hands him her phone.

"Did you take that job?" he asks, keeping the spotlight off himself, as usual.

"I'm going to give it some thought," I say. "Today, though, I'm thinking about you, my friend."

"I'm good. The doctors have convinced me that I'll be better off with a prosthetic lower leg than trying to rehab the crushed, bloodless piece of shit I've got. The only thing that disappoints me is, I was planning to lose twenty pounds in retirement, so I could kick your ass in a triathlon."

"You lose twenty pounds, and we'll train to run a half marathon instead."

"We'll see," he says, sounding tired. "Hey, I almost forgot, what about that article in the *Star Tribune* this morning? For one brief moment, there's justice in the air."

"You're right about that."

"Diane's giving me that throat-slashing motion, so I better sign off. Thanks for the call, my friend."

"I love you, Warren."

I hope he heard that.

I'm calling him J. R. from now on. It feels right. He invites me to spend the rest of the week with him, and I accept. Unfortunately, I have to pay a hefty cancellation fee to Cove Point, but it's worth it. We're having so much fun that I turn my phone off for several hours at a time. On Monday, we run the Gitchi-Gami Trail to Split Rock Lighthouse in the morning, have lunch at the Rustic Inn, and hike in the park at Gooseberry Falls in the afternoon.

He has meetings in Two Harbors on Tuesday in advance of opening the new law office and invites me to tag along, but I've scheduled lunch with Detective Klewacki at her husband's resort on Cascade Mountain. It's clear that Sam MacDonald is her mentor and her hero, which is good to know because she's a super-impressive woman, and the only one I know with a bright-pink scar on her forehead in the shape of a nine-millimeter bullet.

In some ways, I feel like a newlywed. My physical attraction to J. R. scares me. I want to touch him all the time, which is not like me, and I worry sometimes he's not as attracted to me. On Thursday, I become less concerned about that. It's sunny and fifty degrees by nine in the morning, so he suggests we get into dry suits and launch his tandem kayak on the lake. I've never been in a kayak or canoe, but he gives me a quick lesson and assures me my main responsibility will be to enjoy the scenery. We're on the lake for four hours, and I never want to get out, though by early afternoon, black clouds are rolling in and the air is turning cold.

Back on shore, he helps me out of the kayak and, before I can catch my breath, unzips my dry suit and his, and we melt into each other in a hammock stretched between two birch trees near the lake. Later, he grills a couple rib eyes with roasted potatoes and root vegetables, and we have a late-night feast by the light of the firepit. He keeps the fire going while we make s'mores with sea-salt dark chocolate, sip cognac, and gaze at the most incredible star-filled sky I've ever seen.

On Friday, a cold front moves in with high winds and flurries. I thought the variation in weather in the Cities was dramatic, but the winds off the lake up here seem to change things faster and more unpredictably. We dress for the weather and hike up Oberg Mountain, where the views of Tettegouche Park and the lake are spectacular. J. R. carries bottled water and turkey jerky in his backpack, our reward at the summit.

We get back in the Mercedes and continue up Highway 61 to Grand Marais, originally a logging and fishing village on the shore of Lake Superior but better known today for seascape artists, souvenir shops, and quirky restaurants. We stroll the three or four main streets and languish in a couple art galleries, a donut shop—where I can't resist a raised, glazed maple—and a friendly little bookshop, Drury Lane Books, where I pick up *Blood Grove* by Walter Mosley. Easy Rawlins is one of my fictional heroes.

We order a pizza to go at Sven & Ole's and pick up a twelve-pack of Castle Danger Cream Ale at a liquor store near Tofte. I haven't read a newspaper since Sunday, and my cell's been off since Tuesday. I could get used to this life.

CHAPTER 33

'm sleeping better every night and later every morning. One of these days, I'll get up before J. R., but not today. I haven't talked to my mom in over a week, and I need to check on Warren's progress, so I take my phone from the nightstand and peer over the loft railing, looking for the owner. No sign of the man, except for a crackling blaze on the hearth, which means either he's close by or he just left.

I throw on sweats, thinking I need some exercise before a morning shower to offset yesterday's pizza and donuts and head downstairs to tend the fire and get my coffee fix.

There's a handwritten note on a legal pad next to a steaming pot of Sumatra on the kitchen counter.

Got a call from an old friend from Silver Bay who might need a lawyer.
Didn't want to wake you. Be back before noon.

He subscribes to the weekend *New York Times*, so I pour a cup of coffee, make myself a slice of peanut butter toast, and prepare to make some calls and catch up on what's going on in the world. Getting comfortable on a wooden rocker about ten feet from the fire, I see whitecaps on the lake and daydream about our kayaking adventure. At first I don't notice that someone's knocking on the front door, but I jump to my feet when the pounding gets louder and more insistent and quickly stride to the entryway, surprised to see Jake Guzzo through the sidelights.

"Hi, Jake," I say. "What brings you out so early on a Saturday?"

"I didn't wake you, did I?" he says, maybe with a hint of sarcasm. I don't know him well enough to be sure. "Is J. R. around?"

"He's meeting with someone up in Silver Bay," I say. "Can I help you?"

"It's not important. I was on my way to Lutsen, so I thought I'd stop by. On Thursday, when I was building my bonfire stack, I lifted a small chest of drawers from the dumpster and a scrapbook fell out of the top drawer. There were no other books or papers of any kind in the dumpster load, so I got concerned that this got in there by mistake." He hands me a Super One grocery bag. I don't look but assume the scrapbook is inside.

"I'd appreciate it if you'd give this to J. R. when he gets back."

"Of course," I say. "Who knows—maybe it's super important to him." And then I remember Jake's a coffee drinker.

"Thanks, Lincoln. I need to get going, but you should come down to Third Avenue in Two Harbors and see your friend's new office."

"I'll do that, but first you have to try the Sumatra he brewed this morning." I don't wait for an answer and return in ten seconds with a filled plastic mug.

"Thanks, this is great," he says, taking a sip as he opens the front door and then heads up the walkway to his pickup.

I return to the rocker. It's the diary. I had almost forgotten. I lift it from the bag and leaf through the pages—letters, photos, plane tickets, and commentary. I remember thinking how strange and sick it was for him to stalk and photograph his former girlfriend and her family. But I have a different perspective now—a man who can only see his lover once or twice a year has to soak up everything he can during each encounter and then survive on the memories until he sees her again.

So why not keep the diary?

Then I recall reading, "It's over," on the last page. There was nothing else on that page, and I was desperate to know what he wrote on the pages between the *Milwaukee Journal* article about Sara's mysterious death in Mexico and that last cryptic entry. But I had to return the diary to its hiding place before the judge returned to his chambers. Now I have more time and even more curiosity. There are two undated entries, one per page, each in his unique combination of cursive and printing.

The first one is sad but understandable.

> The rage that wells up inside me from time to time, especially when I see her on the news or in the courthouse, is almost unbearable. The irony is, she doesn't make the connection. She doesn't recognize me or even know that Robin Gildemeister is J. R. Campbell. I was never important enough to get on her radar. That she lives and Sara is gone is a travesty. I lost the life I should have had because of her. And then I lost it again.

The second is disturbing.

> I have a recurring dream. I'm waiting for her to leave the house to go for a late-night run. By this time, I know her routes. I meet her on the path, in a dead spot, no lights or homes. I confront her, and she scoffs and blows me off like she doesn't know what I'm talking about. But the look on her face when I plunge the carbon steel dagger deep into her skull is a combination of shock and horror that sticks with me but engenders no remorse. Amazingly, the devil inside her brings her back to life but only for a minute or two. She will rot in hell.

Oh my god. A recurring dream or a brutal murder? I know which one I want it to be. No one knows about whatever this thing is but me . . . and Jake. Did he read it? Would he have given it to me (instead of J. R.) if he had?

Adding logs to the dying fire, I poke, blow, and stoke it into a crackling fury and then hold the diary over the inferno, wanting desperately to toss it in and be done with it forever.

But I can't. I think back to Ollie and the foreign car and the key card, rarely used. Natalie Brinkman got a ride to work; Judge Gildemeister walked from his condo. I hear Warren's voice in my head: "I keep wondering whether your first encounter with the judge was totally random." Then I hear Warren and Sheriff MacDonald and Drostyn Anderberg all giving me the same advice: "RUN."

And so I do. I run upstairs and pack my bag, stuffing the diary in with my clothes. I leave the judge a brief note on the legal pad in the kitchen, thanking him for the great week but saying "something's come up" in the Cities. Worried about a confrontation when he returns, I'm out the door and driving south on 61 in under five minutes.

I call Sherm first, and he picks up right away. "I didn't expect to hear from you today. Are you coming back to work on Monday?"

"We need to meet, Lieutenant, preferably later today. I have some new evidence in the Patterson case. I'm going to hand it over to you, and then I'm done."

"I can't imagine—"

I cut him off. "Can you meet me at the Lake Harriet band shell at noon?"

"I think so, but hold on a minute, Barnes."

"See you then."

Next, I call Sheriff MacDonald, and it goes straight to voicemail.

"It's been a week, Sheriff, and I wanted to thank you again for the offer." I pause for a moment, thinking I see the judge's Mercedes in the rearview mirror, but it's a gold Audi that passes me going about eighty. "I've got some unfinished business in the Cities and want to spend some time helping Warren with his rehab, but if I can start on May first, you've got yourself a new detective."

I'll need to pick up the pace to get there by noon, so I turn off my phone, slide the disk with my dad's playlist into the slot on the dash, and pass the Audi like it's standing still. Just another beautiful day in paradise.